THE EDIBLE HIGHLANDER OMNIBUS

("omnibus" means a "collection" for those less versed in literary terms)

❦

KAREN MCCOMPOSTINE

New Exclusive Omnibus Presage

My dear, dear Fans!

In response to too many requests to count for a complete volume of *The Edible Highlander Saga* I respond with this Omnibus! (Check the title page or the cover for explanation.)

I could have never done this without you. It is you that I have to thank for the great success (I am writing this in the past, but now that you are reading it, it's applicable) of this Omnibus. Now that I have a creative writing degree from the Internet (they sent me a diploma!) I considered revisions on my first two novels out of the three included here, but at the request of a Fan, who begs to remain anonymous, I decided it is more Authentic to my art to leave them untouched. Therefore, no changes or omissions have been added.

There are separate dedications to every novel included in this Omnibus, but I would like to dedicate the complete works (as of time of writing, which, while you are reading this, is in the past) to MYSELF. On the sleepless nights and equally sleepless days, when I slaved over the keys of my laptop computer, often devoid of Muse's inspiration (and sherry) I thought – "Sister Bernadette would say 'of course, Karen, I always told you lovingly that you'd never amount to nothing'," and I continued, as artists do, to create. Her ghost screams from Hell, in which I don't believe but she did, and as we know from the works of Tery Protchett (who was a great author of Fantasy memoirs) once you die, you get what you believed in.

So, nyah-nyah, Sister Bernadette!!!

I love you, my beloved Fans, and I promise to dedicate my next Omnibus to you.

Karen xxxxxxxxx

HAGGIS MACBRAWN'S DISHY SECRET

PART ONE OF THE EDIBLE HIGHLANDER SERIES

This novel is dedicated to Sister Bernadette, who said I would never amount to anything. I am a published author and you're dead. "LOL".

Chapter One

❦

Annabelle wasn't even supposed to work that evening. Her golden heart couldn't say no, though, when Esmeralda called in sick – Esmeralda was eight months pregnant and Annabelle, although she had never given birth, could relate. After all, she had kidney stones removed. They were so much smaller than a baby!

Thinking about the miracle of life, Annabelle approached the businessmen sitting in the corner of Cafe Du Amour. Even though she has worked at the cafe for over three years, nothing prepared her for the brown eyes and ruffled dark hair of the man who... who was saying something to her.

"My apologies, sir," whispered Annabelle, lowering her gaze, which did not help, since she was now staring at his muscled chest, which was even more distracting than thinking about the miracle of life. "Could you please repeat your order?"

"I," said the man, his voice a guttural growl deeper than the ocean, "ordered your phone number on the back of the bill. We're leaving."

"But Haggis," said the other one, "we haven't ordered yet."

"I just remembered the merger," answered Haggis. "I must

complete the procedure before the end of the day, ye ken. And it's already nine twenty-eight. In the evening."

"You're still on London time," said the other man. "It's ten twenty-eight."

"Hurry up," snapped Haggis and Annabelle retreated, her heart pummelling against her chest so hard that she worried it might have been visible through her work uniform, her knees turning into jelly. *Ye ken*. This man was as Scottish as Scotsmen came. A Highlander. She would have never admitted this to anybody, but at the age of twenty-one she was still a virgin, because she was waiting... for a Scotsman. Specifically, for Jiminy from *Outofhander*.

How was she supposed to give him a bill if they haven't ordered anything...?

But he asked for her phone number. Technically that was an order, since she was a waitress and this was a cafe. Bingo!

Annabelle quickly grabbed the nearest piece of paper, which happened to be her own electricity bill, and wrote her number on the back. "CALL ME", she added, then berated herself for her stupidity. Of course he would call, he asked for her number! It took all her strength and a quick shot of whisky to approach the table again and gingerly place the paper in front of Haggis.

"Mhm," said the hunky Scotsman, then dug out his wallet, so filled with banknotes that they were practically begging to be let out for a breather, pulled out a twenty-pound note and placed it on the table. Then he stood up, followed by the other man, whose confused gaze was now fixed on the money.

"Sir," whispered Annabelle. "Your... bill."

"Aye," he said enigmatically. "I will add this to my expenses, ye ken." Before she had time to blush and raise her hand to cover her soft, invitingly open lips, the men were gone and only a faint smell of whisky... ah, no, that was her own breath.

"Annabelle!" yelled the owner of the cafe, an unpleasant man called Donald. "Come here!"

With a quiet sigh, Annabelle briskly dug out a mint Tick-

Tock from her pocket and popped it into her mouth. Maybe Donald wouldn't notice the smell. But of course he did. "I do not pay you to drink at work," he spat unpleasantly. "I pay you to look sexy for our customers. You need to pad your bra, girl. At least the fat one is not here today."

"She's pregnant, sir."

"Pregnant schmegnant! It's a business, not a kindergarten, girl. Go put some toilet paper in your bra, then come back here. The Brutal Bruisers are coming over in ten minutes."

"Bru– bru..."

"You know nothing about rugby, do you, girl? They just won the Cup. You will serve them *all* they ask for. Open the top button of your shirt when you're done with your bra. Off you go!"

Tears rolled down Annabelle's face as she locked herself in the ladies' powder room, then took off her shirt and examined her not very large breasts, which were nevertheless still perky and cheerful despite her age. She did not use the toilet paper, instead opting for paper tissues, which at the very least didn't scratch her gentle nipples. She knew what look Donald had in mind – after all, she had seen the "decoration" on the walls of his office. But there was no way she would be able to replicate the Page Three girls from the *Daily Daily* newspaper. For Annabelle was simply plain, her lips not pouty enough, her hair not shiny enough, her breasts... not quite padded enough yet, despite the tissues. She was not tall either, despite her five-inch heels. Why would a man like Haggis want her number...?

And then she suddenly remembered. She had seen a photograph of Haggis MacBrawn before, on the front page of the *Financial Daily* as she was buying *Glam Girl Daily* for herself, hoping desperately that some of the advice would help her become a beautiful woman, like one of the Real Housewives. He was a billionaire, recently divorced from *the* Margerithe du Lacq, a French countess and Hollywood star in one. Annabelle's roommate, Żaneta, pshawed – according to her, du Lacq's real name was Sarah Lackey and she came from Northampton. But what did Żaneta know? She came from Poland and thought that Prince Albert was a brother of Prince Charming. Margerithe looked so refined and famous, a complete opposite of plain, non-pouty lipped, practically flat-chested Annabelle...

Annabelle sighed and her reflection in the mirror did the same. The tissues did not look good. Neither did her breasts. Nor her waist. She applied some burgundy lipstick and hoped for the best.

Chapter Two

"Well, well, who is this gorgeous lady," roared the captain of the rugby team, one Burr McRogue, known both for his many affairs and the amount of alcoholic beverages he could down in one sitting.

"Keep your hands off her," yelled Seamus O'Shaugnessy, a red-haired Irishman (almost as good as a Scotsman) whose muscles were so massive they threatened to explode through his very tight t-shirt. Annabelle realised, her heart sinking, that it would be another case of meeting her crush and discovering he was an awful person. Seamus O'Shaughnessy was on the short-list of her future husbands. "She is mine, aren't you, babe?"

"I– I would like to take your order, gentlemen..."

A choral cackle interrupted her. "Gentlemen!" panted Rob Stallion. "Gentlemen...!"

"Beers!" growled McRogue. "Lots of beers! And shots! And whatever else you have in this shithole you call a cafe."

"Burgers," added O'Shaughnessy. "Lots of burgers."

"And women!"

"No, Rob, that's not how you order from a sweet sexy babe like her. First you tip."

"My tip?" asked Rob Stallion and the group roared in

laughter again. Annabelle shrunk a bit, even though she was already rather small. Especially in comparison to the hunky rugby players. All she wanted was to go home and buy the *Financial Daily* to find out what a merger was...

As she passed the order to the cook, Brandy, Annabella doubtfully patted her breasts. Or, to be more precise, the tissues. She had a strange feeling that the – now very tight – top made it possible to see that her chest was somewhat angular.

"Burgers," said Brandy in a sepulchral tone. "One day I will be asked to prepare something luxurious, like fries, and I will die of shock." Brandy was very hilarious.

"Ha ha ha," enthused Annabelle. Brandy was not misled, though.

"What is wrong, Annabelle?"

"It's just that they are so *rude,* even Seamus."

"Your husband Seamus?"

"Technically," admitted Annabelle, "it's Geraldine O'Shaughnessy's husband, but if he keeps acting like this, she will divorce him very soon."

"No chance," said Brandy, putting the first twelve pints on a tray that thin-armed Annabelle would have to somehow deliver to the table. "He's loaded beyond belief. And, from what I hear, very lucky."

"Lucky?"

"Some men are born luckier than others, if you know what I mean."

"How... how much luckier?"

"A tripod," said Brandy shortly. "Go, Annabelle. And take those tissues out of your bra, what on Earth are you do– ah, don't tell me. Donald made you." She bent to push in a corner of a tissue which was peeking out.

"Of course," sighed Annabelle, then groaned lifting the tray. She knew this would be a very long night...

Chapter Three

※

Two hours later, she was on her last two legs. Donald closed the cafe, putting a "PRIVATE PARTY" sign on the door. Brenda had no time to talk, slaving over countless burgers and pouring many beers, alternating them with shots of vodka. Rugby players' ability to eat was trumped only by their ability to drink and make disgusting remarks. Annabelle was blushing so often that she started worrying whether it was safe for her circulatory system.

"More women!" roared a player she didn't know. His appearance would have been drastically improved by applying a brown paper bag to his head. "More beer! More everything!"

"I want to go home," squealed Annabelle. It was nearly midnight. Her mobile buzzed twice in the meantime and she considered hiding in the ladies' powder room to check whether it was an incoming call from Haggis MacBrawn, but didn't dare. Donald, her unpleasant boss, was now sitting in his office, no doubt reading *Daily Daily* and smoking one of his disgusting Cuban cigars, but there were cameras all over the place. Not to help in case of trouble, but so that he could keep an eye on his staff. Even in the ladies' powder room. *Especially* in the ladies' powder room.

"No chance," yelled O'Shaughnessy, who somehow heard her voice over the noise duly provided both by his teammates and the stereo system playing one of Ted Shriekran's many latest singles. "Not before one of us got to know you better!"

"Just one?" interrupted Rob Stallion. "So you're not interested?"

The laughter shook the walls and Annabelle briefly closed her eyes, hoping to wake up in the muscular arms of Haggis MacBrawn and discover it was a nightmare. Her future husband Seamus was now completely crossed off her list, leaving an empty space demanding to be refilled. Number two was Jason Moanmoan, who irritatingly lived on a different continent (and was married to somebody else as well). Number one remained Jiminy Frasier of the *Outofhander* fame. As if it weren't bad enough that she had to remove Hunter Thunder from the list very recently, due to the fact that she exchanged a few words with him after his concert two weeks earlier. The words he exchanged with her were indecent proposals.

"I'm going to start putting water in their drinks," whispered Brenda. "They're too drunk to notice."

"I'm scared," Annabelle whispered back.

"Just go there! We'll throw them out at midnight. It's only another hour."

An hour and forty minutes, thought Annabelle gloomily, balancing on her high heels, cursing the paper tissues chafing her soft breasts, her bad taste in future husbands, and the fact that Brutal Bruisers won some sort of rugby Cup. Basketball, she decided. From now on her favourite sport was basketball. They were rich, tall, and... and mostly taken, but...

"Gah!" she managed to scream before the tray hit the floor, quickly followed by Annabelle herself. The men jeered at her rudely. Burr McRogue tripped her on purpose.

"Poor girl," he chuckled. "Her boobs are so big she can't keep her balance! Are you wounded, sweetheart? Come to papa Burr, I'll take a look..."

"Leave me alone!" cried Annabelle, trying to lift herself from the floor, suddenly grabbed by two strong hands – Burr's hands. "Don't touch me!"

"Did you not hear what the lady said?" growled a Scottish voice behind her, startling everyone but Rob Stallion, who dozed off and started snoring aloud.

"Who are you?" asked Burr McRogue, pushing Annabelle aside in a manner that was the opposite of gentle. She gazed at her hands – she cut herself on one of the many pieces of glass covering the floor, which would now be sticky with beer, which she would then have to clean up despite having been injured. Then she raised her huge, green eyes towards the menacing posture of Haggis MacBrawn.

"I just did a merger," announced MacBrawn. "Your team and Feathery Strokers. The new captain is..."

"Feathery Strokes are *women,* you Scottish twat, what are you talking about?"

"A ken they are women. Do you know who owns your team?"

"What does Michael Crumpler have to do with that?"

"Michael is having a sex change," said MacBrawn in a neutral tone, which nevertheless sounded very serious. "Her new name is Michaela Crumpler, and she does not wish to have men in her team. I saved some of your jobs by explaining to her that a gender-mixed team would be a great idea, since we are living in the twenty-first century, ye ken."

"Some of our jobs?" asked Seamus O'Shaughnessy once the collective gasps – sans the snoring Stallion – stopped.

"As long as you get your bits chopped off," said MacBrawn, then turned away from the rude men. "Annabelle," he said, "why don't *you* pick the one whose bits should be chopped off first?"

"This one," said Annabelle without a moment of hesitation, pointing at Burr McRogue's hateful figure. "How do you know my name, sir?"

"It was on your electricity bill, which was overdue, by the way, but it's now paid. Which other ones were rude to you? I know a surgeon who has a two-for-one promotion ongoing."

"I was a gentleman," said McRogue uncertainly.

"Like feck you were!" spat Brenda, who quietly tiptoed over. "You were abusive and nasty towards poor Annabelle, who, I will have you know, is a *virgin*, McDouche!"

Annabelle nearly cried. This was not information that she wished to reveal to MacBrawn! Not to mention a bunch of unruly rugby players! She was now dirty, bleeding, her breasts rubbed raw by the tissues, and her humiliation was clearly going to expand further until it swallowed the entire universe.

"Off with his head," commanded Brenda. "And his. And his."

"I haven't touched her!" protested Seamus O'Shaughnessy.

"Only because you're sitting too far!"

"Mmm," said Haggis MacBrawn. "I'm bored. You're all fired. Annabelle, you're fired too, but I am employing you immediately as my secretary. Let's go."

"Go...?"

"Secretary?" asked Brenda in a disbelieving tone just in time for Donald, their unpleasant boss, to emerge from his office together with a cloud of acrid smoke.

"Who do you think you are?! Get out of my cafe! Leave my employees alone, you... you bully!"

"Ah," said MacBrawn. "Isn't this the famous Donald Huckabee, money launderer, drug dealer, and a runner of sex trafficking circle? The police are on their way. But I must go indeed, ye ken, we're flying to London on the morra."

"We?" asked Annabelle. There was a new girlfriend, then. The *Financial Daily* probably had a word or two to say about that.

"You and I," explained MacBrawn, steering her firmly towards the exit. "I need my secretary at hand."

The silence inside was complete until the door slammed

behind them, after which they couldn't hear anymore whether it was silent inside or not.

"Have you really merged rugby teams...?"

"Don't be daft, wee lassie."

"And... Michaela..."

"I said, don't be daft. I'll give you a ride home. Where do you live?"

"My address is on the electricity bill," she muttered. So he was lying about employing her as his secretary. She would have to go back to Cafe Du Amour in the morning, face her unpleasant bos Donald, mop up the dried beer – it wasn't Brenda's responsibility and there was no chance of Donald doing anything useful.

"It says that you live at Brownhole Street. It's the absolute worst part of this town, sassenach."

Annabelle nodded quietly, nevertheless feeling a jolt of excitement at being referred to as "sassenach" by a muscular billionaire.

"What is someone like you doing working in this dump and living in... in that other dump? Get in the car, Annabelle. Gunther, we're apparently going to Brownhole Street, if this limousine can even squeeze between the buildings. Unless, Annabelle..."

"...yes?"

"Unless, ye ken," said MacBrawn in Scottish accent, staring at her intently in the near darkness as lights passed by outside the windows of the limousine, "you would actually like to be my secretary. I need someone to take notes during my business meetings, to serve coffee, which I believe you are good at. But there is a catch. You would have to travel with me. On the morra. To London."

"Bu– but..."

"You've got time to decide until we reach your place."

"I decided," said Annabelle, oddly determined, barely recognising her own voice, suddenly strong and convincing. "I accept."

"Oh good," sighed MacBrawn. "Gunther, back to the Glitz Hotel we go."

It took Gunther a while to manoeuvre both himself and the limousine out of the street, which was more suitable for old bicycles, like the one which Annabelle left outside the Cafe, unless it was stolen already. Her bicycle, she thought, her four Polish flatmates Kunegunda, Agnieszka, Żaneta and Wiktoria...! Her clothes, her lucky shoes! What was she doing, agreeing to such a ridiculous proposal? What did she know about this man, other than that he was responsible for "mergers", whatever they were, and that he was taking her to London? Suddenly she remembered her favourite novel and shivered violently. Was he one of those men who had Red Rooms of Painful Activities...? Would she be forced to perform deviant sexual acts?

"Your breasts," said MacBrawn enigmatically and Annabelle nearly passed out. "They look different from when I saw them earlier."

"Ah... it's, it's tissues."

His eyebrow wandered up in the darkness, questioningly. "You keep tissues in your breasts?"

"It's– it's– I have to take them out when I... undress..." Every word seemed charged with electricity which was the opposite of static, sparkling between MacBrawn and Annabelle. Or was she just imagining it? Perhaps he really just wanted a secretary to take notes about mergers and serve coffee. But why would he pick up someone like her, when he could undoubtedly pick among all the best secretaries in London?

"Undress," repeated Haggis MacBrawn, again sounding enigmatically. "It might be dangerous."

"Why?" she asked weakly.

"Because I am a man, and I have my urges," he explained politely.

Gunther chuckled.

"One of them is for my secretaries to wear clothes. Tomorrow, I mean on the morra, I will give you my platinum credit card. Your first task in London will be to go shopping and not come back until you spent at least ten thousand pounds on expensive clothes fitting for the secretary of Haggis MacBrawn."

Chapter Four

❦

ANNABELLE ENTERED HARROLDS, WHICH WAS A FAMOUS AND very big store, and stopped, which forced her to apologise to the fellow shopper attempting to follow her inside.

She had never left her small town before. This store was the size of the town itself. Her taste in clothing was nothing like her "uniform" at Cafe Du Amour, but it was also nothing like what she imagined secretaries to be wearing. She mostly wore oversized t-shirts and jeans, ripped at the knees and missing one back pocket, which was luckily back into fashion. The "vintage" look, which she achieved by not having enough money to buy a new pair of trousers.

She was in Harrolds, with a platinum credit card, yet she was still wearing the frankly unsuitable clothes she worked in last night. Annabelle removed the tissues from her bra when they arrived at Haggis's hotel, but her modesty did not permit her to remove anything else. Except her high heels. He just growled a quick goodnight, then disappeared into what was probably his bedroom, leaving her alone. Annabelle didn't get much sleep that night, despite the fact that his suite had four other bedrooms and seven bathrooms, not to mention a drawing room – she had only read about drawing rooms in Jane Austen's novels and for some reason imagined that they involved visual arts and crayons – and at least twenty wardrobes, each of them empty. Not that Annabelle checked, or anything. That would have been weird.

"Excuse me, madam," she said shyly to a woman behind a counter in front of approximately seven billion bottles of perfume. "Where do I buy... secretary clothes?"

"Secretary clothes?" repeated the woman curiously. "Suits and shirts, you mean?"

"I suppose," answered Annabelle shakily.

"With your budget," said the woman coolly, "somewhere else." Then she turned away to attend to a customer who was dressed in something that made Annabelle think of Margerithe du Lacq.

Thankfully, she found what she believed she needed. The clerk, a clearly homosexual effeminate man, assured her that this was what secretaries wore all the time. Subdued, shapely, ageing Annabelle at least to twenty-five. Excellent, she thought. She considered visiting the perfume stall with her many bags to show the nasty woman how wrong she was about Annabelle's "budget", but ultimately found it uncomfortable to walk around with all the purchases. Also, it would have been petty. Also, Gunther was waiting outside.

She just quickly popped into the ladies' powder room, changed into some of the new clothes, looked at her crumpled "uniform", then threw it into the bin. How shocking, she thought, that she had to pay to use the powder room...! Now she understood how Harrolds could afford to employ so many petty and unpleasant perfume sellers. The money they were charging for using the powder rooms must have constituted at least half of their income.

. . .

"Today," said MacBrawn assertively to the eight people gathered at a conference room, "we are going to discuss the merger."

"Not again," groaned one of the near identical suited men. "You're obsessed with it."

"That's because I closed it last night," announced MacBrawn and a hushed, excited whisper briefly encircled the table, followed by weak applause.

Annabelle sat in a corner, her legs crossed, a legal pad in her lap, wondering what exactly she was supposed to write down. Just in case, she started writing down every word as fast as she could, assigning her own names to the seven men and one woman. The first man, she decided, would from now on be called Grumpster. The woman who sent Annabelle a quick, sour glance before proceeding to ignore her completely became Lemony. Annabelle was busy hastily writing down the words of Pinkerton, whose face and shirt were the identical shade of piggy pink, when Haggis interrupted her.

"Annabelle," he said. "Can you please re-read what Jason said in the beginning?"

Annabelle blushed furiously.

"Jason," repeated Haggis with a slight undercurrent of impatience. "Jason Johnson, the owner of Jason Johnson Corp. Here."

"Ah," breathed Annabelle with relief, "Grumps– that's Mr Johnson. Of course."

"Grumps...?"

"In our annual report," she quickly started, "we have reported an operational profit of twenty-one point eight per cent..."

"See, Jason," said Haggis in a triumphant voice, "the wee lassie knows it all. So stop telling me that all of a sudden you can't afford to buy extra stocks. Thank you, Annabelle."

"You're welcome," she whispered, but MacBrawn was already grilling Mr Jason Johnson, who looked even grumpier than before. His cold glare made Annabelle understand that she just made a very powerful enemy.

"You've done very well," said MacBrawn on their way back to the hotel. "And I like your clothing. Although it doesn't look to me like you've spent ten thousand pounds."

"I– I didn't dare."

"First lesson. When I order you to do something, you do it. Understood?"

Annabelle felt her cheeks heat up again. He was such a manly, masculine, macho man, with this unbearably erotic Scottish burr. No, not burr, she thought, shivering with repulsion at the thought of Burr McRogue. Growl. That was more like it. What was Scottish for growl...?

"I beg your pardon?"

The blood vessels in her face were in danger of exploding, Annabelle realised. She had accidentally said that out loud. "Nothing, mister MacBrawn."

"It's also growl," he said, his tone impenetrable. "Only with a rolling 'r'. Grrrrrowl. Stop laughing, Guntherrrrr, focus on the rrrrrroad."

"Yes, sirrrrr."

"He's my cousin," explained the muscular businessman. "So many times removed that I lost count, but he always comes back. We fly to Amsterdam on the morra, wee lassie."

"M– m..." stammered Annabelle, completely blown away by being called a "wee lassie", unable to stop imagining Haggis MacBrawn wearing a kilt and nothing else. Was his chest hairy? Did he have tattoos...? No, he was definitely not the type who would ruin his muscular body with tattoos, unlike Annabelle's first and only boyfriend Fat Joe, who kept trying to get into her panties only to laugh cruelly and push her away when he saw them. Annabelle was aware of the existence of Wintouria's

Secret. She even memorised the address of the store. To make sure she wouldn't accidentally enter it.

"M-msterdam," helped the grrrrowly Scot. "Indeed. We will be closing a transaction involving a... ah, who cares. As long as you join me for dinner tonight, then we can discuss the important business matters."

Gunther cackled.

Chapter Five

ANNABELLE KEPT LOSING TRACK OF THE CONVERSATION, hypnotised by the movement of the muscles under the skin covering Haggis's forearms, embellished with golden hair which positively sparkled when he gesticulated, excitedly talking about the important business matters.

"Sir," she interrupted when he paused for breath. "I think... you must be mistaken. I am not a secretary. I am but a modest waitress. I have never studied. I am uneducated, plain, boring. There is... I don't even know the names of those people."

"Grumpster and Lemony? Works for me."

She cried in surprise.

"I went through your notes," explained Haggis, "after all, I hired you to take them. You don't need to write it down when they ask for a glass of water, but feel free to assign any name you want to each of them. Next time I'll point at the person when I need you to read what you wrote down. I memorise every word anyway, since I have an aural equivalent of photographic memory, but they don't need to know that. Sometimes it's a useful business tactic to make yourself look foolish and have to ask your secretary to repeat what was said. So that they can see it was written down, ye ken."

Annabelle nodded, still unable to speak, her shame on full display.

"You are perfect," he continued. "You don't look threatening or too intelligent, but there are depths in those emerald eyes of yours which reveal that your mind is quick and silly."

"Thank– silly?"

"Ye ken," chuckled Haggis. "Wee lassie. You watch too much TV. Am I Scottish enough for you or do I need to read some sort of slang dictionary? If the answer is yes, you must get it for me. I'm overeducated and spoiled, wee lassie, ye ken. Rrrrrrr. But I do wear kilts, aye..." His laughter died for a moment and he threw Annabelle a darkened look, surprising her, since she hadn't even said anything about kilts.

It was a good thing that Annabelle wasn't holding a glass of wine, because she would have dropped it.

Chapter Six

"Tell me about yourself," demanded Haggis.

They were sitting on the sofa of the hotel, elegantly drinking white wine. Annabelle was still wearing her business suit, which earned her a polite, yet very masculine scolding – MacBrawn apparently expected her to buy other clothing as well, not just two modest secretarial suits. Her lunchtime task, as the whole day would be occupied with meetings, would be to go and spend more money on clothes for herself.

"There's not much to tell," she said, looking at the wine glass. She had no idea whether the wine was expensive or not, but suspected that the only cheap thing in the hotel were her shoes. "I'm twenty-one. I am an orphan, raised by the nuns. I live with four flatmates..."

"Used to."

"I– yes. I used to live with four flatmates. I worked as a waitress at Cafe Du Amour for the last three years, trying to save some money, but it's just so... so difficult." An unwelcome tear rolled down her cheek and she briefly hoped that Haggis would reach towards her face to wipe it off, but the sofa was so wide he would have had to walk over.

"What are your hobbies? What do you do in your spare time? What are your dreams?"

"I... I like watching TV."

"I understand," said Haggis after what felt like an eternity, whilst Annabelle continued blushing. "I suppose that answers the first two questions, but what about your dreams?"

How was she supposed to explain? She felt like she was in a dream right this moment, holding a glass of white wine like some sort of refined lady, sitting at not very large distance from a man who wiped the memories of Jiminy Frasier *and* Moanmoan The Samoan (who was a famous actor) from her mind. "I'm expecting to wake up any moment," she blurted out. "Do you travel to a different country every day?"

"Not always. Sometimes I stay somewhere for two or three days. It's a joke, wee lassie, I am in a difficult period right now. My old secretary eloped and sent me a text message from Hawaii wishing me all the best. I'll work you to the ground once your trial period passes."

Annabelle only managed to hold on to the glass because her hand – and the other body parts – froze.

"One month," said Haggis, looking at her curiously, then he glanced at his watch and visibly stiffened. "I must go to my room."

How odd, she thought, still sitting motionlessly with her fingers wrapped around the glass of wine, except for her pinky which she kept in a certain distance from the stem of the glass for that certain je ne sais quoi, as he saw himself out. He didn't even go to the bathroom, he didn't say goodnight.

The clock produced a soft sound as midnight struck.

Chapter Seven

THE NEXT FEW DAYS BECOME A FEVERISH BLUR IN Annabelle's confused mind. They changed cities every twenty-four hours, yet somehow every day seemed similar. Haggis kept encouraging her to buy more clothes, wined and dined her, asked her a lot of questions, only to disappear before midnight not completely unlike Cinderella. Somehow it always coincided with the moment when Annabelle tried to ask *him* a question.

She had seen him bare-chested and bare-backed once when he thought she was still asleep. He literally tiptoed to the bathroom, clearly doing his best not to wake her up, unaware that her gaze was longingly following him. There were no tattoos, no chest hair, just a muscular body which made Annabelle feel painfully inadequate. He was wearing loose black sweatpants, which somehow managed to be tight around his... his... his much lower back, thought Annabelle, already feeling an approaching blush. There was no chance of her getting another second of sleep afterwards, not when she was guiltily imagining his legs under those sweatpants. She was too modest and shy to imagine anything that was below the waist and above the undoubtedly muscular legs, but she didn't need to imagine his wide shoulders, six-pack abs, and massive chest anymore. She just had to recall what she had seen, which was easy, since she could barely see anything else, including her own reflection in the mirror.

"Annabelle MacBrawn," she whispered, just to test how that would feel. It felt good. And silly. She was just an orphan, a waitress who somehow managed to escape her dull life and travelled between London, Amsterdam, Berlin... and some other place she forgot. Oh. Yes. Her own hometown, Annabelle thought darkly. Where they would be going either tomorrow or in two days. She felt ashamed, since she believed it was her duty as Haggis's secretary to keep track of their upcoming whereabouts.

Annabelle had no plans to visit the cafe, but she had to go back home, pack her things, pay her part of the rent... The only problem was that she had no cash and didn't dare to ask Haggis for a penny. He was giving her his platinum credit card already, one so posh that it didn't even have a number, just a piece of expensive looking metal with his name on it and some sort of electronic chip. The very sight of the card made the clerks in the stores pale a bit.

"Go," said Haggis, "I don't need you today. Buy yourself some other shoes."

"Why, Mr MacBrawn? Why are you doing this? Giving me your card? I could run away with it, buy – I don't even know – a... a car, or a plane ticket to Hawaii, why do you trust me?"

"It's your eyes," he said in a serious tone. "No, wee lassie, this card is traceable using a GPS navigation app on my smartphone. If you were to spend a dime without my permission, you'd get arrested within hours, no matter where you tried to hide. Now, off you go."

Annabelle shrunk for a moment. Her old unpleasant boss Donald said "now, off you go" quite often. Those words were invariably supported with a slap on her bum. But Haggis just smiled, revealing his perfectly white teeth. Hers were neither perfect nor completely white, as dental care cost money.

What am I doing, she wondered, going through the racks with discounted clothes out of sheer habit, before moving to the shoe section. She was aware that as a woman she practically had a duty to be fascinated with shoes and desire hundreds of pairs, but she only liked high heels – the higher the better – and slippers. Although... now that she was thinking about it... Annabelle picked a pair of leather boots, which she had seen somewhere, probably on the perfectly formed feet of Sheryl Fernandes-Borsini-Coll-whatever her latest husband's name was. She could buy them now. But then Annabelle glanced at the price tag and gasped. They cost as much as her part of the rent in the old apartment. Assuming she decided to pay for a year in advance.

No, Annabelle decided, putting the boots away. She couldn't allow Haggis, no matter how perfect his abs were, to pay her wages in boots and suits. She needed cold hard cash.

But the boots were calling her name. "Sheryl," they sang... oh, no. "Annabelle. You must take us with you. We are so lonely here. Those other boots only talk about Love Island. We are classy and sophisticated, like Sheryl Fernandes-Borsini-Coll-whatever her latest husband's name is. TAKE US."

Her hands shaking, Annabelle approached the counter, carrying the shoes as gingerly as if they were made of platinum, like the card, which she then handed to the woman behind the counter, whose face predictably paled a bit.

"I'll be right back," she said sharply, then disappeared, taking the card along.

Annabelle didn't like that at all. For all she knew the woman could have been using the card right now to pay for her own furs and diamonds, even though the shoe store didn't sell any. A minute passed, then another. The next customer was waiting and Annabelle was becoming restless enough to contemplate bursting through the door and leaving Haggis's traceable card behind, when two strange men suddenly grabbed her arms.

"Leave me alone!" she cried. "What's going on?!"

"It's best for you not to say anything," said one of the men coldly.

"I haven't done anything!" shrieked Annabelle. They ignored her pleas, pulling her, kicking and screaming, into an empty storage room. They took her handbag, then violently threw her inside. Annabelle heard the sound of a lock and she was alone.

Her phone was in her handbag, Annabelle realised. She couldn't call Haggis to tell him what was happening. "Oh no," she exclaimed aloud all of a sudden, realising there was an *even* worse problem. She didn't have his number. He had hers, but when he called his number displayed as "unknown caller"... It was only then when she suddenly understood. She was being a victim of an elaborate prank, most probably concocted by a YouTube influencer.

Annabelle didn't understand why anybody would spend so much money on such a cruel joke, taking her to foreign countries, making her buy clothes she would never see again. Would he now ensure that she would remain imprisoned in this room forever...? Would she be thrown into the street of... where was she today... it was probably Amsterdam. Yes, definitely. Unless it was Berlin. Or Denmark. In any case, it was a foreign place where she knew nobody.

Annabelle was about to burst into frustrated tears of powerlessness when the door opened so brutally it nearly flattened her against a wall, even though she was standing by the window on the opposite side of the room.

"Where did you get this card?" inquired a man in a uniform.

"I haven't done anything," she cried.

"Where did you get this card?"

"From Mr MacBrawn himself. I am his secretary."

"The police are on their way," said the uniformed man coldly. "We have your name, your passport, we know you stole this card."

"If it's his idea of a joke, tell him it's not funny at all...! I haven't stolen it!" Annabelle paused as an idea arrived. "Call Mr MacBrawn! Tell him what you are doing to me!"

"Oh," said the man, "the bank is already notified, and once Mr MacBrawn picks up his phone he will be notified as well." Then he left and shut the door.

Annabelle was being loaded into the police car, barely conscious due to anxiety and anger, when Gunther arrived and rescued her.

"Really?" asked the same uniformed man, but his tone was now completely different. "Our... our sincere apologies... I thought..."

"Whatever you thought," informed him Gunther, "will be best kept until your court appearance."

"I haven't done anything...!" cried the man and Annabelle couldn't stop a smirk.

"You have brutally assaulted Mr MacBrawn's fiancé, kidnapped her, imprisoned against her will, taken away the credit card that she is using completely legally," said Gunther, counting on his fingers. He scowled. "I've got one more finger left. Annabelle, were your human rights violated?"

"Definitely," she agreed.

"That will be five," he said, satisfied. "Officer, please take this man's personal information. It will be necessary for the lawsuit."

"We– I– maybe we can settle...? Maybe we can somehow apologise?" The uniformed man, no longer menacing, seemed to be on the brink of wetting his pants.

"Annabelle?"

"I have a hobby," Annabelle immediately decided. "I love boots. I've seen ten or so pairs that I really liked."

"All yours," the man responded, "madam. Please just point which ones."

"I believe that the future Mrs MacBrawn also enjoys furs," said Gunther.

"We– we are a shoe store. We don't have furs..."

The officer who was still holding Annabelle's arm suddenly realised what was happening and let go so quickly she nearly fell.

"I will take the boots," Annabelle announced, massaging her arm and glaring at the officer, whose face turned a tasteful shade of green. "You will also be so kind as to show me your latest collection of shoes. I love high heels. The higher, the better."

"As long as they're classy," said Gunther quickly, then noticed her expression. "I mean, expensive."

And this was how Annabelle was driven back to the hotel in a limousine, escorted by a police car, the back seats completely filled with bags and boxes, the platinum card safely in her pocket.

Chapter Eight

"Let me ask some questions," Annabelle demanded once Haggis stopped laughing. She was now barefoot, relaxed again, wearing her new (Guchi) jeans and a crop (Guchi) top. "You know everything about me, I know nothing about you."

"I don't know a very important thing," Haggis purred. "Your name."

"It was on the bill."

"I would prefer it if you told me yourself."

Annabelle blushed again, wondering whether she was misjudging men with multiple burst vessels whom she always assumed to be drunks. She was also wondering whether it was possible to buy some sort of cream against this constant blushing. "It's an old-fashioned name."

"That's perfectly fine."

"Why did Gunther introduce me as your fiancé?" she decided to ask, changing the subject sneakily.

"Ah," said Haggis, taken aback. "Did he? Well, I suppose the cat is out of the bag then."

"You're not even protesting," Annabelle said in disbelief once a moment of silence passed and it became clear that he had no intention of saying anything more. "Am I somehow your fiancé? I don't recall being asked."

"You're becoming more assertive, I like that."

"I thought you played a prank on me," Annabelle complained. "I thought I would go to prison or become a laughing stock for the benefit of a YouTube influencer. And you tell me that I am your fiancé now and that I am assertive? That won't do, Haggis MacBrawn."

It was his turn to blush and avert his gaze, which confused her. "I'd prefer it if you could use my middle name."

"Oh? What is it?"

"Angus."

Annabelle didn't manage to stop herself from snorting and Haggis Angus MacBrawn gave her a wounded look. "Of course," she said, quickly composing herself, "A-Angus. My name, as you well know, is Annabelle Elle Ellendeling. Go on, laugh."

"I don't laugh at people's names, Annabelle."

Oh no, she thought, I will *not* blush, but her body didn't listen. "I don't either, generally, I– I don't know why I laughed. Please don't be angry, Mr MacBrawn."

"I couldn't be angry with you, wee lassie. You're so wonderful. So, aye, I suppose I should have asked... Please put that glass down."

Automatically, she listened.

"Would you marry me?"

"Why though," Annabelle croaked once she could speak again. "Surely you can't love me?"

She kept his gaze until he looked away. "No," he muttered. "I don't. Not really, not the way you deserve to be loved. But... I've been... I've been cursed, Annabelle."

"Cursed...! Is proposing to me a joke to you?"

"I am not joking. I've been cursed. I... I have a secret. I would rather not reveal it to you until we are married."

"I can't marry someone who keeps secrets from me," Annabelle snapped, then picked the glass again and emptied it.

"This is not what marriage is about! You're supposed to tell me everything, that's how it works, no? Am I wrong?"

"You're not," said Haggis sadly. "Look... I have to go."

"No! Not before you told me your secret!"

"Annabelle..."

She didn't even know when she grabbed his hand. "You can't go, not now...!"

Both of them froze. This was the first time their hands touched, *really* touched rather than just brushed in passing. Annabelle regretted not having paid attention to physics, because maybe then she would have been able to explain the jolt of electricity that connected them and made it so difficult to let go. As if their hands were glued, only by electric current, or perhaps chemistry, which she also paid very little attention to at school. "Oh," she whispered. "Oh, Angus..."

He jerked his hand away and practically ran towards the bedroom, slamming the door shut a moment before Annabelle's phone'd display went black, like it always did at midnight.

Chapter Nine

※

She couldn't sleep, despite the fact that Haggis seemed to always rent an entire floor of a hotel just for himself, Mr MacBrawn. And now for both of them. The MacBrawns...

He *proposed* to her. Then he ran away, but not before letting her know that he had a secret he intended to keep. This was not how she imagined it would turn out. In Annabelle's dreams, which repeated more often than she would have wished to admit, his handsome face hovered over hers before their lips connected in a kiss so intense that it would shatter the double-glazed windows of the selected bedroom. His muscular fingers caressed her nipples, which stood proudly like soldiers guarding the Queen, before his hand wandered down, then further, towards the soft, dark cave which hid secrets of its own...

Annabelle sat up and refilled her glass with shaky hands, no longer caring whether the wine was expensive or not. She couldn't tell whether she was in love with Haggis, but she knew that she was definitely drowning in lust, her dreams both moist and slightly sticky. He definitely didn't love her, he said it to her face, so – why?

There would be a pre-nup, of course. She would probably get a separate account with some sort of pocket money to spend. Sometimes she would be sent to Harrolds together with the platinum card to buy another dress or ten pairs of shoes to please Angus. Haggis. Angus. Couldn't he have had a normal name, like Jax or Hunter or at least Jiminy? Kilt, though... They didn't wear underwear, thought Annabelle and nearly crushed the glass in her hand in unsavoury excitement. There was something breathtakingly e-e-erotic about men speaking with a Scottish accent, wearing nothing underneath their kilts, and in Scotland they would have unlimited quantities of those men, not that she wanted more than one...

"Oh no!" Annabelle exclaimed aloud, then looked worriedly at the closed door of Haggis's bedroom. She understood everything. The "curse". The "secret". The proposal.

Haggis was gay.

Margerithe du Lacq must have gotten bored with a sexless life, whether she was hanging off the arm of a possibly kilted Scottish billionaire or not. Haggis needed to marry someone desperate, poor, ugly, undemanding, just to get rid of people asking him when he was going to present a wife. Annabelle's flatmate Kunegunda escaped Poland to live with Agnieszka – although Annabelle couldn't quite figure out why anybody would move to *Brownhole Street* out of all the places in the world – because her grandparents wouldn't ever stop asking the same question. But Angus was in for a disappointment, thought darkly Annabelle, who knew what would happen next. Kunegunda eventually produced a fake boyfriend, a gay man who was undergoing the same interrogation on a regular basis, at which point the question was replaced by another one. "When are you going to get married?" When they made it clear that they never intended to marry, the question changed again: "when are you going to have a kid?". The next stage would be "when are you going to have more kids", probably followed by "why do you have so many kids?". Annabelle might have been a virgin, but she was streetwise, well acquainted with the ways of the world filled with well-meaning, nosy grandparents.

What would she do if Haggis asked her to have a kid?

With certain wine-fuelled difficulties Annabelle forced the vision of a little kilted Jiminy away from her mind. This wasn't TV, this was real life, as unreal as it felt. She was being asked by a high-flying businessman with a platinum, traceable, electronic-chip-equipped credit card to marry him, so that he could go on being gay without – so he thought, poor Haggis – being constantly questioned.

It would make Annabelle rich, at least to some degree. Haggis's wife would have to live in a suitable house. If those were his hotel suites, what was his house, farm, mansion, or maybe palace like...? A different bedroom for every day of the year? She would probably just get one, the remaining 364 reserved for Haggis and his gay lovers... although, undeniably attractive that he was, nobody had *that* much time, especially with all the travelling and mergers and whatnots. In any case, she would be more than happy with just one bedroom and one bathroom, far away from her unpleasant boss Donald and his cigars. Haggis could keep as many lovers as he wanted in the remaining 364 bedrooms. Annabelle, as said previously, was a streetwise, modern, open-minded woman, whether she was raised by nuns or not.

It's just that she was also incredibly attracted to her gay fiancé...

Chapter Ten

❧

Annabelle was rather hungover when they were boarding the plane, and the loud announcements gave her a headache.

"Haggis," she muttered, once she realised they were going to be alone in the first class. "I have to ask you for something. No, no personal questions, don't worry. I already figured out your secret and it's safe with me, I just need..."

"What?!"

Annabelle winced at the outburst of fury, then took a closer look at the angles at which his face was currently contorted. It wasn't as much fury as fear. "It's okay, really..." she said meekly.

"You entered my bedroom! You did not respect my privacy! Even though the door was locked!"

"Angus..."

"Sir? Madam?" interrupted the stewardess and both Annabelle and Haggis stiffened. "Is everything okay?"

"Absolutely," said Annabelle, sounding slightly strangled. "Couldn't be better."

"Aye," confirmed Haggis after a mortified pause. "What the wee lassie said."

"Don't you 'wee lassie' me now," hissed Annabelle the

moment the stewardess disappeared. "If your door was locked, how did I enter?"

"I don't know," he whispered back, "but you should never have done it."

"I haven't. I just guessed. It's fine, you can have as many lovers as you want, I..."

"What *are* you talking about?"

"Angus," said Annabelle, trying and failing not to raise her voice, "it's *fine* with me. I'm happy to marry you if it helps with your grandmother."

"I– What grandmother?"

"The one who minds."

"Who minds what?"

"Your secret," repeated Annabelle. "You don't need to act like you have no idea what I'm talking about, as I said I understand and it's perfectly fine. We can talk about it later, but Haggis, I must..."

"But what do you understand and what is perfectly fine? Annabelle, don't be daft."

She pursed her lips and pretended to stare at the window. He was doing it again, not letting her ask any questions, turning them against her. Annabelle's anger slightly subsided as she realised how difficult his life must have been, remembering Kunegunda's bitter confessions. Poor girl had to constantly swerve to avoid the interrogation, come up with lies explaining why she was not at home, finally producing a fake boyfriend. Even that wasn't enough. Kunegunda introduced Agnieszka as her "friend", "just a friend", but still needed to remember not to look at her with too much tenderness, not to accidentally hold hands where somebody could see them... Haggis would calm down once they were married, at least until his grandmother would start inquiring about children. As for Annabelle, she would happily prove to him that she was not interested in him in the sexual way, even though she was...

"I need money," she whispered, trying to stop her imagination, which by now took her all the way to giving birth to their third child, produced using a turkey basker. "That's all. Not much. I have to pay my share of the rent at the old place. That's it. I'm so sorry to ask. It's okay if you don't want to, it's just that..."

"Annabelle," said Haggis. "Look at me. You are really weird this morning. Of course you will get money. You're working for me, at least for now. You get wages. Just give me your bank account number."

"I... I need cash. That's how it's arranged. We... we're not really... oh, I'm not telling you, you have your secrets, I have mine. Sixty quid is all I need, then I won't ask for anything more, ever. And you don't have to buy me things..."

"Sixty quid?" Haggis repeated questioningly. "I thought you were going to ask for sixty thousand." He seemed almost disappointed as he pulled out his wallet, then opened it, frowning. "That's euros. That's Icelandic kronur. That... I don't even know what it is... ah, there we go."

"What's this?" interrupted Annabelle, noticing something that definitely wasn't an example of monetary currency accepted in any of the countries in the civilised world.

"Just a picture," he said, looking down at the photograph as if it was the first time he has ever seen it.

"Can I see?"

Without a word, Haggis handed it to her, then looked at the window, his lips tight, forming an expressionless line.

So this was his lover, thought Annabelle. He actually looked like Haggis, just younger, bearded, and undeniably kilted. If she didn't know... but she did, so she handed the picture back, in exchange for a few banknotes none of them bothered to count. She didn't comment on the picture, but their gazes met and there seemed to be something to Haggis's stare that gave her a strange feeling, as if he wanted her to ask. Annabelle made up her mind, though. If he wanted to keep his "secret", he could. She was only half-angry. The other half pitied him. The poor, gay billionaire, Annabelle thought, but it didn't seem as funny as she would have expected it to be.

They didn't speak to each other until the plane landed. Annabelle couldn't decide whether the better cure for a hangover was paracetamol or a drink, so she asked for both and found herself slightly inebriated again, since she had forgotten to eat breakfast. She tripped twice and both times Haggis's hand was there to stop her from falling. How symbolic, Annabelle thought after the second time.

"So I guess I'll go," she said when they made it out of the airport.

"Meet me later at the Glitz Hotel," he just said.

Chapter Eleven

"We were so worried!" repeated Kunegunda for the third time.

You could have called or texted, thought Annabelle for the third time, but said nothing.

"Kunnie," she said instead, "would you consider marrying a man so that you could be with Agnieszka?"

"But I am with Agnieszka."

"No, I mean, if you were still in Poland and your grandmother kept asking?"

"I'm happier here, to be honest, because I don't have to lie or hide. Only from Andrzej."

"Who's that?"

"Wiktoria's boyfriend. He thinks lezzers are hot," said Kunegunda, rolling her eyes. "If he could, he'd invite himself in. He thinks being gay is simply about not having met the right man, and of course he is the one. For both of us. And Wiktoria as well, I suppose. Lots of stamina for a thirty-year-old. Why do you ask, why now?"

"I... I met a man," said Annabelle, blushing both modestly and shamefully at once. She needed to look up creams for that.

Or to start wearing as much make-up as Wiktoria. She still didn't know what Wiktoria actually looked like.

"Oh, that's nice. Please don't try to hook us up, I'm not interested."

"No... it's something else. He's gay and wants me to marry him."

One of Kunegunda's eyebrows wandered up.

"He's very rich," muttered Annabelle and the other eyebrow joined the first one.

"How very rich?"

"*Very* very rich."

"And your question is...?"

"Should I...?"

"Annabelle! How is this even a question? If you don't want a *very* very rich gay man to marry you, I changed my mind, hook us up right this minute. I'd kill to move out of Brownhole Street."

Annabelle just nodded, then excused herself. She wanted to pack before Żaneta returned home. Żaneta was a gossip queen. By now she probably knew everything anyway, possibly including the name of Haggis's kilted lover... Annabelle's movements slowed down, then stopped once she realised *what* she was packing into a plastic garbage bag.

Granny-style underwear. Bras with wires sticking out into random directions. Stretched sweatpants. T-shirts with tomato sauce stains or rips under the armpits. Make-up samples, the few that were so awful even Żaneta hadn't deigned to steal them. And... her lucky shoes. Heels that made her tall enough to marry a basketball player, as she used to joke. Used to... it wasn't that long ago. Two weeks? Was it even two weeks? It felt like years since Haggis asked for her number.

"The electricity bill is paid, I forgot to mention. Anyway, I'm leaving everything. Except my lucky shoes."

"We're not in Kansas anymore," said Kunegunda automatically. "Or something."

"Feel free to keep whatever you want..." Annabelle's voice broke. Who would want that crap? "Throw away the rest. Here's rent for two months... three," added her guilt. "I'll miss you," she lied.

"I'll miss you too," lied Kunegunda, then they performed the compulsory hugs and air-kisses, and Annabelle was free. Free to sit somewhere and think about her engagement, which didn't even deserve the name "relationship". She could go to a cafe – *not* Cafe Du Amour, never. Or to the Glitz Hotel, knowing that Haggis would be stuck in meetings – the charade of her being his secretary was as good as over – and snoop through the few things he brought with him whilst perusing the mini-bar's contents...

Chapter Twelve

❧

Her spy mission at the Glitz Hotel proved to be less entertaining than Annabelle had hoped. It was the same suite, except this time she was led there by a maitre d' – or some sort of butler, she wouldn't know – who bowed every thirty seconds until she finally got rid of him by giving him ten pounds and telling him not to spend everything at once. The glare she received in response was definitely worth a tenner.

Haggis only brought one small suitcase on wheels, which contained two neatly folded shirts, the sweatpants, two pairs of socks, two pairs of underwear, a book, which Annabelle checked for a dedication – none. Underneath all this hid a black metal box and she immediately got excited before opening it and discovering a shallow, wooden tray.

Annabelle picked it out of the packaging and examined carefully, turning it around, knocking on it, trying to find some hidden compartment. But it was just a wooden tray, something between a very flat bowl and a round plate with raised edges. No decoration. It somehow managed to look both expensive and useless. Why on Earth Haggis would drag something like this along in his hand luggage was beyond her.

Annabelle returned to the book, called *Storytellers*. She

flipped through the pages, searching for underlined passages, a bookmark, even a bent page corner, something that would help her see a hidden meaning. But there didn't seem to be none. It wasn't even a gay romance, just some sort of boring historical novel with an admittedly pretty cover. Nothing along the lines of "with love from Jiminy" anywhere. Annabelle went as far as to open the book again and shake it, upside down, hoping that something would fall out. Nothing. Frustrated, she threw it back in the suitcase, then examined the metal box itself, turning it around, knocking on the top and bottom, then its sides. But it was just as plain as the bowl. No suspiciously thick parts that could be hiding drugs or false passports or scented condoms. The suitcase had no double lining, or if it had she couldn't figure out how to find it, much less access it. If only he had left his mobile phone. Together with the PIN code. Or at least his laptop, with password on a post-it...

Annabelle put everything back, closed the suitcase, sighed, looked at the clock, which suggested it was lunchtime, then decided to descend upon the mini-bar. It was loaded not just with alcohol, which she expected, but also with all sorts of chocolate. Very soon she was in satisfying state of half-coma, having mixed milk chocolate, dark chocolate, filled chocolate, hazelnut chocolate, and whisky.

"So I'm not refined," she said to the suitcase, slightly slurring. "I'm not a lady, I don't have edumacation, I'm not even sure whether electricity is a chemical or not. Is it? If it flows in wires? Anyway, I think I'll marry him. Why not?"

The suitcase didn't answer.

"Do you think there are courses to become a refined lady of the house?" Annabelle asked the suitcase. "Like one of the Real Housewives, only Scottish, ye ken?"

The suitcase remained silent.

"I like you," confessed Annabelle, then hiccuped. "You're a good listener. Do you know what you need? A name. I will call you... I will call you... Jiminy..." She reached out to wrap her arms around the surprised suitcase, then passed out in a very uncomfortable position, surrounded by chocolate wrappers.

The lights switching on and the sound of the door slamming shut brought her back to life.

"Annabelle," said Haggis with that growl which would have caused her knees to turn into jelly had she not been mostly horizontal already.

"I can explain..."

He sighed irritatedly. "You've been spying on me. There is nothing you can find here."

"I know. I mean, you're wrong and I haven't done anything like this at all!"

"Annabelle. Please. Have you eaten anything but..." He gestured at the bed. "Those?"

Annabelle unglued hair from her cheek, realising how awful she must have been looking even for her already low standards, then looked at the wrappers in surprise. "I'm not happy," she thought, only the words came out aloud.

"You're not happy?"

"Oh... I didn't want to say this, just think... ignore me. I– I will go."

"Where will you go? Stay with me, Annabelle," said Haggis softly, then glanced at his watch. Annabelle automatically checked the time as well. Half past nine! She wouldn't get a minute of sleep at night. "Is it because I didn't give you enough money? Did your flatmates say something?"

"It's not always about money, Haggis! You proposed to me, told me you didn't love me and that you had a secret you wouldn't reveal, you've never answered even *one* question I asked you..."

"I see," he interrupted, then ran his strong fingers through his attractively shiny hair. "Go on. Ask me your one question and I will answer it to the best of my ability."

Annabelle opened her mouth, but no sound came out.

One question. That was not a lot. Which one should she pick? She knew his secret, she even saw the man on the photograph. What else was important? "Why do you want to marry me? Don't tell me I'm so special, tell me the truth."

He even scowled handsomely. "You *are* special and that is the truth. But I am changing my mind, Annabelle. I am already hurting you. It would be even worse if we were to get married. I am a liar and I am cursed. The only thing that can take the curse off me is the love of the right woman..."

"Haggis!" Annabelle exploded. "Surely you don't believe that! Kunegunda's grandmother would say a thing like this, but it's twenty-first century! You don't get cured of 'being cursed' by the love of the right woman!"

"You know nothing about my life," he said. "You have no idea how difficult it is to lie to everyone, to hide who you really are..."

"Cry me a river, Haggis," said the whisky, borrowing Annabelle's lips without her permission. "I don't mind your 'curse', what I mind is that you won't just... emancipate yourself, permit yourself to be as you are! You can't even say it to me, can you? You just repeat the word 'curse' as if it was so bad, which it isn't!"

"Annabelle..."

"Annabelle this, Annabelle that!"

"Annabelle," he said, his growl changing from the polite, friendly sexy into the dark, brooding sexy. "Do you think you could love me like this? A good-looking Scottish billionaire who sends you shopping with a platinum card?"

"No," she immediately answered. "I want a man who tells me the truth and opens his heart to me. I had enough encounters with rich, good-looking men from the rugby team, although they were not Scottish and probably not billionaires. I don't care about your card, it almost got me into prison, Haggis.

I want to know the real you, and once I do then maybe, maybe I could love you."

He closed his eyes and swallowed, his Adam's apple pointedly underscoring the emotions storming inside his heart. Annabelle swallowed too, but for a different reason. Tired, slightly dishevelled Haggis seemed even more appetising than his usual, already sizzling self. "You are dangerous," he groaned, "because you are so beautiful."

Alarmed Annabelle looked around, expecting a dangerously beautiful kilted man to appear behind her.

"I should give you a million or two," Haggis murmured thoughtfully, "send you home... no, not send you home, buy you one very far from Brownhole Street. Then ask you to forget about me forever. I should. But I want you, Annabelle, I wanted you since I saw you..."

She was nearly melting when she was brutally jerked back into the moment when he first saw her indeed. "You paid my electricity bill," she spat.

"Pardon me?"

"I did not ask you to do it. You, you used your financial leverage..."

"I helped you escape this bunch of testosterone-laden brutes. Was that also the wrong thing to do?"

"Who? Ah, the rugby team?" Annabelle calmed down, pinching the inside of her hand, which she heard could have been helpful with the blushing problem. "Fair," she admitted reluctantly. "It still doesn't give you the right... I'm a stupid cow. Thank you, Angus. I appreciate you paying the electricity bill. But next time when you want to bestow financial favours upon me, please ask."

"You are very different from Margerithe," he whispered.

Annabelle winced. She didn't want to be reminded that she was nothing like a French countess, who was also a Hollywood star. But he wasn't finished.

"The only way to keep her around was with money,"

Haggis continued. "This was when I understood how the curse actually worked, that I needed a woman who would really love me as I was. The *right* woman, Annabelle, not just 'a' woman. Margerithe did a good impression of loving me, she is an actress after all, but at the end she was only in love with the credit card. That was also why I gave it to you, to see what you were going to buy and how much you would spend. I kept pushing you to buy more..." His voice trailed off. "Annabelle, my secret is not something you could comprehend, hell, even I can't really comprehend it. It is a real curse."

Annabelle, who was becoming slightly blurry with delight, snapped back into reality again. The approaching blush was the angry sort. "Curse," she repeated coolly.

"You just won't believe me," said Haggis darkly. "It's... I hoped that you would fall in love with the money, then perhaps with me as well, that maybe you would find me attractive in some way..."

Those words made Annabelle understand what she had to do to force him to reveal his badly obscured secret. "Oh, Angus," she whispered. "I find you attractive in absolutely every way. Please, ravish me. Call me your sassenach and a wee lassie. I beg. Wrap my weak, feminine body in your strong arms," she added, her courage fuelled by the whisky, and waited to see the reaction. She expected him to pull away, possibly scream and run out of the room. Instead, Haggis removed his tie, then stopped to cast a smouldering look towards Annabelle.

"Annabelle... what this woman said about you being a virgin... was it true?"

This blush nearly caused Annabelle's internal organs to shrivel and die from lack of oxygen. "Yes," she whispered, looking into her lap, where she folded her shaky hands, trying to obscure them from Haggis's penetrating stare. "I am indeed. I have been saving my... my virtue for a man like you."

Haggis started unbuttoning his shirt, which caused

Annabelle to stop breathing, then he paused again, which made her want to cry. "Wouldn't you want to get married first?"

"You don't love me," croaked Annabelle, forcefully pushing air through her strangled throat, pushing away the thought of Sister Bernadette. "What does it matter? Oh, Jiminy, I mean Angus, possess my body right here and right now, I can't take another moment of waiting!"

"Stand up," Haggis demanded, somehow managing to cram a rolling "rrrr" into those two simple words.

Annabelle followed his order, still expecting him to demand that she switches off the light and talks in a manly voice, but instead he threw the duvet off the bed, together with all the chocolate wrappers. "Come herrre, wee lassie," he growled. "I will remove your outer garments, if you insist on speaking like they do on TV. Aye, so I shall do before I impale you on my throbbing manhood..."

"It's a mangrove, please," she whispered.

Haggis turned into a statue for a moment.

"I don't think I can stand it if you talk dirty. It's too much all at once. Although..." Annabelle hesitated. Because the words "throbbing manhood" uttered in his low, nearly menacing voice were nearly as disturbingly moistening as "wee lassie".

His shirt was off and she took a sharp intake of breath, studying the perfection of his body. He still hadn't asked her to switch off the lights. His gaze wandered up and down her insufficiently curvy figure, and all of a sudden Annabelle understood. "You only like my breasts," she whispered, "because they're small."

"Annabelle, if you don't take your clothes off right now, I am not responsible for my actions. We only have forty-five minutes."

"Until...?"

"Until my secret is revealed and you leave me."

Chapter Thirteen

IF HE WAS WILLING TO REMAIN STRAIGHT FOR FORTY-FIVE minutes, thought Annabelle, ripping off her top and sending buttons into the air, she would use the opportunity to introduce his mangrove to her lady garden. She could already see the shape of his Hammaconda through his trousers, which were suddenly tighter than a minute ago, especially around his possibly already throbbing manhood... This scared her and Annabelle stood in front of him, paralysed, her hands inadvertently covering the sweet entrance into her moist garden of pleasure (to be confirmed, since as a virgin she couldn't be sure).

"Will it hurt?" she whispered modestly.

"I will be gentle," Haggis promised, but his voice carried a menacing hint of throbbingly brutal impaling he had mentioned not long ago. "Forty-three minutes."

"I... I don't remember..." she whispered, afraid of the vision of masculinity displayed in front of her eyes.

"You don't remember what?"

"How to take off my bra. You have to help me."

"Turn around," demanded Haggis and Annabelle had to listen. His muscular hands slid down her shoulders, then arms. She could feel goosebumps appear on the areas he touched.

"Mmm," he said when his hands enclosed her (maybe small, but still perky for her age) breasts. "I wonder if this is how you take it off?"

"Oh," groaned Annabelle. She could *feel* his mangrove pushing into the small of her back, even though there were still multiple layers dividing their lower parts. "Ohhh. Oh."

"I don't think so," murmured Haggis, then turned her around with a brutal, masculine tug and their lips connected, removing all further thoughts from Annabelle's mind. She could feel his experienced fingers fumble with the hooks of the bra until the hooks gave up under the attack. He tasted of woodsmoke, wilderness, and whisky, although there was a chance the whisky taste was simply still lingering in her own mouth, which he was now expertly exploring with his frisky tongue, its playful and energetic actions reminiscent of a puppy running around a newly redecorated living room...

"Do you want me to slow down?" he asked, seemingly worried, removing his mouth from hers and destroying the physical connection which Annabelle expected to last forever, or, if that was not possible, at least for forty minutes, give or take one or two.

"No," she gasped. "Do it again."

And he did, somehow managing to keep their lips glued together even when he was removing her jeans with his hands and her boots with his toes; when he lifted her into the air; when he gingerly placed her body on the bed, bending into positions she had always believed to be impossible for anybody but highly skilled circus artists. "Thirty-six," he muttered a moment before flinging his trousers away, followed by his boxers, so tight now that they must have been hurting his... his... HIS...

Annabelle did not dare to look towards his mangrove, but despite the fact that she laid flat on the bed her eyes were drawn towards the imposing appendage, too massive to be simply ignored, its shadows dancing playfully on the wall in the light of flickering candles which he must have lit when she wasn't looking. "It won't fit," she whispered, wishing that she had consumed more whisky.

"Don't worry," assured her Haggis. "I know what I am doing. And I use medium-sized condoms."

"This is... medium... sized...?"

"For Scottish standards, sassenach," he muttered and Annabelle experienced her first ever orgasm, throwing all her senses violently around the room, the pleasure like a re-enaction of the Guy Fawkes' Night inside the quiet privacy of her lady garden, every cell of her body demanding more Haggis. She was nearly crying with impatience as he fought the medium-sized foil package. Annabelle technically used a condom before, as in buying one, filling it with water under the tap and gasping at the amount of liquid that fit inside the thing before it exploded so loudly that both Kunegunda and Żaneta ran into the bathroom to check what happened to the gas boiler.

As if paralysed, Annabelle permitted his throbbing manhood to find its way to the entrance of her sweet cave of ecstatic pleasure (to be confirmed very, very soon). There would be stains, a messy thought ran through her head, before she felt his lips on one of her nipples, gently caressing it as if it were a lollipop handed to a particularly patient child. Yet the sweet cave was still only filled with gaping emptiness, which was a great metaphor for the state of her life before she met Haggis. "Hurry up," she begged, out of breath, "take my virginity, you medium-sized Scot, oh, oh, don't stop, no, I– oh, please go on, no, I– oh, oh, oh, OOOHHH!!!!!!"

"I'm sorry," said Haggis, "I am trying to be as gentle as I can..."

"Is there blood?" asked Annabelle weakly. "There always is in the movies."

"Annabelle, my love, this was my pinky."

She was so blown away by the words "my love" that she briefly blacked out. Yet despite the emotional tornado

Annabelle was caught in the physical sensations she was experiencing enforced a brisk return to reality, which was so magical it was practically a best-selling novel in the "Escapism" section of a dark, dusty bookstore; a reality where Haggis's sword was securely placed inside the sheeth of her lady garden, massaging its fleshy walls in ways that she imagined have been developed in cooperation with Marge— no, this was not the right moment to think about Margerithe du Lacq, the cold, money-grabbing bitch, not when the majestic billionaire Highlander's appendage was curiously exploring her slightly sore and definitely no longer virginal sweet cave of ecstatic decadence. "Sassenach," he muttered and Annabelle exploded in another orgasm, one that made the previous one barely a gentle tickle to her senses, all of which screamed "HALLELUJAH" in perfect unison, together with her own voice which had never risen to such volume before. Who cared about Margerithe, Seamus O'Shaughnessy, or even Haggis Angus possibly being gay when he could do *that* to her body...? ...and then he suddenly withdrew, tearing the condom off his massive trouser-or-rather-kilt-snake, cursing nastily.

"Goshdarnit! At least I'm naked," he spat. "Annabelle, this is your last chance, you have two minutes left. You can still leave before my secret is revealed to you."

"No, no," she begged, her still insufficiently explored body demanding the mountain man's return, confused by how extremely she desired an experience she had never even imagined before. Although that was a lie, since she imagined it many times, not knowing how limited her wildest dreams were. And not before she left the confines of the orphanage, of course, since it would have been inherently wrong to imagine such elaborate productions with Sister Bernadette under the same roof. "Please stay."

"I will," said Haggis darkly, opening his small suitcase and removing the black metal box. "I will, Annabelle. Please promise... promise... no. Don't make promises you can't keep. If... if you decide to leave, remember that I love you with my heart and soul." Naked, he placed the wooden bowl in a corner of the room, then squatted on it.

"Ha– Angus...?" asked Annabelle, staring at him in confusion. A moment later her scream, tuned very differently from those she emitted just before, shook the walls before she passed out, her mind refusing to accept what it was seeing, especially after having had to absorb the bodily sensations which exhausted its capacity for newness.

Chapter Fourteen

❧

"This is a dream," she repeated to herself, guzzling the little wine she did not spill after she ran to the mini-bar right after she regained consciousness. "This is a nightmare, or a dream, it doesn't matter, I will wake up in a moment."

"No," said the contents of the wooden bowl sadly. "You won't. This is what I really am, Annabelle." Its voice was repulsive, each syllable emerging in form of a squelchy gurgle.

If only Haggis was gay, thought Annabelle dizzily. She would have given anything and everything to return to the previous day and re-live it, even that awkward plane flight; she'd be willing to spend the next ten years listening to her unpleasant boss Donald; anything at all if she would have been able not to see what she was now perceiving with her own eyes, which must have been lying to her.

"What are you?" she asked weakly.

"I am a haggis," said the blobby object, then sighed. Annabelle couldn't see how it was speaking, so she took a closer look, then tried to retch discreetly before nearly biting through the glass to empty another mini-bottle. It was gin, which she despised, but right now it didn't matter. Annabelle briefly considered the option of pouring bleach into her eyes, but even when they were shut she was still seeing the haggis as clearly as if her gaze was still glued to its bulgy surface.

"I thought... haggis... was just... a fairytale to keep naughty children from straying from their healthy, plant-based diet."

"Definitely not," sighed the haggis. "This is the curse I tried to tell you about. Every night, precisely at midnight, I turn from Haggis to haggis and remain this way until six a.m. The only thing that can rescue me is the love of a woman who would accept me, all of me, even when I am like this. I can't see you, Annabelle, because most of my body parts are currently either minced or replaced with onions and toasted oats, but I can hear your voice. You are repulsed and I can't blame you."

"Why– what– how..."

"I used to be the CEO of a company which went bankrupt," haggis squelched. "I had to fire the employees one by one, I was forced to be ruthless and heartless, even though I cried into my pillow every night due to frustration and powerlessness over the brutal machinery of capitalism. A certain woman, one of the thousands who had to be let go, shed many tears, explaining that she had eight hungry children at home, that her husband was a violent junkie, and that she needed the money to leave him and start a new life at a convent that would accept someone with eight children. At this point, I must admit, I became angry. I accused her of lying. Who would have believed that? I was not even a billionaire yet, only a multi-millionaire, I couldn't afford to keep anybody on the payroll, since the company went bust. But she refused to understand the reality of the capitalist market despite my repeated explanations. 'Your name is Haggis, you merciless swine,' she said, 'and so you shall turn into haggis every night, between midnight and six a.m., until you find a woman who will love you exactly for what you are. And so will your twin brother.' Then she disappeared in a cloud of smoke. I opened the windows and the smoke...

Annabelle, the cloud of smoke took shape of a crow, which flew outside, cackling in a way that made me understand I was the victim of a witch's ancient curse. Blub."

"It's not possible," she whispered, her lips as pale as the off-white, silky bedsheets, which were most probably produced by women like her slaving over sewing machines up to twenty-two hours a day for pitiful payment, then purchased by Mr and Mrs Glitz at a place which made Harrolds look like Don Corleone's Pizzeria.

"You can touch me," sighed the haggis squelchily, "but please don't poke me. You see, I am very mortal when I am like this. Very. One bite or one poke with a fork, even a toothpick..." Its voice died out. "Annabelle, my brother's name used to be Tartan."

"The man on the photograph," she guessed flatly.

"Tartan had a girlfriend. He didn't warn her about his secret, he just slipped sleeping pills into her food to make sure she would never find out. But one night he must have forgotten and she found herself unable to sleep, a well-known side effect of using sleeping medication for a time longer than declared safe in the leaflet. She was surprised not to see my brother in bed, so she got up and wandered around, only to find a roll of tartan resting on the floor. It surprised her to see it, as you can imagine. So she decided to surprise my brother. At least I can speak, although I have to do it carefully so the filling doesn't get out. She..." The haggis blubbed in misery. "She was a tailor, very skilled and extremely fast one, so she decided to surprise my brother in the morning with a new kilt."

Annabelle swallowed loudly.

"The funeral was an extremely awkward and sad affair," continued the haggis, sobbing slightly, its greasy tears smelling of various spices she couldn't identify. Annabelle's stomach was at once demanding to be fed and to get emptied into a toilet. She was dizzy both from the drink consumed on an empty stomach — oh God, a haggis *was* a stomach — and the view, contrasting so extremely with the vision of Angus's muscular body and throbbing manhood, the memories of which were still slightly throbbing here and there, but mostly there. "Some of his body parts were found in the garbage bin, others sewn together in ways impossible to explain. The family paid a doctor willing to testify that he died of natural causes. His girlfriend was diagnosed with paranoid schizophrenia and placed in a dark asylum for the rest of her days. This was when I realised that the curse put on me was not just disgusting, but deadly. I remembered what the witch said. I had to find a woman who would love me exactly as I was. But how does a haggis find anybody who even likes it at all? I mean, have you *seen* haggis?" The dish paused. "Don't answer that."

"I'm going to be sick," croaked Annabelle, then ran out of the room and barely made it into one of the many bathrooms, but not before encountering a few more luxurious bedrooms.

Scottish to the bone, indeed, although a more precise phrase would be "Scottish to the innards"... She retched violently again, her still naked body shaking in uncontrollable spasms completely unlike those she was experiencing barely minutes, yet many ages ago. Annabelle had no clothes to put on apart from those left on the floor, on a lamp, and probably over the massive plasma TV in Haggis's... oh no, oh no, she thought, surprised to find out that there was still anything left to vomit. Angus's. Angus. His name was Angus. It was definitely not anything else.

Oh, how bitterly Annabelle regretted having found out...! She should have never pried into his privacy. She should have just married him, he could have slipped her sleeping pills... But then she would have never loved him for what he was, Annabelle realised with a sad startle. This was why and how Tartan died. He had never revealed his true self to his girlfriend, who was now going to spend the rest of her days in a dark asylum, plagued by the realisation that she had cut her beloved into pieces, sewing some of them together, only to... No, Annabelle couldn't even begin to imagine it. Things were bad enough without visualising a Frankiltstein.

Annabelle called the room service, ordered lots of tea and scrambled eggs, wrapped her nudity in a hotel gown, then waited, staring into space, until the ordered products appeared. She told the maitre d' or some other waiter to add ten pounds to their bill, then sent him away. She could still smell the admittedly mouth-watering herbal, greasy tears of Angus. The scrambled eggs threatened to leave a few times, but once she forced enough tea into her poor, suffering stomach she felt well enough to return to the room which had already generated enough memories to last her a few lifetimes.

"Angus," she said.

"Mhm."

Annabelle didn't know it was possible to belch out a sound like "mhm".

"I– I don't know what to say. I have to think. But I am not leaving."

"No?" asked the haggis tearfully.

"Please don't cry! I just ate."

"There is air conditioning in here. Just turn it up. The remote is on the side table."

"Ah," muttered Annabelle, "that's where my bra was." Once she found the right button there was no sound or even a LED light blinking to confirm that she had undertaken the correct action, but a lively cool breeze seemed to go through the room, replacing the smell of Angus's tears with the freshness of white snow and glaciers found in Scandinavian countries. "Can I ask a personal question?"

"Ask me anything."

"How did Margerithe react?"

"At first," said the haggis sepulchrally, "I slipped her sleeping pills as well, but then when Tartan... I stopped. I realised she might wake up hungry one night. I don't go cold, you know."

"Angus, I really just ate...!"

"I'm sorry. See? You will never love me as I am, sassenach."

"Angus – please. Don't. Not right now."

"I knew it," muttered the haggis. "Margerithe used the curse to blackmail me, to get more and more money. I had to buy her a superheroine role in a blockbuster movie."

"Ah! I've seen that! The one where she played a Superpanther!"

"Superlynx, yes. The movie was tanking, so I had my people buy tickets for months. I spent a small fortune, but her blackmail didn't stop there. She demanded more and more, in fact she was shameless enough to suggest or rather order me to fund a remake of *Go With The Winds* starring her as Scarlet Fever. I paid her half a billion and finally got rid of her. My heart shut down, avoiding all feelings, as I was consumed... constantly overcome by fear. You would be afraid too if you were aware that you will always turn into a... into this, that you will always be alone until you die. That you can't afford to fall asleep without locking the door, because you risk that someone might poke you with a fork."

"Oh, Angus, that is so sad."

"You know now," belched the haggis miserably. "You can blackmail me as well. You know everything, you can kill me any moment, even now. I've seen your fingernails, you wouldn't even need a fork."

I would never touch you, thought Annabelle, barely stopping herself from saying it out loud. Not even with a lot of onions, haute cuisine mashed potatoes, and the tastiest sauce, assuming haggis was served with sauce. "I won't hurt you," she promised instead, her throat constricted by tears, anger, disgust, pity.

"But you won't love me either."

"I... I don't think... Angus, I wish I could say 'maybe', but I just can't. You told me not to make promises I wouldn't be able to keep."

"Will you still want to see me in the morning...?"

The smell of his tears rose into the air again. "I have to sleep now," Annabelle croaked, then escaped the room, making sure to close the door.

Chapter Fifteen

LIKE SHE COULD POSSIBLY FALL ASLEEP, ANNABELLE THOUGHT darkly, then switched on the lights and her thoughts became a bit lighter, too. Luckily, she already got her regular eight hours during the day. It was *hours* ago, Annabelle realised with a shocked startle. Hours ago she was a girl, now she was a woman, one that was broken-hearted and changed forever, having experienced the best and the worst moments of her twenty-one years long life.

Annabelle desperately wanted to speak to someone. But what would she even say? "Hello Kunegunda, my rich fiancé is a disgusting Scottish dish, I *know*, Sheryl Fernandes-Borsini-Coll-whatever her latest husband's name is wishes!" Margerithe, she briefly thought, before disgust stronger than that she felt at the smell of Angus's tears overwhelmed her.

She lost her virginity to a stomach filled with onions and oats, and only God knew what else. It was safer not to look up recipes.

In a few hours he would probably emerge from the room, wearing his sweatpants, then run to the bathroom, probably to wash off the greasy stink. Then he would put on a suit and tie before either flying to another country or firing a few thousand people. Some of them, no doubt, mothers and fathers of multiple children, spouses of violent junkies. If only his mother had named him "Moanmoan the Samoan MacBrawn"...! It would have changed *everything*. Then again, with a cruel sense of humour like that, she could have named him "Toilet Paper Hung The Wrong Way Round"...

Annabelle briefly imagined herself killing the haggis Haggis right now, in cold blood. (Ew.) Just poke him with the silver fork she used to eat her scrambled eggs. Then she would take the platinum card. She would take out all the money from all the cash dispensers she could find before buying a ticket to somewhere luxurious, like Paris. She would be disgustingly rich and she would learn French. She would wear green velvet suits, smoke Gaeuoluises, read French poets, and never wash her hair. Like Harlot Groinsburg, who was a famous French movie star *and* a pop star *and* also the daughter of Louis de Funnies.

But Annabelle wasn't the killing type. Or the blackmailing type, for that matter. Or a thief.

She didn't even know which country all her expensive clothes currently resided in, except for the boots. Which were in the same room as Angus. If she wanted to escape, she had to go back there and pick them up... Or she could call the room service. According to movies, it was possible at places like Glitz Hotel to order a full wardrobe to be delivered over within five minutes.

"Jeans," she said to the surprised person on the other side of the line. "A top. Something elegant. Ish. What size? Oh, uh, er, four. I mean, six. Okay, eight. You know, just get me a white t-shirt, size M. And a bra..." Annabelle hesitated. Bra sizes were tricky, no matter what your credit card was made of. "No, I don't need a bra. Underwear, though... no, skip that too, just get me jeans and a t-shirt really fast. And..." She sniffled at the thought of the boots, before her eyes landed on her lucky shoes, their heels so high they could have been used for pole dancing by vertically challenged people. "And that's it."

Time passed slowly as Annabelle waited, more and more impatient, her skin unattractively covered in goosebumps and cold sweat. She would have sworn that most of the time time passed much faster. Especially when she pressed "snooze" on her alarm clock. As long as she would be able to leave before six, she was safe, if disgusted and broken-hearted by her dishy Scot's secret.

Maybe she could convince the girls to take her back into the apartment at Brownhole Street. She would beg her unpleasant Donald to take her back as well, so she could work at Cafe Du Amour again... The thought alone made her skin crawl, which was a very unpleasant feeling. But Donald's advances, if sexual harassment could have been rephrased this way, were preferable to marrying a talking haggis.

At least she was not a virgin anymore, Annabelle thought miserably just in time for the maitre d' or some other waiter to deliver the jeans and a t-shirt so white it put the lights in the room to shame.

Annabelle left the suite as quietly as possible whilst wearing very high heels.

Chapter Sixteen

ANNABELLE REGRETTED HER CHOICE BEFORE THE BUTLER OR some other doorman even said "goodbye" to her. His tone indicated he was taking her for a prostitute of ill repute. And perhaps in a way she was one, her lady garden still pulsating in a way she had never experienced before, not even during the special time of the month.

"A pair of jeans," said Annabelle darkly to a lamp post, "and a t-shirt. I'm cheap."

The lamp post didn't answer, which was reassuring to someone who had recently undergone a difficult conversation with a traditional Scottish dish.

Brenda. She needed Brenda, the sweet no-nonsense cook from Cafe Du Amour. Brenda was a skilled chef who once almost passed the eliminations for Mastercook North-Eastern Britain. She probably knew what to do with haggis... yeah. How to prepare and serve it to an unsuspecting victim.

Annabelle sat on the pavement and burst into tears. She had never felt so alone and hurt before, but the tears were for poor Haggis and Tartan, especially the latter, cursed for something he had nothing to do with, cut and sown into a kilt by a well-meaning girlfriend, who might have even loved him to some degree, despite her accidental cruelty, which she was now paying for, locked at a dark asylum. But Annabelle's tears dried out all of a sudden when she remembered Margerithe Du Lacq playing Superlynx. The worst was that Annabelle enjoyed the movie.

Poor Angus, she thought. It wasn't his fault that he had to fire all those people. It was his job, which he hated. That witch was just evil for no reason. Annabelle didn't believe for a second that there were eight children and a junkie husband involved. If she was a real witch, and she clearly was one, she could have just either magicked a few million quid or blackmailed Angus, like any reasonable person would have done. But then... would he have believed her? It was a rhetorical question. Nobody would have believed something so outrageous. Her evil was so great it led to poor Tartan's death already, no doubt as a warning to Angus.

Annabelle got up and continued her walk of shame for approximately eleven steps before gasping in horror. She had forgotten her handbag. She had literally nothing right now except the jeans, shoes, and the t-shirt that she was wearing. No passport, not a penny, no burgundy lipstick, not even a tissue to dab at her luckily eyeliner-smudge free tears. She had to go back to the hotel and face Angus again. Sniffling, she turned back, nearly breaking a heel of one of her lucky shoes, which was the best indicator of the fact that she had made a horrible mistake.

"I am staying with Mr MacBrawn," she was soon repeating for the fourth time to the completely uninterested night porter. "No, I don't know the room number, but surely you've seen me walking out? I just went for a short walk, to get some air."

"Miss," said the porter, "I understood you the first, second, and third time. I've called his room three times, but he is not picking up. You don't have any form of identification. I can't just let you in."

"I don't have any form, because my handbag is in the room!"

"I'm very sorry, miss."

"He will be very angry," threatened Annabelle without much conviction. If Angus would be angry with someone, it would be her.

"I'm very sorry," repeated the porter. "I understand your situation, but unless Mr MacBrawn picks up the phone, there is nothing I can do. You don't even remember the room number, Miss."

"I am not a hooker!"

"Nobody said you were, Miss."

Annabelle left the hotel defeated, crying, but nevertheless unable to feel the full extent of her sadness as long as she had no eyeliner on for that fashionable raccoon look as seen on TV. She knew her face was puffy, though, which was not something recommended by TV. She *also* knew that if she were to go back to Brownhole Street and tell the girls that her rich boyfriend dumped her, they would let her kip on the sofa. At least. Maybe. But she couldn't face them, not after she told them to throw away all her belongings, giving them all her money but twenty pounds, which were currently located in the pocket of her other jeans, strewn carelessly on Angus's bedroom floor or on top of the plasma TV.

"I'm stupid," she said to herself excitedly, suddenly and conveniently recalling that Brenda lived nearby, at the exact spot where the surroundings changed from Practically The Inside Of The Glitz Hotel Itself into A Dumpster Fire. This wasn't Brenda's exact address, but Annabelle visited her once and remembered herself chuckling at the fact that Brenda's surname was Frasier.

Chapter Seventeen

"Darling," said Brenda, opening the door, "this is a bit of a surprise."

"All I need is to kip on your sofa," sighed Annabelle. "I haven't planned for my boyfriend to– for me to leave."

"Oh no!" gasped Brenda, shocked, raising her hand to cover her full lips. "Did he hurt you?"

"In a way," said Annabelle reluctantly. "Let's talk about it in the morning."

"I work in the morning."

"Can I come along?"

Brenda stared at her impenetrably for a moment. "Of course you can," she finally permitted. "I'm going back to bed. Right now I'm not even sure if you're real or a dream."

Annabelle, who was absolutely certain she would never sleep again, closed her eyes for just a moment before Brenda shook her shoulder, announcing it was time. It had never occurred to Annabelle that Brenda started so early. The coffee and bagels and, for certain clients, cheap beer which Annabelle served starting at nine had to be prepared in advance. Except the beer, obviously. Reheating coffee in a microwave was only possible when the coffee was already waiting. The burgers, as Annabelle soon found out, had to be bought at the Russian/Hungarian/Communist store on the corner, which apparently always had some leftover food which they either forgot to refrigerate or changed the expiry date twice and didn't dare to do it again. The bagels, which would soon be placed under a heating lamp, came from a baker who was pleased not to have to throw them away in the evening, but instead – as Brenda briefly explained – offer them to an orphanage.

"Wow," breathed Annabelle, impressed, when she found out that the freshly pressed orange juice she so proudly served consisted of own-brand syrup, water, and discarded silicone implants expertly ground by Brenda to create the illusion of orange chunks floating in the liquid.

"Yes," said her friend huffily. "All this must be ready before anybody else comes in. Can you imagine what the Health Inspectorate would say? Oh, Annabelle, you are so naive. You should watch the news sometimes, not just *Outofhander*. We are simply preparing for the inevitable financial crisis in advance."

"I watch the news! I even read *Financial Daily*!" Annabelle quickly crossed her fingers behind her back.

"Oh, do you? Who is the prime minister?"

Annabelle swallowed. "Some bloke or other, I don't pay attention to politics, I am *vegan*, Brenda."

"That's new. No breakfast for you, then. The only vegan food I have are the silicone implants."

"Ugh! No, thanks. I am politically vegan, Bren. Please give me a burger."

"What exactly happened?" asked Brenda, scraping the green parts off before throwing the burger into the deep fryer.

"I, ah, found out that my boyfriend had a secret," said Annabelle, then strategically filled her mouth with a stale bagel. What was she supposed to say? "He is gay," she finally decided.

"Don't you say! I would have never guessed that MacBrawn was gay! Ruthless, nasty, cruel – yes. Gay, though? I didn't get the vibe..."

"Nasty? Cruel? Why would you say that?"

"Annabelle, I thought you were his secretary."

"Uh," mumbled Annabelle, her mouth full of stale bread, then refused Brenda's offer of freshly squeezed orange juice. "Sometimes. Why?"

"MacBrawn's job is to merge companies," explained Brenda. "Bugger, I forgot to add food colouring to the juice..."

"Ah, yes, the mergers. Been there," said Annabelle in a tone suggesting that she was practically a financial mogul herself.

"Do you know what it means?"

"That they make more money, Bren. I can't believe you have to ask me that."

"And how do they make more money?"

"Um... because of being merged?" tried Annabelle.

Brenda put away the plastic pot which apparently contained food colouring, then took a critical look at the orange juice before deciding it was suitable to be served to customers. "He takes two companies, each of which employs, say, five thousand people, then turns them into one company, which employs six thousand. Where do you think four thousand people go? They go on the dole, Annabelle. Whether they have children, mortgages, loans, they go on the dole. And your ex-boyfriend takes all the money the company would have saved."

"He used to do it, Bren, but he got punished for it. You must believe me, he is a good man."

"Not good enough not to try and hide his sexual orientation from you," huffed Brenda, topping up vodka bottles with tap water. "I wish him all the worst, to be honest. Almost forgot! Your burger is ready."

If only you knew, thought Annabelle darkly. "I lost my appetite. What time does our unpleasant boss Donald actually arrive?"

"Oh," said Brenda, somewhat sheepishly. "He doesn't."

"He doesn't? Why, is he sick?"

Brenda chuckled, then coughed, which was due to the fact

that she smoked cigarettes. "That's one way of looking at it. He's been arrested. Imagine! Your ex-boyfriend was taking the piss when he was talking about merging rugby teams, but it was true about Donald! He did call the police! And Donald *was* a money launderer, drug dealer, and a runner of sex trafficking circle!"

Annabelle gasped. She should have guessed. After all, he was smoking cigars.

"Ding dong, Donald is gone," sang Brenda. "Looking at twenty-five years, I think. Which will be shortened to twelve, then they will let him out with a bracelet on his ankle and tell him not to leave the European Union as long as we all haven't left it, but still, this place is now mine. Ish. I don't own it, but I keep it running and financially safe and sound." She patted an extra silicone implant pointedly.

"Brenda! That's fabulous news! Uh... Do you happen to need a waitress?"

"Why," laughed Brenda heartily, "I do! Especially since Esmeralda gave birth. And since Seamus O'Shaughnessy keeps asking for you."

Annabelle would have dropped something if her hands weren't empty. What a wasted opportunity. "Seamus? The Seamus?"

"Yes, your future husband Seamus, once he divorces Geraldine. He seems to be quite upset by your absence, actually. Not that I know why, but he keeps asking about the virgin girl..." Brenda chuckled.

"Well," said Annabelle coldly, "he needs to look elsewhere, because I am no longer a virgin."

"Annabelle! You don't say! Actually, I don't know why I'm surprised, I'd have slept with this chunk o'hunk in a minute!"

"With Haggis MacBrawn? Didn't you say he was a monster?"

"Oh, darling, he may be a monster, but those arms! This chest! It's not like I would be marrying him. Is he hung?"

"Brenda!!!"

"I'm very sorry, my apologies, so is he?"

"Maybe," admitted Annabelle. "Is there a cream for blushing?"

"A cream... what do you mean, maybe? You're not sure? Is it because he's gay and couldn't get it up?"

"He says he's medium," answered Annabelle, choosing to ignore her friend's tasteless remark.

"Aha," said Brenda, disappointed.

"For Scottish standards."

"Aha," said Brenda, less disappointed. "What does that mean?"

"Let's put it this way," said Annabelle, blushing modestly and looking down at her unfinished breakfast. "If it's true that they were nothing underneath their kilts, he would need a very long kilt."

"Annabelle...!"

"I can't help it, Bren."

"If he wasn't gay I could eat him," said Brenda dreamily and Annabelle lifted a fork just in time to drop it.

Chapter Eighteen

The day was boring, which was pleasant. Annabelle has had enough surprises for a while and she was enjoying serving coffee to older couples and morning beers to younger couples. Her mind, however, was occupied by both Haggis being a haggis and Seamus O'Shaughnessy asking about her. She had asked Brenda four times and every time her friend confirmed that Seamus came over every afternoon.

"No, sir," Annabelle said politely, "we don't have whisky and soda." They did, but not for Mr Toodeloo, who came over every single day, demanded the same every single day, and every new waitress's training involved being informed very strictly not to give him one.

"Bitch!"

"Thank you, sir. Is there anything else I can give you?"

"There is," said Mr Toodeloo, staring at Annabelle's breasts, even though she did not pad them with tissues. "But I don't think I can afford it, you sexy minx." He sighed. "What time do you leave work, love?"

Annabelle couldn't resist the chuckle. She could recite the conversation from memory. Mr Toodeloo suffered either from dementia or Alzheimer's — she didn't know which one was which – and he was cute in a disgusting sort of way. "Very late, sir."

"What a shame. Then I might have to say 'toodeloo' before you go, sweetheart. Can you get me a..."

"Yes," said Annabelle automatically, straightening up. Her eyes were glued to the man who stood in the door and his face changed the moment he saw her.

The Seamus O'Shaughnessy. If there was ever a "chunk of hunk", it was Annabelle's future husband Seamus. Compared to him, Haggis was a stick insect. "Sea– Mr O'Shaughnessy," she exclaimed excitedly, then berated herself for doing so.

"Miss," he said solemnly, bowing.

"Excuse me?" boomed Mr Toodeloo. "You are taking my order, bitch!"

Seamus's handsome face darkened and he was already on his way to, most probably, tackle Mr Toodeloo in a rugby manner, when Annabelle placed herself between the two. "Sea– Mr O'Shaughnessy, please allow me. You have already ordered, Mr Tood– sir."

"Have I? Oh. What have I ordered?"

"A coffee, black. And a burger, your favourite, together with one of our f-fresh... fresh bagels with cream cheese." Oh God, thought Annabelle. She had no idea where the cream cheese came from, but immediately resolved to become allergic to dairy.

"That's right," mused Mr Toodeloo. "My favourite. Ho-hum. Thank you, sweetheart."

"Coming right up," announced Annabelle, sensing the warmth of Seamus's muscled body despite spatial distance between them. He noticed her. Even if he was married... and a bit rude, which could have been attributed to drink and the company he was forced to keep due to his job... Perhaps he and Geraldine had an understanding. Or perhaps he just wanted to laugh at her again. But he looked very serious. Oh, thought

Annabelle, her face dropping. He probably just wanted to say sorry.

"Can I talk to you for a minute?" asked Seamus O'Shaughnessy, all seven feet and four inches of him appearing in front of her so suddenly Annabelle's face nearly bumped into his navel.

"Ah, oh, I, yes, of course, be right back, just getting Mr Toodeloo's burger."

"Mr Toodeloo...?" asked Seamus O'Shaughnessy, visibly confused, but Annabelle was already running as fast as she could in her lucky shoes, their heels so high they were sometimes mistaken for street lamps.

"Brenda!" she hissed, even though the name "Brenda" did not contain any hissing consonants. "Seamus is here!"

"Yeah, saw him. So?"

"And a burger for Mr Toodeloo, his favourite with the cream cheese, on the bagel, not on the burger, please don't tell me where you get it from, the cream cheese, I mean," babbled Annabelle. Seamus, Seamus, number two on her list of potential future husbands now that Haggis's cursed existence provided a new opening.

"What do you mean? I get it from the shop. Where else would I get it?"

"Don't tell me the sell-by date. Seamus..."

"It's perfectly fine, Annabelle, you can look in the fridge. Do you think I am some sort of monster?"

At the very thought of seeing what else was in the fridge Annabelle shivered impatiently. "Seamus wants to talk to me for a minute!"

"Oh God, Annabelle. Go and talk to him for a minute then."

"But I am not wearing any make-up...!"

"Darling, he is a *man*. They don't notice this sort of thing. Maybe run to the bathroom and put some tissues in your bra, though?"

"Ha ha," hissed Annabelle, then returned to Seamus, who was deep in conversation with Mr Toodeloo.

"This young man here tells me he plays rugby," announced Mr Toodeloo excitedly. "I told him that if he's lucky and works hard, he might get places one day."

"That's right," confirmed Seamus. "Thank you, Mr Toodeloo, I am delighted to get your advice."

Annabelle opened her mouth, but no sound came out.

"You are welcome, Mr Whatsit," answered Mr Toodeloo without a blink. "Now, off you go to talk to your wife."

"Off I go," nodded Seamus, took Annabelle's arm without asking her permission, and led her into the farthest corner of the cafe. Despite the masculinity which was practically dripping from Seamus, Annabelle could only think about the fact that this corner was where she first saw Haggis.

"M– Mr O'Sha..."

"Call me Seamus. May I ask what your name is?"

"Annabelle," managed Annabelle.

"Let me be clear, Annabelle," said Seamus without unnecessary hesitation. "I would like to ask you out."

"But Mr O'Shaughnessy! You are married to Geraldine O'Shaughnessy!"

Seamus winked. "She doesn't need to know. What you don't know can't hurt you, eh? We all have secrets."

Annabelle shivered. She had asked – repeatedly – about Haggis's secret and now she wished she hadn't. Maybe Seamus was right. "Secrets," she said darkly.

"Come on," said Seamus, smiling, his handsome eyes metaphorically shooting through her skin with laser beams of desire. "Just one little dinner at a little place. One which isn't this dump. What do you say?"

"Why do you even come here?"

"Because you work here, duh."

"Shouldn't you be away in... I don't know, wherever you play rugby?"

"The season ended. We won the Cup. I'm having a break."

More ashamed of her lack of knowledge of rugby than of her lack of knowledge regarding the current prime minister Annabelle agreed, handed Seamus her phone number, forgetting that her phone was currently in Haggis's possession, then made up for her mistake by accidentally revealing that she would be free this very evening.

"Then I don't need to call," said Seamus, masculinely crumpling the paper and throwing it on the floor. "I'll pick you up at seven o'clock," he added, then tickled her chin. "I'll be here, princess. Toodeloo!"

"Too– bye, Mr O'Shaughnessy."

"It's Seamus for you. Or 'daddy', if you prefer. Bye, Annabelle."

Chapter Nineteen

❦

SEAMUS O'SHAUGHNESSY WAS PAINFULLY PUNCTUAL. UNLIKE Annabelle, who spent the last two hours in the ladies' powder room putting on Brenda's make-up, furiously rubbing it off her face, trying to do something with her hair, deciding to add some more make-up, sticking tissues in her bra, then removing them just in case Seamus would like to take a look at the aforementioned garment. Not that she intended to let him see anything on the first date, of course, but he was a (very) big strong man and could easily overpower her.

"You just lost your virginity," Annabelle berated her reflection, which didn't even have enough self-respect to look guilty. In fact, her reflection looked radiant and way more excited than she had the right to be, considering the fact that her virginity was taken by a traditional Scottish dish only last night. "You slut," chuckled Annabelle, then blushed furiously. She was, after all, raised by nuns at an orphanage where "my bum is itchy" was enough of a reason to be deprived of dinner (celery sticks and water) for three months. "You woman of ill repute," she corrected herself, but still couldn't stop beaming.

Seamus O'Shaughnessy. Asking her, Annabelle Elle Ellendeling on a *date*. A secret date, but still...

To her slight disappointment, he took her to a pizzeria behind the corner. True, he promised a little dinner at a little place, and Don Corleone's pizzeria definitely satisfied the latter requirement, but there was very little romance to be had over garlic sauce and pepperoni slices. And *pineapple*, thought Annabelle darkly, watching the monstrous concoction on his plate. He was one of *those*. Pineapple must have been good for rugby, she reassured herself solemnly.

"So," he said cheerfully. "Annabella."

"Annabelle."

"Can I just call you Anna? It's shorter."

"Of course, Seamus." She couldn't help but wonder whether Geraldine referred to him as "Seamus" or "daddy". Or just as "ravish me, you big and strong Irishman"?

"I've got a hotel room," he murmured seductively. "It's waiting for you."

"What?!"

"Just in case you wanted a glass of wine in a nice company."

"A glass of wine," said Annabelle flatly, understanding the badly hidden meaning behind those words. Seamus imagined that he could buy her with pizza, get her drunk, then use her body in all ways imaginable. He was, of course, right, and could have skipped the pizza. After all, he was Annabelle's future husband, even if he was cheating on his wife.

Angus would never cheat on his wife, a thought appeared, and Annabelle had to pick a piece of pineapple flirtingly from Seamus's pizza to focus on him again.

"Do you work out a lot?" she piped.

"Six times a day," said Seamus proudly. "I mean, a week, but it feels like six times a day. I'd love to relax. Mmm. With a little massage, maybe. Do you know how to massage a man like me?"

"I– I can't, I don't, I mean."

"I'll tutor you, sweet innocent Anna."

Sister Mary appeared in sweet innocent Annabelle's head. What would sister Mary have had to say about this situation?

"Ride 'im," that's what. Sister Mary's collection of Marlon Brando photographs and movies could put a Marlon Brando museum to shame. As for Sister Bernadette, she was fortunately dead and couldn't comment on Annabelle's sexual escapades involving married rugby players.

"I'd love that," she grinned, then ate a slice of pepperoni before pushing the plate away. Seamus was all too happy to finish her meal, his manly jaws crushing the crust (and pineapple) and making Annabelle shiver with anticipation.

Chapter Twenty

❧

It was all wrong.

Seamus lifted her in his arms, which were so muscular even his muscles had muscles, pinned her against the door of the elevator, then kissed her so greedily Annabelle had a feeling he was trying to suck out any bits of pepperoni that could have embedded themselves between her teeth. This was not how Angus kissed her, but Angus was past now.

The hunky Irishman threw her on the bed, his eyes burning with fierce fire of desire, and his clothes were off before she had a chance to say "ouch". There was a lot of Seamus, but not where Brenda would have checked first. In Scottish terms he was most probably somewhere around size zero.

"Grrrr," he actually said and Annabelle had to bite her lip not to burst out laughing. "Oooh, I like it when you bite your lip," Seamus growled and Annabelle immediately stopped. "Let's see you naked, shall we?"

"Seamus..."

"Come on. Take your clothes off. Ah! Forgot, you're a virgin. I'll help you."

"No, I mean..."

"Shoes," he said, and her lucky shoes hit a wall. Annabelle

gasped in shock. Those heels were not made of iron and for obvious reasons she only had one pair of lucky shoes, as luck didn't come at 85% discount every day. "Stockings. No stockings? Oh well. Saves me time. Feck me gently with a chainsaw! I didn't think you're the type to go commando!"

"To be honest," said weakly Annabelle, covering her lady garden with her hands, "I didn't either."

"Roar. No bra either?"

"No."

"Oh boy. Oh girl. Are you sure you're a virgin? Because..."

"No, Seamus, I'm not a virgin."

She hadn't expected the change. His facial expression ran a quick slalom between handsomeness, desire, surprise, shock, then... anger. "You're leading me on."

"No, I am not. Just because Brenda said..."

"Get out of here, slut!"

"Wha– but Seamus!"

"Don't you 'but Seamus' me, slut. The bet is off."

"The bet?"

"Oh yeah. Why do you think I would even bother to look at you twice? Get dressed, I'm going home to my dumb wife. I had a bet with Rob Stallion that I would seduce the virgin within an hour, including dinner. I would have won a crate of beer, I still had ten minutes! You just want to sleep with a famous sportsman, that's all you sluts want."

"Seamus," said Annabelle huffily, pulling on her jeans, "first of all, do not use the s-word in my presence, since I have been raised by nuns at a very respected orphanage. Second, you're hardly a famous sportsman just because you and your disgusting friends won the Southern Eastern Anglia Cup For Men Aged Between 30 And 32."

"Bitch!"

"I hear this all the time from Mr Toodeloo," said Annabelle, her hand already on the door knob, very far from a shrunken, wrinkly knob of Seamus O'Shaughnessy, "but at least he's cute.

You use too many steroids, Seamus. Remember Haggis MacBrawn? Now *that's* a real man. You..." She paused, then chuckled quietly. "Oh, Brenda will love this. Everyone will know by tomorrow."

Seamus was still trying to come up with a semi-coherent answer when Annabelle slammed the door behind her, then ran down the stairs, holding her shoes in her hand, tears flowing down her face. For all her fake bravado she could only think about one thing. Or rather person. And a traditional Scottish dish. She had to go back to Cafe Du Amour and wait there. If there was one thing she knew about Haggis, it was his chivalry. He would be back to bring her belongings and Annabelle would be there, even if it meant working sixteen hour days and sleeping on the dirty floor.

Chapter Twenty-One

Two weeks later Annabelle's certainty that she would see Haggis very soon began to melt. Perhaps she misjudged MacBrawn's pride.

Her thoughts returned to the conversation which took place two weeks earlier. Once Brenda stopped laughing at Annabelle's poetic description of Seamus O'Shaughnessy's wrinkly Irish appendage, she returned to her gloomy stories about what a monster Haggis was.

"He helped me," protested Annabelle.

"Then he threw you out."

"I left him."

"Sure you did."

"I did too! Why would I lie about that?"

"Was he even smaller than Seamus 'Not A Tripod After All' O'Shaughnessy?"

"N-no. He was... different," said Annabelle weakly.

"Ah!" exclaimed Brenda. "Forgot he was a homo. Girl, you don't have much luck with men, do you? I should introduce you to someone."

"Bren, last time you introduced me to someone it was Mr Toodeloo."

"I would not introduce you in *that* way, silly. A cop? A soldier? A fireman? Maybe not a stripper, let's wait with that. Irish, Scottish, Aussie? Bearded, shaven, a hipster? Black, white, Latino, Asian?"

"Bren," said Annabelle after a pause, "you are kidding, I hope?"

"Nah, had them all, but I get bored easily."

"Uh... how easily?"

"Sometimes during," sighed Brenda. "I would become a lesbian, but I like cock too much. I'm sorry. Mangrove. That's the word, isn't it. I love me some good, well-kept mangrove."

"That's enough," huffed Annabelle. "I'm going to mop the floor."

Maybe she, too, could become lesbian, Annabelle mused. Like kb long and Helen DeGenerous. They were rather glamorous, although obviously not as much as Sheryl Fernandes-Borsini-Coll-whatever her latest husband's name was, but there was very little chance of Annabelle performing lesbian activities with Sheryl Fernandes-Borsini-Coll-whatever her latest husband's name was... Annabelle sighed melancholically and rested on the mop. She wished she had never left Haggis, even when he was a haggis. During, as Brenda would have no doubt phrased it.

"I love him," she told the mop.

"What?" asked Brenda.

"Nothing," muttered Annabelle wistfully, raising her longing gaze towards the door, wishing that Haggis would kick it in, run inside, take her into his arms, then declare her to be the love of her life. No such thing happened, of course. It was Annabelle's own fault, since it was she who had left him. Haggis was not like Seamus. He wouldn't chase her against, as he no doubt imagined, her will. He was probably in Vienna or Paris or some other Denmark by now, merging ruthlessly and firing thousands of people. Possibly some of them were even witches. And since she was still missing her phone, she couldn't even call him, not to mention that the only thing she knew regarding his phone number was that it displayed as "unknown".

"Bren," said Annabelle. "Have you ever met a witch?"

"Oh," said Brenda, "many times. Remember Kylie?"

"No, not a witch as in stealing your boyfriend, one that does... magic."

"Annabelle, magic doesn't exist. Stop stealing whisky when you think I'm not looking."

"I don't steal it! I just borrow some every now and then."

"Will you return it then?"

"Brenda," said Annabelle in a deadly serious tone, "I *could* return it even now, but you will clean that up."

"Annabelle! Where have you learned language like that?"

"I haven't used any dirty word."

"Fair enough," admitted Brenda. "No, I haven't met a magical witch. Why, do you need her to cast a spell on Seamus?"

"There's no need. Once you've seen the little Seamus... there is really nothing worse a witch could do to him." If only his name was, say, "Poop" or "Pineapple On Pizza", added Annabelle, but only in her thoughts. "Just make sure everybody finds out."

"Oh," said Brenda dreamily, "that's going well, Annabelle. I told The Babes, but made sure they knew it was a secret and they could never, ever tell anybody."

"Great," enthused Annabelle, who knew eThe Babes, also known as Brenda's flatmates, wouldn't stop until even Mr Toodeloo and *Daily Daily* knew about the very little Seamus. "I forgot what we were talking about."

"You were asking me whether I met a witch and I said no. But now that I think about it... My mummy was a bit – ahem – unusual, although not as much as our daddy, who was a violent junkie before he overdosed and was found in a dark alley with a syringe sticking out of his arm, exactly one day after we last saw mummy. Almost as if she could have predicted that."

Annabelle froze.

"Mummy kept talking about revenge over Haggis MacBrawn," continued Brenda. "The monster, she called him, then cackled in evil laughter. Me and Brendan, Brandon, Bran, Bronn, Brandy, Brendoline, and Gertie were quite shocked. She truly hated MacBrawn more than anything and anybody on Earth. But then, imagine that, mummy just disappeared."

"In a cloud of smoke," whispered Annabelle.

"She smoked a lot," agreed Brenda. "But ultimately we were scr– in a bad place, because she told us she had life insurance and we should cash it once she kicked the bucket. She also bought life insurance for daddy. Except the insurance people said – no body, no money. And obviously daddy's death was not the sort that can be insured. Which is why I work at this dump and feel compulsive need to save as much money as possible. Haggis MacBrawn was the last person who saw mummy, but he told the police she left his office and hasn't returned. There was an investigation against him, actually. But they found nothing." Brenda shrugged. "You try to arrest a billionaire, although he was only a multi-millionaire, and charge him with murder of an old woman whose body was never found."

"Do you think he really...?"

"No, Annabelle, if Haggis MacBrawn tried to lay as much as a fingertip on Mummy *he* would have disappeared in a cloud of smoke. She was not somebody you'd want to mess with. Her only fault was loving daddy. And the cackling. Anyway, she's gone, I have to make freshly squeezed orange juice out of discarded silicone implants, and MacBrawn is a monster."

"You never said anything."

"When was I supposed to say anything? He came by, took you away on his metaphorical white horse, then disappeared. But then, he also got rid of our unpleasant boss Donald, which I can't complain about." Brenda shrugged. "To tell you the truth, apart from the money problem we weren't that upset about our mummy's disappearance. We were concerned about her mental health after she poisoned the neighbours' dogs, because they kept scaring Satan and Lucifer, our sweet kittens. Anyway! Those times lie in the past now. Want to have a little drinky? It's on the house."

"Gladly," said Annabelle.

"Once you finished mopping the floor," added Brenda professionally and they both guffawed heartily. Brenda was very hilarious.

Chapter Twenty-Two

※

ANNABELLE SPENT HER DAYS IN A HAZE, WISHING SHE COULD forget Haggis Angus MacBrawn. It was difficult. Not just because she dreamt about him every night. Sometimes even about his human form. Mostly because of the paparazzi pictures of Haggis and Margrethe du Lacq appearing on the front pages again. She was apparently going to feature in a new superhero movie, where she would reprise her role of Superlynx. The movie would be financed by a mysterious, private investor. But even *Daily Daily* wasn't stupid enough not to guess the identity of the investor. Annabelle knew what that meant. The bitch – she didn't even scold herself for thinking such a dirty word – was blackmailing Angus again.

One night Bren went out, returned home with two bodybuilders. They said hello, then promptly disappeared in Brenda's bedroom. After a few hours of very noisy physical activities Brenda shook Annabelle's shoulder to announce she was bored and ask whether Annabelle would like to switch places. She took celibacy vows, answered Annabelle. Brenda was very convincing, though. Unfortunately ten minutes later, for this was how long it took Annabelle to decide that she could restart her celibacy vows tomorrow, they discovered that the bodybuilders got so deep into conversation about various protein powders and the difference between creatine and creatinine that they haven't actually noticed Brenda's departure. The next morning Annabelle asked whether she would be permitted to sleep in the cafe for security reasons and Brenda didn't seem too upset by the request. Annabelle's new bedroom was Donald's old office, still stinking of cigars, but at least free from bodybuilders, rugby players, firemen, cops, soldiers, heavyweight boxers, and for some inexplicable reason the elderly TV presenter, John "Johnny" Walker.

"Young men have stamina," explained Brenda when Annabelle gathered enough courage to ask.

"I'm asking about Mr Walker. Who will need a walker quite soon."

"Now," said Brenda dreamily, ignoring the insult aimed at her elderly lover, her eyes slightly blurring, which was very unsettling considering that the pupils were black and the irises blue, "older men have technique, patience, and difficulties finishing, if you know what I mean."

Annabelle blushed so furiously that her burgundy lipstick became the only lighter spot on her face.

"So they take forever," purred Brenda, unconsciously touching her long, blonde hair. "Long enough. And then long enough again. And then..."

"Yes," interrupted Annabelle in panic, "I get it, thank you, no more information necessary."

"How old was your gay boyfriend?"

"Angus? Uh, I actually don't know. I never asked. Very old, though, at least thirty-five."

"You keep calling him Angus. Why? His name is Haggis. It's not a nickname, his name *really* is Haggis."

"Uh," answered Annabelle. "Would you want people to call you 'Haggis'?"

"God forbid! It's bad enough that my name is Brenda Joan Spares. Almost, but not quite, like Britney. OMG!"

"What, what's going on? Is Mr Toodeloo...?"

"It's him," hissed Brenda dramatically. "Don't look!"

So encouraged, Annabelle immediately looked, then gracefully passed out, just slowly enough for Haggis to grab her in his muscular arms and stop her head from hitting the floor.

"Leave her alone, you gay homosexual!" heard Annabelle and her consciousness immediately returned.

"I don't know what your problem is, female woman of the opposite sex, but if there is one thing I'm not..."

"Stop fighting," said Annabelle weakly and blinked a few times in a manner that she hoped conveyed her powerlessness against Haggis's powers of seduction. Then she blinked again, in surprise. He looked thinner, his face covered with thin stubble, yet the electricity between them was just as chemical as always. Even though he looked resigned and was dating, if that was the correct way to phrase it, Margerithe du Lacq.

"Annabelle," he whispered.

"Angus."

"Sweet, innocent Annabelle."

"My dear Angus."

"Oh, for Christ's sake," snapped Brenda. "I'm going for a smoke. You have five minutes."

"I couldn't go on knowing how you must have felt," confessed Haggis.

"Oh, no! It's my fault, my Angus."

"I had to come back."

"I am so glad you did, my Angus."

"After all, you couldn't just go on without your passport," he continued miserably. "And phone. And the boots. I gathered everything you bought and brought it here, or rather Gunther brought it here. It's all still in the limousine. We went to Brownhole Street, but apparently you don't live there..."

"Hold on a second, Haggis Angus MacBrawn!" said Annabelle in a completely not fainty way, channeling the tone of Sister Bernadette's response to Annabelle's childish question regarding the meaning of the word "fanny". Haggis Angus would not be getting dinner that evening. "My passport? My boots? Is that why you came here?"

"Why else...? I didn't really want to disturb you, I respect your choice, but... but... I am a horrible liar, Annabelle. All I wanted was to see you just one more time. I did not expect to be as lucky as I am, holding you in my arms. Thank you for passing out."

"You're welcome, you..." Annabelle closed her eyes and inhaled before saying the bad word. "You big silly. I love you, Angus, exactly as you are, in any shape or form. I would be more than happy to marry you. That is, assuming you are still interested. I know you now, although I had to leave you in order to really get to know you. I was stupid. I regretted it before the door even shut, but they wouldn't let me back in."

Haggis nodded. "You wanted your handbag."

"I wanted *you*, you big silly!" Phew, she thought, relaxing a bit. It was easier the second time. Then she saddened. "My apologies, I forgot that you were back with Margrethe du Lacq."

"Sarah."

"I beg your pardon?"

"Sarah Lackey, her name is Sarah Lackey, Annabelle. She comes from Northampton. Her father is a plumber, which is how they could have afforded Sarah's expensive education, and her mother is a cat lady. Do you think you would be able to stand without my help now? My arms are about to fall off."

"That would be a shame," muttered Annabelle, composing herself, "because they're very nice arms. Why are you with that wi— woman?"

"The usual," sighed Haggis. "She wants more money. If she

doesn't get it, she will reveal my secret, but not just to anybody. Her cruelty knows no bounds. She will call the room service at Glitz Hotel and tell them to remove the food rotting in the second master bedroom from the right. What do you think they will do if they find screaming haggis? If they just throw me in the garbage, I will be a very lucky man, sassenach. A very lucky traditional Scottish dish, I mean."

"A man," said Annabelle with determination. "Forever. Because I love you with all my heart and all my soul. And my body."

"And your lady garden?"

"And my– my lady garden too," she admitted, blushing. "Therefore, you are saved from fate worse than Margrethe's poisonous embraces. You will not turn into haggis ever again. I will marry you. I can't wait."

"Will you?" cried Haggis. "Will you, my sweet Annabelle, the apple of my eye, moon of my sun, Mars of my bars?"

"Yes!"

"OMG!" shouted Brenda. "I leave you alone for five minutes and you're getting married all of a sudden! I will do the catering."

"No!" yelled Annabelle. "You will absolutely not!"

"Annabelle! I did not expect this! Is that how you thank me..."

"You will be my bridesmaid," Annabelle quickly continued. "What else could I have possibly meant?"

All of a sudden, she was drowning in Haggis's – Angus's, she would never call him anything else – muscular arms once more, safe, delighted, happy, nearly fulfilled, since her lady garden needed a lot of attention before she could consider herself completely fulfilled. So her future husband was neither Jiminy Frasier nor Seamus O'Shaughnessy. Not even Moanmoan The Samoan. She would marry a Scottish billionaire, the dishiest of them all, his taste unforgettable. A Scottish wedding! In

Scotland! Surely, with the right amount of therapy, Angus would agree to wear a kilt for her!

If only Annabelle had known that the future held *many* more surprises in store for her...

TO BE CONTINUED

Acknowledgments

I couldn't be happier that you have finished reading my first novel!

I would like to thank my sister from another mister Pell, who was a great inspiration and muse for writing *Haggis MacBrawn's Dishy Secret*!

I would like to thank my soulmate Naff, whose work inspired me almost as much as pictures of J. F. (I can't use his real name due to not being able to afford a lawyer.) The one from the TV show and you know which one!

I would like to thank my bestie Jessica for introducing me to the magical world of kilted Scotsmen! Especially J. F.!

I would like to thank YOU for reading my novel! Please leave me a review on Amazon!

Lastly, but mostly, I would like to thank my husband for not reading this, because I would be in so much trouble if he knew about this side career! (My name is not really Karen McCompostine. I am writing in cognito to avoid recognition.)

HAGGIS MACBRAWN'S (A SHADE) DARKER SECRET

PART TWO OF THE EDIBLE HIGHLANDER SERIES

This novel is dedicated to J. F.!!!!! but not to my husband. Take that, Gunther! (Name changed.)

Chapter One

❦

"Of course you can have your old job back," exclaimed Brenda, looking at her best friend, Annabelle Elle Ellendeling with sadness and sympathy due to the fact that Annabelle, who had entertained dreams of becoming the wife of an international, high-swinging Scottish billionaire who was also a haggis *and* called Haggis, which Brenda, who had great sense of humour, found very ironic, had to return to her old job at a greasy cafe called Cafe du Amour.

"Oh, Brenda!" sobbed Annabelle. "I am such a horrible monster due to ruining Haggis's chances of turning back into a full-time human being, since he is currently a werehaggis who at midnight turns into a traditional Scottish dish, because I did not love him well enough."

"Annabelle! Don't you dare insult my best friend like that! Jokes aside, you are the most loving and wonderful person I know. You wouldn't even sleep with my two bodybuilder friends due to you subconsciously wanting to remain faithful to Haggis when you left him for being gay."

"I told you he isn't gay! He is the wonderful, kind man I met. It's just that when cries and repeats it's not my fault his tears *smell*. Of grease. And... I can't even eat haggis, not even to try..."

"Why would you want to do that?!" interrupted Brenda, who despite Annabelle's protests felt that Haggis must have been gay. After all, people didn't just turn into traditional Scottish dishes.

"Well I don't, but if I wanted to, it would feel like... like... cannibalism...!" groaned sadly Annabelle and burst into tears again, sneakily drinking a little glass of whisky to rehydrate while Brenda left the room to bring over more paper tissues.

"Darling," huffed Brenda seriously upon her return. "It's better for you to make him look gay in the public eye. How would you expect the readers of *Daily Daily* to believe he was a werehaggis... no, sorry, that was a bad example. They believe Borys Johanson, our prime minister, exists, when everyone knows Domald Tramp created him using mirrors and holograms. How would you expect the readers of *Persons* and perhaps even Operah to believe it? No. Gay he is. I will tell The Girls and you will be fielding calls from reporters left and right."

"He isn't gay! And I don't want any calls!"

"I understand," said Brenda slowly. "You are a broken-hearted practically virgin, due to him not taking your virtue, due to him being gay. I'll tell you what, I will be your manager and take the calls for you."

"I... I don't want to talk about him to the press."

"Darling," hissed Brenda, who even possessed the ability to hiss "I". "The press will pay you for dirt on the ex-husband of Margerithe du Lacq's, who is a famous actress and French countess despite the fact that her real name is Sarah Lackey and she comes from Northampton. In fact... perhaps I can get Margerithe to join you, although she doesn't get any more money than you. You know a standard manager contract is 85%-15% split, right?"

"I know."

"But," said Brenda, "I am your friend, not just a manager, so I will only take 75% and you get whole 25%."

"Thank you, Brenda. You are such a great friend. But I really don't want to talk to the press," managed through the tears Annabelle. "Just– I don't want to smear his name. It really is my fault."

"It can't be," said truthfully Brenda, "for I have seen your face when he lifted you in his strong, homosexual arms. You love him as he is. But! You don't love him being gay."

"Brenda, he *isn't* gay and no matter how many times you repeat it he won't be!"

"Then there is only one explanation."

Annabelle's tears hopefully dried. "What is it?"

"He has another, even darker secret. You can't love him exactly as he is, because you still don't know exactly who he is. Do you understand my point?"

"You're right," whispered Annabelle in disbelief. "It's the only sensible explanation. But I have watched him all day and night. He doesn't change into anything but haggis."

"It might be a boring secret. Not everything has to be about... what's the plural, haggises or haggi? About shifting into traditional Scottish dishes. It might be something very simple. Perhaps he has a Pink Room of Pain..."

"He doesn't!"

"It's a *secret,* Annabelle. That means you don't know it. Even if you snooped through his entire house, which I know you would never do..."

Annabelle snorted, then quickly sobbed again.

"...you still wouldn't find it," said Brenda triumphantly. "But it might be something even different. Does he like pineapple on pizza...?"

"Don't be ridiculous! Only Seamus 'very small throbbing pole of dubious pleasure' O'Shaughnessy likes pineapple on pizza."

"Does he hang the toilet paper the wrong way?"

"Brenda! First of all, I would have noticed and cried until he fixed it. Second of all, he is not an absolute monster. That's not it either. He showed me press cuttings explaining, or rather not explaining, Tartan MacBrawn's – that was his brother – mysterious death. Some of them think he is still alive and works at a gas station in Texas."

"That's Elvis," sighed Brenda. "We can only do one thing. Contact Margerithe du Lacq."

"But Brenda, how are we going to do it? Haggis financed *Superlynx,* her solo movie in the *Supereverything* franchise. She is acting, or maybe a better way to phrase it is that she is often present on set. In the breaks she is a famous supermodel and appears on the news as an expert on health and economics."

"Fecking Sarah Lackey got far," barked Brenda. "But darling! You, too, are now famous, since you appeared on the cover of *Persons* numerous times due to your relationship with Haggis MacBrawn. He's a billionaire and he's hot. I mean, uh, my many gay friends say that. His spokesperson announced his engagement to you to the press in a press release, darling. You are famous enough to have press releases, most people have to tell others over a pint of voddy."

"Doesn't help me much," said Annabelle sepulchrally. "I have no money."

"Did he just throw you on the street?!"

"First, I left him for his own good, so that he can find the right woman who will love him exactly as he is. Second, no, he didn't. I now own a penthouse in London and a bank account with a round million on it."

"Annabelle!!! That's great news!"

"I am not taking any of that. He was nothing but good to me..."

"Unlike to my dead mother," uttered Brenda, "whom he had the indecency to call a witch and who had to deal with a violent junkie husband, my seven brothers and sisters, and possibly the worst – me."

"This is not about your dead mother, who might actually be alive..."

"Please don't say you believe she works at a gas station in Texas!"

"It's about ME! And I have morals, Brenda."

"No," said Annabelle's best friend coldly. "You are stupid. You have all the chances to make tons of money and you prefer to work illegally at Cafe du Amour for the minimal wage? Annabelle, I don't understand you."

"Even I don't understand me," sighed Annabelle.

Chapter Two

❧

ANNABELLE WAS IN THE MIDDLE OF MOPPING THE VOMIT OF various rugby players from the floor, having first spent many hours resisting their "advances", which were mostly attempts at grabbing her ass and booing "you famous woman, bring us more beer", when suddenly someone knocked on the door.

Her heart stopped.

It must have been Haggis. Even though she couldn't possibly go back to him, she was his best hope.

But he had a secret...

Annabelle quickly ran to the ladies' powder room, where she non-expertly applied some make-up to her pleasantly relatable, by no means supermodel-like face. Then she opened the door and saw...

Seamus O'Shaughnessy.

A rugby player who was missing in action today. Annabelle assumed his absence was correlated with shame related to the fact that he attempted to take her virginity as a bet with his "friends", then upon discovery that she was not in fact a virgin he threw her out of the room. Or rather she left, which filled her with pride. But this time she might not be able to resist his...

"Dear Annabelle," whispered Seamus shamefully. "I brought you flowers and a little present."

"Present? For me?" squealed Annabelle, who actually intended to say something about his minuscule, steroid-eaten plunger.

"I can't believe you work here as a waitress again. I did not join my homeboys tonight for a simple reason: I wanted to speak to you in person."

"Then you did," said Annabelle coldly and nearly continued, when she remembered all of a sudden. "Present? It better be impressive."

"Speaking of impressive," grinned Seamus, "I stopped using steroids, which miraculously enabled my manly equipment to return to its previous size! There is doubt on your face, my dear Annabelle, and I can't blame you, but I have never forgotten your harsh, yet truthful words. This, unfortunately, is why Geraldine and I are getting a divorce. It will be all over the papers tomorrow, but I wanted you to know first."

Brenda harrumphed and went into the kitchen.

"M-me...?"

"Yes, Annabelle. Not many women, by which I mean not even one apart from you, have ever refused the presence of my tubular organ inside their caves of pleasure. I don't even swear anymore. I am truly a changed man."

"Sounds like he's been reading Shakespeare," boomed a voice from the kitchen, which had a large open window to enable Annabelle to pick up the orders without opening the door. And to eavesdrop. It was a very smart idea of Brenda.

"I like Shakespeare," yelled Annabelle, then lowered her gaze and shyly steepled her fingers at the level of the aforementioned cave. "Seamus... thank you for the flowers."

"That's it?"

"Yes, that's it. My heart has been broken. Go home."

"I don't even have a home!" cried Seamus. "I live in a motel.

I am glad that we have no children, because no doubt Geraldine would demand a lot of money and full cursory."

"Isn't it called custody?"

"Do you see, Annabelle? I don't even know the word, which is a proof of how very much I have no children."

"Yes," said Annabelle somewhat impatiently, placing the enormous bouquet on the nearest table. "That's great for you. But what do I have to do with it?"

"Isn't it obvious? You have stolen my heart and changed me into a good man! For you I am willing to convert to any religion..."

"I'm agnostic," muttered Annabelle.

"Haven't you been raised by nuns?" yelled Brenda, slamming pans and pots against each other for no other reason than to be obnoxious.

"Exactly," answered Annabelle, her voice set to middle volume. "So, yeah, no religion. Goodbye, Mr O'Shaughnessy."

"Please call me Seamus."

"Not 'daddy'?"

He winced in surprise. "This was... the old me. Before I became a changed man. I would *never* say a thing like this again. Which is yet another reason why Geraldine and I are getting a divorce."

"I'll check all that," announced Brenda, reappearing and briskly walking towards surprised Seamus. "Lift up that cardigan. Oh," she continued, doubtfully patting his somewhat rounded midsection. "Yeah. Um. No steroids. Well, don't call *me*, O'Shaughnessy."

"What... what do you want?" asked Annabelle, her knees getting softer. The truth about her reaction to gorgeous, ripped men – including, at the beginning, Haggis – was an unwanted, repeating thought in her head: "I'm fat I'm fat I'm fat I'm fat". Despite the fact that she actually wasn't, according to the BMI index. But nobody has ever seen Annabelle and any sort of exercise equipment in the same room. She was allergic to iron and the smell of locker rooms.

"Please give me another chance and go on a date with me. To a *nice* place."

"Four stars!" shouted Brenda. "Or a Michaelin star. Or two."

"There are no Michaelin stars in this dumpster of a town," yelled back Annabelle.

"Paris," gently corrected Seamus.

"Pa– that's a name of a restaurant?"

"Annabelle! I will fly you to Paris tomorrow. We will have a typical French dinner: frogs' legs..."

"Ewww!"

"...or coques d'oueille, which means caviar."

"Ah," said Annabelle in a different tone. She has never even seen caviar. "Tomorrow?"

"Not before seven!" roared Brenda.

"I'll pick you up at seven zero one," said Seamus and flashed his unmistakably knee-softening smile. He didn't know it at that time, but he was already back to Annabelle's list of potential husbands, and storming up towards the top. "Thank you, Annabelle."

It wasn't until he departed, singing a hit song "Belief" by Sher, an old-fashioned pop singer popular in the 1970s, that Annabelle realised she never actually said "yes".

Chapter Three

※

It was a short flight. He took economy class tickets – Seamus was no longer a man who wanted to impress the world with luxuries, he explained, and Annabelle felt somewhat disappointed, as she never had a chance to impress the world with luxuries. When she was at the Glitz Hotel with Haggis, the only people who saw here were its employers... oh, Haggis...

Haggis Angus MacBrawn. There was absolutely no way to avoid the truth, which was that Annabelle still loved him. Just... she swallowed tears that began to rise in her throat. Just not enough to help him stay human, which, as the witch announced, would happen when a woman would love him exactly as he was... This meant he had another, darker secret, remembered Annabelle and scowled.

"Is everything alright?" asked Seamus worriedly.

"No," she responded. "You had a bet with your team that you would take my virginity. What bet is it this time?"

"Annabelle," he just said, then handed her a copy of *Daily Daily*. It was true. The entire cover was dedicated to a classy simulation of their wedding picture torn into two and the title, large enough that Annabelle could read it in the middle of the night inside a room with blackout curtains. (And without any lamps.)

"SEAMUS AND GERALDINE ARE NO MORE-INE!!!"

"This gross tabloid," sighed Seamus. "They offered me ten thousand pounds to tell my side of the story. Of course I said no."

"You have morals!"

"Morals? Annabelle, they offered me, *the* Seamus O'Shaughnessy, ten *thousand* pounds. I don't even get out of bed for ten thousand. Except for you, Annabelle, I will always get out or into bed for you. And you get a 100% discount!" His famous grin was a bit less pleasant, though. Annabelle began to feel butterflies in her stomach, but they were actually moths.

"What if I said I want to go home without dinner?" she snapped.

"Have you been a bad girl then? Sorry, sorry! It was a joke. I am trying to lighten the atmosphere."

"It's not working," Annabelle muttered, her mind full of Angus, as she preferred to call Haggis for obvious reasons. "But it's not your fault. This better not be a French version of Don Corleone's pizzeria."

But it wasn't. It was a restaurant right on top of Eifla tower. It was what the French call *bijou* – only four tables, three of them unoccupied, one covered with silk and waiting for them. Annabelle couldn't stop herself from gasping. Angus was only living a life of luxury where people *could* see him, during his business trips. Although, how would she know? They spent the night before their departure for Scotland at the Glitz Hotel. Then he departed on his own, possibly heading for his castle, which he described as a "small farm". There was nothing farmer-like about Haggis Angus MacBrawn, except for his hands... his real man hands... Annabelle shivered at the thought of what those magical hands could do to her body, then shook her head, trying to get rid of the vision. Those hands were always cruelly withdrawn when midnight was about to strike and naked Angus needed to crouch over a wooden tray in order not to stain everything when he turned into a haggis.

Werewolf, she sighed lustfully. Why didn't his parents name him Wolf? She wasn't sure whether vampires could also be werevampires and she did not really expect that any parents on Earth would have named their son "Vampire", but still. The witch's curse caused Haggis to turn into haggis, his brother Tartan into tartan and, as Annabelle found out before leaving him for his own good at midnight his sister, affectionately known as Potty, became... never mind.

"Panther," she whispered to herself. A werepanther could be interesting. They could go for walks in the neighbourhood together...

"Pardon me?"

"Oh no, Seamus," exclaimed Annabelle, but was interrupted by a waiter, who brought her coques d'oueille, which as she found out to her shame – Seamus apologised a hundred times – were actually called "hors d'oeuvre" and meant appetisers.

"I am an Irishman," he confessed unnecessarily, his ginger face stretched sideways in a boyish grin. "We don't have French food. Spuds and Guinness, Annabelle, and pineapple for the pizza. That's all I used to eat. But now, for you, I will become a worthy rival of Haggis MacBrawn, that bastard."

"He's not a bastard."

"Don't tell me you still love him, Annabelle. He invited you to his house, used your body in frankly easily imaginable ways, then threw you out. I know, because it's on page two of *Daily Daily*, I am so sorry, but it really is. If it weren't for me and Geraldine, you would have been the front page."

"Phew," sighed Annabelle, who didn't want her disappointment and shame spread over the millions of copies of *Daily Daily* sold daily to people without class, except of course herself and Seamus. The Irish rugby player presented her with his award-winner's smile again and she nearly forgot about Angus. When she was with the Scottish billionaire, he had never once done anything modestly and she had never dared to complain. How could she possibly complain about the food being too nice and the accommodation too pleasant...? But she always felt out of place. It was best evidenced by the smirk of the porter at Glitz when she tried to return to pick her handbag after she left Haggis for the first time.

Annabelle picked nervously at her cuticles. She was a bad person. She misled Haggis Angus into thinking that she loved him just as he was, yet somehow she didn't. A secret, said Brenda, one that made it impossible for her to know who he really was. But what if there was no secret? What if it really was as simple as Annabelle not loving him how he deserved to be loved...? What if her disgust with his tears was the reason those greasy, well-seasoned tears kept flowing freely?

She was in Paris, at the very top of la Eifla tower, sitting by the window from which she could see lights of Paris, and she was unhappy.

Chapter Four

❦

"Would you like to fly home tonight," asked Seamus, his handsome face innocent and free of bad intentions, "or tomorrow? There are hotel rooms waiting."

"Ah," muttered Annabelle, immediately reminded about Angus again. "Hotel room. How nice."

"No, Annabelle, rooms. Separate ones. I will only touch you if and when you permit me to. You are worth the wait."

She gave him an incredulous look. "Am I really?"

"Absolutely," he said with the crackle of wood fire in his voice.

"In this case," said Annabelle slowly, enjoying the tortured expression in the muscular (even if not ripped anymore) rugby player's eyes, "I am happy to share the room with you."

"Really?!" His eyes were now those of a puppy, happy as if handed a bone. Probably hardly daring to dream of Annabelle handing his bone, which is a metaphor. "I... I couldn't say no, but only if you are absolutely certain that this is what you want?"

"I am absolutely certain," whispered Annabelle. He was so sexy in the light of candles standing on their table flickering in his mischievous, but good eyes. Seamus O'Shaughnessy was getting a divorce because of her. Seamus O'Shaughnessy deserved to get lucky tonight. If, and that was a big if, he had learned in the meantime how to please a full-bloodied woman that Annabelle aspired to become one day.

She was ceremonially served a large amount of caviar, which to her disappointment didn't taste so different from tinned sardines. The champagne was more to Annabelle's liking. Seamus dug into his French pizza with pepperoni and pineapple, proving that not everything about him changed. Annabelle elegantly gulped some champagne and let her imagination fly freely.

It was true that Seamus was Irish, not Scottish, and therefore not quite who she wanted to be her husband. But perhaps Angus was the best medication against her allergy to all men who were not on her list of potential husbands, which until yesterday still, sadly, consisted only of Angus. Now that Seamus made a return, Annabelle remembered her other potential husband, Moanmoan the Samoan, but unlike the burly, muscular (if not ripped) rugby player, whose testosterone-laden voice caused her anticipating chocha to become moister than usual, he was not getting a divorce.

Annabelle quickly excused herself to visit a ladies' powder room, then flipped open her smartphone. Moanmoan was most definitely not getting divorced, as she found out by perusing a well-known search engine website. She quickly looked up "Jiminy Frasier divorce" as well, the one and only J.F. from *Outofhander,* before remembering he was fictional. This left her with a very short list consisting only of two entries. Unfortunately she couldn't quite push Haggis Angus off the top. But perhaps once she saw the non-steroid-shrivelled manly prod allegedly carried by Seamus these days...?

She returned to the table, wiped her hands in the serviette, which was made of very fine, white fabric, possibly the best cotton in the world. Or something even more expensive. But not silk, because silk was very impractical as a serviette. Then she smiled, noticing that Seamus finished his pizza and the remains of the monstrosity were now removed.

"I'm not so fond of the caviar," Annabelle admitted.

"Tried it on pizza once. Never again. Would you like a dessert?"

"Gladly! Oh," remembered Annabelle, who was a devout reader of women's magazines. "No, not at all, I am on a diet."

"Annabelle, you look perfect and you are perfect. How about sharing with me, then?"

She shyly nodded and Seamus ordered a massive chocolate and a whipped cream cake. They didn't eat all of it, of course, although they gave it their best try. He tipped the waiters a generous 100 French Euros for the mess they left on the table, then, giggling, ran down la Eifla tower, carrying Annabelle in his strong, muscular arms. And the thoughts about traditional Scottish dishes disappeared from her head.

Chapter Five

THE HOTEL WAS NOT GLITZ. IT WAS WONDERFUL, ALSO something the French would call *bijou,* in its unassuming, luxurious, but not too luxurious glory. Seamus ensured a few more times whether she wouldn't have preferred a separate room. Annabelle repeatedly refused, realising the cake sponge was soaked with liquor she did not taste. Her head was spinning and she was unsure who exactly the man in front of her was. Angus. Seamus. It kind of rhymed if you mumbled. Which she was now doing.

"Dear Annabelle," cried Seamus. "You look exhausted. Let me get you to bed."

"Blorp," answered Annabelle, ashamed of how unromantic the night was being after all. But she knew that there would be many more nights. And surely the changed, God-of-her-choice-fearing Seamus would not insist on anything sexual, when he could clearly see how inebriated she was.

She was wrong.

"Let's get you naked," muttered Seamus, positively salivating. "Mmmm. You are so beautiful, Annabelle. I can't believe what a prick I was that first time. It will never happen again."

"I want to sleep," she mumbled.

"Look," he boasted, presenting her with his tough column. Annabelle gasped. Until now she didn't really believe that the shrinking effects of steroids were reversible. The triumphant lamppost (but without a lamp) was the proof that she was wrong. "Is that big enough?"

In Scottish terms, she thought vaguely, it would be closer to S than M, but since she didn't want to give him ideas by mentioning the letters S and M in close proximity she just nodded.

"I will wear a condom," Seamus promised and soon enough his body was all over Annabelle's, who immediately woke up, struck by a lightning of desire which awakened all her senses. The most amazing was the smell of a real, muscular, slightly sweaty, but showered before dinner man. He was – she couldn't deny – delicious. When his face hid between her breasts, which despite her advanced age of almost twenty-two were still perky, even if also closer to S than M, she groaned with ecstatic abandon. Then his face, together with the remaining parts of his head descended down her body until his frisky tongue entered her lady garden, finding a nice spot right next to the fountain, and Annabelle's screams of joy and fulfilment shook the walls of the hotel. They would have to leave a big tip, she thought dreamily, then felt a big tip very near *all* of the fences of the lady garden.

If it wasn't for Seamus's hand, which playfully landed on her mouth, her screams would have alerted the police, which she believed was called something else in French, but Annabelle couldn't focus her thoughts as the train of his manhood entered the tunnel of her womanhood only to withdraw and enter it again and again, as if undecided which route was the right one, as Seamus's handsome eyes laughed warmly. Since he was a sportsman, he managed to bend in a way which allowed his lips access to her nipples whilst his tubular organ still massaged the spot by the fountain. "Oh, oh!" she cried. "Ooh la la," she quickly added, since they were in France.

This playful game of love-wrestling lasted for hours, and when confused Annabelle – still a bit dizzy, but not from the cake sponge any more – tried to figure out how huge a tip they would have to leave, she ran out of numbers she had learned at school. If this was a bet, she thought through clenched teeth, she definitely won it. Although maybe producers of condoms won it. Quite a considerable number of rubber protective items was used during the night. But what would he be like in the morning?

Annabelle would have sworn that she didn't get a moment of sleep before Seamus's alarmingly iron-like baton woke her up by poking her in the leg. More condoms were used up and she noticed that they were super extra thick. Such was the fate of a professional sportsman, she thought, feeling sad for Seamus's boyish beauty which had to be so carefully guarded against gold diggers, who wanted nothing more than to get pregnant in the arms of a professional sportsman. When they were finished and ready for some breakfast, les baguettes and les croissants with low-calorie cream cheese and jam, she noticed with a corner of her eye that Seamus gathered all the used condoms strewn around the room into a small plastic bag, which he then carefully placed in his small hand-luggage-sized suitcase. This was also because of the gold diggers, realised Annabelle with a sigh. *Daily Daily* had devoted many column inches to that sad topic. Although it mostly provided instructions for the gold diggers rather than ways to escape for the poor (although they were really rich, but it's not all about money when it comes to feelings) professional sportsmen.

After their breakfast, which was served with a glass of red wine as French like to eat their breakfasts, Annabelle wanted to go shopping for a traditional French beret, but Seamus seemed to be in a hurry. A taxi drove them to the airport and she noticed he seemed very quiet.

"Are you quiet because of Geraldine?" Annabelle asked sympathetically. She knew everything about broken hearts by now. Despite the fact that her frankly sore tunnel, so brutally pillaged by Seamus's undecided train, currently hurt (in a nice way) more than the broken heart.

"No, no. It's just that..." Seamus sighed. "I will tell you when we are not on an airplane where, as a celebrity, I am being listened to. It's a bit of a secret."

Annabelle's heart sunk at hearing the dreaded word. She did not wish to experience any more men with secrets. But she was also noticing that Seamus seemed to actually be willing to talk about his, once due to his celebrity status he was not being listened to anymore. This alone made him extremely different from Angus, who hid his dark secret for a long time, and if Brenda was to be believed, he had another one – even darker – left. Maybe two? Ten? A hundred?

Since Seamus wasn't saying much, Annabelle's mind flew towards nervous ruminations over Angus's secret, despite the fact that her warm lady garden was still sore from the repetitive, expertly directed thrusts of Seamus's not-so-little-anymore little Seamus. Perhaps Haggis liked wearing pantyhose. Or used drugs, such as cocaine and heroin. He might have had a wife locked in a room, a la Mr Ranchester in a book by Janet Austin, who was a famous writer in the medieval times. Perhaps... no, she would never find out unless he was ready to tell her, and Annabelle didn't even know whether there was a secret other than the one which she has unwisely shared with Brenda, who had a lot of contacts in the media and an unfortunate tendency to gossip.

Brenda would have been delighted to find out that Haggis had a secret, thought Annabelle sadly, before gasping in terror when they arrived at the airport and the front page of *Daily Daily* struck her eyes.

"HAGGIS MACBRAWN IS A GAY HOMOSEXUAL MAN. ANNABELLE ELLE ELLENDELING SEEN WITH FAMOUS RUGBY PLAYER SEAMUS O'SHAUGHNESSY

BEFORE 12 HOURS PASSED FROM HER BREAK-UP WITH MACBRAWN. THE SLUT!"

Okay, thought Annabelle as Seamus studied the cover without a word, attracting looks from fellow passengers going to and fro around the airport. In fact, she has only imagined the last two words. But guilt and shame, instilled by the fact that she was raised by nuns at an orphanage, were already dancing an Irish jig inside her stomach.

"Today's news," muttered Seamus in his sexy Irish accent, then walked on, holding her hand, nearly causing Annabelle to trip since she was wearing her lucky heels, so high that they were often taken for street lanterns, "tomorrow's bin lining."

Annabelle cheered up a bit, nevertheless deciding to buy a few copies. She would just cut out the bit about Haggis and keep the photograph of herself and *the* Seamus O'Shaughnessy being seen in Paris, holding hands. The lighting was not exactly the most flattering, Annabelle thought absent-mindedly. She knew that she was no great beauty, her relatable face perfectly matched with her job as a waitress, but even Seamus looked fat and ugly. There would be an article inside, she realised. It would inevitably be nasty towards poor Seamus. Her future husband. For Annabelle had no doubts that once the divorce was over they would elope and very soon her name would be Annabelle O'Shaughnessy. It was true that she was not chic like the participants of *Love Iceland* TV show, which was actually not about Iceland at all, but Annabelle was nothing if not brave. She was already entertaining visions of the fellow gold diggers and real housewives following her style, described by *Persons* as "a mix between Ana Winter's more inspired moments and Luis Vuitong's expensive, one-off creations". Which she bought at a second-hand store.

Life was good, Annabelle decided, half-fascinated, half-repulsed by being on the cover of *Daily Daily* and being dragged by Seamus towards the exit, where they could catch a taxi before a paparazzo blew their cover of being in cognito. This could jeopardise the divorce's result and she did not want to marry a bankrupt rugby player, who – it needed to be said – was already past his prime, age-wise, nearing the age of twenty-five. In the world of business and finance, which surrounded Angus like the greedy arms of Margerithe du Lacq, he would be only starting. In sports, he was heading towards retirement.

There was something strange about this whole event, though... How did the paparazzi know? Did they hack into his credit card on the Internet in order to follow their itinerary? It would be quite a coincidence if they guessed that Annabelle and Seamus would be dining at the *bijou* restaurant on top of la Eifla tower.

Poor Annabelle, so often recently disappointed by men, was about to learn another lesson about the mischievous acts committed by the rich and famous...

Chapter Six

"It's been nice," said Seamus as he dropped her outside Cafe du Amour, the one where Annabelle worked. "I'll be in touch."

"Wait! Do you still have my number?"

"Of course," said Seamus, but he averted his fiercely masculine gaze and Annabelle realised with terror that he was lying. He had no intention of ever seeing her again.

"Why, Seamus?" she whispered. "Tell me the truth. I will neither blackmail you nor attempt to contact you. I know you've used me. Why? Surely not for my body."

"No," Seamus admitted, still looking away, "but I wanted to humiliate Geraldine. To show up on the cover of *Daily Daily* with a plain-looking woman like you. So Geraldine would realise how lowly I valued her if I was willing to replace her, a famous person, with a waitress."

Crying, Annabelle ran inside, searching for solace in the embrace of Brenda, who was not a lesbian, therefore Annabelle felt safe in her arms.

Chapter Seven

※

"How do we humiliate *him*," mused Brenda. She decided not to open the cafe, which Annabelle greatly appreciated, knowing that Brenda needed to save money, but then Brenda explained that it meant Annabelle wouldn't get paid. Which made Annabelle even sadder, but it was completely reasonable. "There must be something wrong with him. I mean, except for what is already wrong with him and he won't even bother to deny it. Pimples in sensitive places? Three nipples? Come on, Annabelle, there must be something."

"Not at all," uttered Annabelle sepulchrally. "He is perfect. Except, of course, for being a nasty person."

"You should run to *Daily Daily*, now you have two stories to tell. They will cover you in millions!"

"Oh, Brenda, don't you understand? My reputation must already be in tatters. I ran from the arms of a billionaire Scottish businessman into the arms of admittedly very attractive Irish rugby player in the middle of a divorce. I would have shown myself as the sluttiest of sluts and my face would be plastered on the cover, together with my full name and possibly my smartphone number, so that nobody could possibly miss that. What would sister Bernadette say?"

"Isn't she dead?"

"Yes, a horrible case of syphilis transmitted by mosquitoes. I mean, theoretically. No, no, no."

"Then you will spend the rest of your life mopping spilled beer from this floor," said Brenda with a sigh that was so deep it seemed to have come from the basement, which would have been very strange, since the cafe didn't have a basement.

Annabelle had no idea that yet another blow was coming her way.

The next day, on her way to work, she caught the front page of *Daily Daily* and gasped in shock. Her face, which was at least well lit and possibly photo-shopped to enable her to look vaguely attractive, was on the cover. "THE BEST FRIEND SPILLS THE BEANS," said the cover this time. "EXCLUSIVE! ROMANCES OF MACBRAWN AND O'SHAUGHNESSY ON PAGES 2, 3, 4, AND 17."

Annabelle bought a copy, her hands shaky. The owner of the newspaper stall stared at her with a mixture of disgust and curiosity. She was plain, as Seamus said, and she knew that. Why would she out of all people be printed in millions of copies on the cover of *Daily Daily* for two days in a row? But the worst was when she actually read the newspaper, sitting on a bench which happened to be placed near Cafe du Amour. Because Brenda – obviously not identified in any way other than "A. E. Ellending's best friend" – yes! with a typo! – *lied* her big bosoms out. Not just because she assured them that Haggis was gay and in love with his cousin many times removed but always returning, Gunther. And that Seamus's a*s*s – this was the word the unclassy journalist of the newspaper used, for Annabelle would have called it his much lower back – was wrinkly and covered in boils.

Annabelle raised her head when she heard a loud rumble of a motorbike engine. It was a man dressed in leather with the unmistakeable insignia of the club on his back. The rugby club. Another one roared past her. They were heading towards Cafe

129

du Amour, no doubt expecting to catch her there and exert violent revenge. Or, worse, laugh at her for sleeping with someone whose much lower back was wrinkly and covered in boils.

She hid her face in her hands, the newspaper falling to the ground, less to cover the tears which weren't there, more to protect her identity. This was terrible. Within days, she lost a potential real husband, a potential dream husband, a friend, and a job. For there was no chance of Annabelle ever stepping inside Cafe du Amour again, not when it was owned by her hilarious, but treacherous ex-best friend Brenda and when Annabelle was being hunted by a brigade of chunky hunks on motorcycles.

Annabelle was trapped in a hole so deep it had no bottom and reached China, where she could probably crawl out, but Annabelle didn't know any word in Chinese apart from "ni hao" and she didn't even remember what it meant. So she didn't go. If only she paid more attention at school, she quietly whimpered. All her things were in her old flat, where Żaneta and Wiktoria welcomed her as if she never left, announcing that Agnieszka and Kunegunda bought an expensive, yet tasteful villa in Spain and now Żaneta and Wiktoria had to scrape together pennies to pay the rent, which did not decrease. They were all too glad to have a flatmate again, even though they were very disappointed when it became clear that the flatmate was absolutely skint despite having dated a billionaire and having been granted access to a bank account with a million on it.

"I am dumb," cried Annabelle quietly, which happened when she was still sitting on the bench and not yet in the old flat, not to be noticed. "I am so, so dumb. I will never believe a man again. Even if it's Jiminy Frasier from *Outofhander*. I will become a nun myself, since I have expertise in the subject having been raised by nuns. If they permit a fallen woman like me to join their throng!" But her tears soon dried out. She knew the sisters would welcome a fallen woman. They loved nothing more than sinners. In fact, it would have been ideal if she could commit some more sins before coming in, not to disappoint them by her insufficient level of fallenness.

"No," she said to a black cat, who ominously ran in front of her. "I will commit no more sins, kitty. I will become a respectable citizen." Annabelle sighed deeply. "Once I change my identity and get plastic surgery."

Chapter Eight

A YEAR LATER

Brit-xit was completed and Annabelle was now living in France, specifically in Paris, where she had a job at the *bijou* restaurant. Everybody else who worked there, surprisingly, was gay and homosexual. It was a proof that the gay mafia existed, she realised, then wondered why they hired her, as she was not a gay man at all. But she soon found out that it was her impeccable manners (luckily the information arrived by email and nobody heard her snorts) during the dinner with that awful, yet buff (Jean-Pierre's words) Seamus O'Shonessie (also Jean-Pierre's words). (Jean-Pierre was her future boss.)

The job was wonderful and not just because the restaurant employed four cooks, four waiters, and had four tables. The pay was lousy for French standards, but the gossipy queens, as the gay men called themselves, were even more hilarious than Annabelle's EX-friend, as she always emphasised, Brenda. She learned French very quickly, luckily, even though she had no talents for learning anything whatsoever, but discovered that French came to her as naturally as liking for *Love Iceland* and French wine she classily consumed at breakfast.

Annabelle was not dating anybody and not just because all

her friends were suddenly gay and homosexual men. In fact, Bruno, who was either Jean-Pierre's lover or one of Paolo, a Brazilian expat who was constantly present at the *bijou* restaurant (the funny thing was that the name of the restaurant actually was "*bijou*", in italics and without capital B) despite not working there. At one point, when Annabelle and her new friends were sufficiently inebriated, she asked them playfully if they could draw her a graph explaining who was whose lover exactly. When Annabelle weakly asked Jean-Pierre to maybe start wrapping it up he said, upset, that he wasn't even halfway through yet. Gay men, as Annabelle found, were very promiscuous, making her look positively virginal in comparison. Then again, what right did she have to judge others, having jumped from one man's bed to another and being immortalised on the front pages of *Daily Daily* (which she got laminated, but not before cutting away the not nice parts of the titles)?

Those were the ways of the world, ruminated Annabelle over the four-star cake prepared by her friends for her birthday. She was now a bilingual woman, one who was living in a foreign country, working at a restaurant so posh its name was even said in italics. She was, in short, a woman of the world herself. Somehow Annabelle felt that her exploration of the world wasn't over yet. And she couldn't refuse feeling a very un-nun-like pang of excitement when Paolo told her that he knew a straight man who would be just perfect for her.

"Is he famous?" Annabelle asked in French.

"Not at all. He is a model, of course, since I do not have unattractive friends," said Paolo also in French, "but nobody is perfect. Ha ha!" he laughed, and Annabelle joined, for Paolo was very hilarious. "Anyway, you are straight, he is straight, you will have a lot to talk about!"

"Will he come here?"

Paolo snorted. "Very few people can afford to come here. And you need to book a year in advance."

"But there is nobody tonight," observed Annabelle. "All the tables are free."

"That's why you signed a document saying that you would never, ever tell anybody how many clients *bijou* actually has, silly girl. If they allowed people to find out that you can in fact enter without reservation any time, this place would be o-vah. We charge such prices that one person who dines here pays monthly wages of one of us. When we get over eight patrons, everything else goes either into Jean-Pierre's pocket, or to pay the rent. You can probably imagine how much rent is on the very top of la Eifla tower!"

"True," admitted Annabelle. She was learning a lot from working as a waitress at *bijou* restaurant. One day she would surprise a suitable man with the knowledge she acquired simply by being a woman of the world, surrounded by glitz (not the hotel) and glamour (and the room she was renting together with three others, all of whom were sex workers, but nobody needed to know that either and they didn't bring work home). She now had a secret as well, Annabelle realised with a surprised gasp.

Perhaps it was as simple as everyone having a secret? Maybe Haggis's farm was in fact a hole in the ground and he wasn't a billionaire at all? No, that was nonsense, the paparazzi would have figured it out... Suddenly Annabelle slapped her forehead with more force than necessary to convey the fact that she was stupid. With shaking hands she flipped her smartphone open to look at Internet, searching for "haggis macbrawn farm".

No.

It was not a hole in the ground.

Haggis Angus MacBrawn owned twenty five horses and, by the looks of it, half of Scotland.

"I should have never looked," muttered Annabelle to a coat hanger. She liked to talk to objects, because they never laughed at her, made bets to take her virginity, or betrayed her and took money from *Daily Daily*. A bit like dogs, actually, but without all the pooing and peeing.

She was so sad and not feeling ready at all to have a date with the straight man whom Paolo knew, a model or not. But she wanted to go and be entertained by something else than her dark thoughts and her sex worker roommates gossiping about their clients.

And so she went.

Chapter Nine

As Annabelle soon found out, the straight man's name was Ricardo. He was Paolo's stepbrother. He was, indeed, very good looking and Annabelle immediately started to feel self-conscious, but it transpired she didn't have to, since over their fourth glass of Chardonnay Ricardo confessed in a very loud whisper that he was actually more straight-curious than straight.

"And Paolo said you look like a man," he continued, not aware that he was stabbing Annabelle in the heart with every cruel word. "That you have small breasts, even though still perky for your age which is by now approaching twenty-three, and that you do not wear make-up. And that you wear trousers. I wish you wouldn't have worn this dress. It's a bit... vulgar."

"Mhm," answered Annabelle, unable to produce an actual word. He was correct. The dress was borrowed from Monica, who complained that the thing shrank in the laundry. Which was also correct. But Annabelle didn't realise that the fact that the dress shrank both horizontally and vertically, which made it look so short it was practically a very stretched (downwards) bra. Now her modesty was suffering and it was her own fault.

"So would you like to come to my house?" asked Ricardo. "I

have a jacuzzi, a 84" plasma TV with multiple channels delivered by cable, including a channel with straight-curious adult movies to get us more in the mood. I also bought a bottle of champagne to celebrate my attempt at turning straight thanks to you."

"Over my dead– jacuzzi? No, non," snapped Annabelle, moderately excited for a moment at the idea of spending one night away from her flatmates, but a jacuzzi reminded her of her many hotel stays with Angus at the Glitz Hotel, where every bathroom – and there were many – came with at least one jacuzzi. "You offended me, Ricardo," she spat, already getting up. She threw the napkin at her plate and stormed out, secretly happy at not having to decide whether she should offer to split the bill or not.

Annabelle wondered whether the Internet had a form allowing her to find out how long it would take her to become a virgin again if she entered all the dates at which she had sex and her number of partners (two). Apparently an average woman had six partners in her life. That meant she was most probably due to experience three more horrible ones before Jiminy Frasier from *Outofhander* would ride into her life, shirtless, due to being allergic to clothes which were not kilts, and on a horse. Obviously by then she would have to live at a farm, with her Scottish husband whom she loved with her whole heart, Haggis Ang–

"Donnerwetter!" screamed Annabelle in French, but nobody turned their head. Parisians were very laissez-faire about women screaming their lungs out. They simply thought that her date didn't go well. And they were right.

Chapter Ten

It was an evening like any other when Annabelle arrived at *bijou*. She no longer found pleasure from staring at the lights of Paris or even from taking an elevator taking her to the top of la Eifla tower, to a place most people didn't know existed at all, and even those who did know couldn't afford to as much as come inside to use the powder rooms.

"We have a rich one," said excitedly Jean-Pierre. "Dinner for two. But he booked the entire restaurant. Nobody is going to find out that we don't have many guests *and* he will pay four times more."

"Who's doing his table?" asked Annabelle.

"You," said Jean-Pierre. "Whatever tip he leaves will be yours. He's very rich and very spoilt. Do you remember when the Backhems visited? He's like that, only a thousand times more, so I read in *La Daily Du Daily*. When the fashion Backhem woman asked me to serve her one leaf of spinach, steamed, without salt or any other spices, and a grape to look at as dessert, I nearly quit. Then I remembered I am this place's owner. They are now on our black list."

"No!" gasped Annabelle, who never forgave herself for being

sick due to her feminine problems on the one day when Backhems, who were very famous, came to dine.

"Oh la la, oui, merci."

The black list was very short. It now included four people, two of whom were Backhems, the supermodel Noemi Campy-Belle who threw a napkin at the window so hard the window (double-glazed, bullet-resistant) broke, and Mr Eifla himself, but that was due the fact that he was dead and Jean-Pierre was afraid of ghosts. Annabelle's un-made-up face darkened. She would never meet Backhems now. She could tell everyone...! But of course the only friends she had left were the waiters and cooks here at *bijou* and they would have known.

Poor whichever cook was told to steam one leaf of spinach and find the perfect grape for the fashion Backhem woman to look at it after her "dinner" was finished...!

"Here he is," gasped Paolo, who inexplicably was here again and Annabelle wished she would have allowed Jean-Pierre to finish the graph, so she would have known whom Paolo was dating. Perhaps all of them, or none, simply misleading them in order to be allowed to spend time at the *bijou* restaurant? He apologised profusely for the fiasco with Ricardo and Annabelle believed him, since Ricardo clearly kept his straight-curiousness a secret. Except now that Annabelle shrieked it out at Pablo in the presence of everyone else Paris was practically shaking due to loudspeakers announcing Ricardo's name, address, and sexual confusion. Yes! Annabelle now used the word "sexual", encouraged by her slightly perverted, but very nice friends!

Nothing could have possibly prepared her for the shock when the guest arrived.

"I can't serve this table," said Annabelle, her lips white in shock. "I can't serve this man. I know him well."

"He requested you personally."

"Did he," said Annabelle flatly, then suddenly her face turned red. "Did he now!"

"Annabelle!" yelled quietly Jean-Pierre, hoping that the

guest wouldn't hear. "Wait until he pays before you cause a scene!"

But she didn't. "Haggis," she spat in English.

"Annabelle, my beloved," growled sexily Haggis Angus MacBrawn.

"You have two hours and forty-one minutes."

"No. My curse is on London time. It's three hours and forty-one minutes."

Annabelle's slightly nervous mind suggested that it was in fact *one* hour and forty-one minutes, but she was not a billionaire Scottish businessman, so what could she know? Not to mention the fact that the curse already changed its working hours during winter and summer time.

"Sit down, my love," Haggis begged.

"No, Angus. I am serving you. I work here. You can't just tell people what to do."

"But you said you are serving me?"

"That's true. Any hors d'oeuvres?"

"If you are serving me, wee lassie, then I order one sassenach sitting on the chair in front of me."

Unable to resist his Scottish charm, Annabelle plopped ungracefully into the chair. A moment later Paolo, his face a mask of curiosity and excitement, appeared with a bottle of champagne inside an ice bucket.

"I don't like champagne," said Annabelle, although in fact it wasn't true and she was simply being contrary.

"What do you like?"

She tried to remember what was the absolute most expensive thing they had on the second menu, the one for the VIP guests, not the one for just guests. Backhems didn't know that, but Jean-Pierre refused to show them the second menu. Not that it was needed to serve one spinach leaf. "I like Milanese-oak-aged, 75-years-old whisky produced by monks in Guatemala at midnight during a moon eclipse."

"Very good choice," said Paolo excitedly. Since he was now

the waiter, he would get the tip. "There was only one bottle ever made and we have it."

"If there was only one bottle ever made, how do you know you like it?" asked Haggis with genuine curiosity on his face.

Annabelle blushed. She had forgotten how she used to blush every two minutes back when she was young. Now, over two years later, she was a woman of the world, but Haggis affected her in a way no other man ever had. "I have a good feeling about it."

After one sip, once she stopped coughing, she ordered a fizzy drink with caffeine. Paolo's handsome gay face became a mask of terror. Annabelle realised she made a mistake when she heard a thud. She could guess it was Jean-Pierre fainting in shock. She would be fired very soon. Unless she came up with a very good story... Once she added the fizzy drink to the whisky glass and managed to actually drink some of it, Annabelle relaxed. This would be a very good story. Because she wasn't done.

"You left me," said Haggis bitterly. "And it is nobody's fault but mine. I... apologise. And I am here to right the wrongs. If you don't want to ever see me again when I am done, I will not try to stop you from leaving, Annabelle."

"Oh," she just said. All of a sudden Annabelle realised that it should be Haggis taking his revenge on her, not the other way round. She left him, after all. Shyly, she ordered some caviar on baguette, since she has by now developed taste for it. Haggis ordered an egg and a bottle of their very best French red wine, explaining that he didn't like champagne either. Poor Annabelle was stuck with the whisky mixed with a fizzy drink and honestly would have preferred boxed wine they drank with her flatmates.

"How are you?" he asked, genuine concern in his voice.

"I'm good," said Annabelle, "Hag..." She paused. It was her Angus, calling him "Haggis" would be cruel, since she was one of the two people who knew his secret. She loved him. No, she used to love him. She still loved him. "Thanks," she lamely finished. "You?"

"I'm bad," he responded, looking away, then his gaze met Annabelle's and imprisoned it in a metaphorical tight grip. "I can't live without you. I know why you left me."

"Because I didn't love you exactly as you were."

"No, indeed. But that is my fault." Haggis paused to thank Paolo.

"Cameras off," demanded Annabelle. "And microphones. I know where they are. If I notice any of them is on, I will destroy them and they were super expensive."

"Cameras...?" repeated Haggis, surprised.

"How will you know?" asked Paolo.

"Because I have the special *bijou* app on my smartphone too and I can check, Paolo. I just don't have the administrator rights."

"Very well," Paolo huffed and Annabelle discreetly opened the *bijou* app to check on it every now and then.

"We are safe now," she said.

Haggis poked his egg with a fork. His face darkened. After all, he could be killed with one poke of a fork when he was in his haggis form. "You see... you didn't know who I really was. I tried to keep a secret from you. It was the wrong thing to do, but I knew you would leave me. And... you still left me."

"Aha?" said Annabelle, very curious.

"How is your caviar on a baguette?"

"Delicious. Tell me."

"I think we should eat first," said Haggis sadly, "otherwise you will storm out and refuse to finish the meal. And let's face it, I know how much everything here costs. And I happen to be close to bankruptcy."

"Oh no! I am so sorry! I will send this whisky back!"

"Too late," he answered gravely. "It's open. Let's make the best of it. I'm going to have a taste, then cork it again and sell it on a popular auction website for 75% of the price. Annabelle, it's true. I gave up my business job and gave everything I owned to Margerithe du Lacq. I want to become a good man. For you. All I kept is my small farm..."

"The one with twenty-five horses?"

"You have no clue how much work twenty-five horses are when you let all your employees go," observed Haggis, but did not elaborate further, which Annabelle should have felt was ominous. But she didn't. "Among all the people I have hurt the worst was the witch, who, as I found out, was the mother of your best friend Brenda."

"Brenda went to the papers and told them you were gay," murmured Annabelle. "And that I slept with Seamus O'Shaughnessy."

"Did you?"

Annabelle coughed. "Go on."

"I created special funds to help people in need who lose their jobs," said Haggis, "but most importantly I have transferred a hundred million pounds to Brenda's account."

"So about twenty-five thousand euro," said Annabelle.

"The exchange rate is not my fault. She can buy half of the country for it and you know it's true. Any more and I would have destabilised the financial system. But this is not all. When I transferred the money, the clerk was dishonest, took it all, and tried to escape to Bohoma. He didn't realise, like you do, because you are smart, that it was just twenty-five thousand euro and that he would have needed to wait eighteen months for a visa."

"Duh!" said Annabelle, whose eloquence was currently limited by the whisky and sheer impatience.

"Exactly," confirmed the no longer billionaire. "I got him arrested, so that the money would all go to Brenda and her seven siblings. I did not realise that getting the clerk arrested was also an evil deed – no, darling, please don't interrupt with platitudes, as kind as your golden heart is, it was an evil deed. He lost his job and that was how I started my fund. He was the first to receive financial help. Initially I decided that the fund would only cover this country, since it wouldn't cost me much. You see, I was still greedy. But then I remembered that my business techniques have hurt people in all the countries I have ever visited. I axed jobs left, right, and centre when I was merging and consolidating." Haggis sighed. "Eat your caviar, you look too thin."

"Do I?" squealed Annabelle before realising that she did not enjoy strange men – and Haggis was being very strange – saying things like that.

"So I started funds in all the countries I ever visited, paying the average wages to every employee who lost their job because of me."

"And..." Annabelle paused, the heaviness of the pause hanging so heavily over the table it nearly knocked the whisky bottle off. "How many countries would that be...?"

"Seventy-four," sighed Haggis. "My accountants were furious, claiming that they didn't put all my money into dubious funds located in tax havens transferring them twenty-one times to avoid paying any taxes, but I was strong and my resolve impossible to break. I needed to make it up to you."

"Make what up?"

"Order the main course, dear."

Annabelle ordered Jean-Pierre's famous kale hamburger endorsed by the website Doop belonging to a famous female entrepreneur and actor, and Haggis ordered a pancake with chocolate sauce. She managed to persuade him to add whipped cream, so that Jean-Pierre wouldn't be too upset by such a simple order.

"I am down to just enough money to pay for this meal, although to be frank I did not expect you to order this bottle, to fly back to Scotland, and pay for upkeep of my farm for a year until I collect the first crops with my own bare hands, like the honest man I now intend to be." Haggis sighed so heavily a napkin fell off the table. "But I just had to see you before I go. I will never be able to afford a plane ticket to Paris again."

The food was delivered, but Annabelle lost her appetite, even though – or despite – the fact that her hamburger was decorated with a discreet microphone. She picked the thing and broke it under the heel of her new lucky shoes, which came from Guchi.

"Eat," said Haggis in a little, broken voice. "Or don't, so you can throw it at me when I tell you my secret."

Annabelle took a bite of the hamburger, which was wonderful, almost as good as the one in MacDolands, which despite the name was not a Scottish restaurant.

"I have been truly ruthless, Annabelle."

"But you created the financial funds to make up for it."

"True, but some of those people are no longer around. I also fired old people over the age of forty, ye ken. I was cruel and all I thought about were the stockholders and, I will honestly admit, my own credit card bills. I have accommodated so many sins that if Devil exists I will not even fit through the door to Hell with all this baggage. You see... the witch... her name was Jane Smith. How am I supposed to find the right Jane Smith to apologise to her for all the damage I have done...?"

"But I knew all of this," interrupted Annabelle, "except for her name, which indeed doesn't help."

"Yes, my darling Annabelle. I know you know. I am not finished, though. I knew that she really had a violent junkie husband and eight children, but I felt that it was her own choice that brought her there and that she was earning too much – can you imagine I thought that? Yes, I was still only a multi-millionaire, but she was earning a minimum wage, which had to stretch to pay for all her bills and food. And her junkie husband's drugs. I did not care. She cried, pleaded, begged, then threatened to turn my brother Tartan into a weretartan. I did not believe her. How ridiculous does that sound? I threw her out of my office. A few days later I called my brother, since

I had a bad feeling, and asked whether anything was wrong. 'How would you know?' he asked. 'I had a bad dream,' I said, 'one in which you turned into a roll of tartan at night'. He cried, my poor brother, then demanded that I tell no-one about my dream. But he refused to confirm whether it was true or not. So when Jane Smith returned to my office, to beg for her old job, I threw her out, but not before she threatened to curse my poor, late sister..."

"What was her name?" whispered Annabelle, feeling the cold tentacles of horror wrapping around her golden heart, which was now beating very fast.

"Potty."

"Oh. This sister. I am so, so sorry. But she's alive," said Annabelle confusedly.

"Would you like to be alive and be a werepotty...? She forced me to pretend that she was late. My sister never leaves her house, she lives alone in the middle of a thick forest, hoping that nobody will ever break into the house between midnight and six a.m. and... and use her. Still. I called her a week later and said that I had a bad dream, but I couldn't squeeze it out. Wrong phrase. I couldn't say that I worried she was turning into a potty, Annabelle, surely you understand. So Potty said all was perfectly fine, but she decided on a whim to become a hermit for no particular reasons. She said it's always been her dream, but she and I used to be very close. I knew her actual dream was to become a professional curling player and compete at the Olympics."

"Can women be curling players at the Olympics?"

"Annabelle, please listen to me further. So I allowed Jane Smith to turn my brother and my sister into a weretartan and a werepotty, but still, I refused to give her back her job. Out of principle, I said, since I was furious with her. I demanded that she removes the curse. She demanded that I give her the job back first. I said, truthfully, that due to the merger her job no longer existed. 'You are a multi-millionaire,' she cried, 'why can't you just give me some money?' I answered that if I were to do it, I would have gone bankrupt with the number of people whose jobs I was... consolidating. And so, sassenach, Jane Smith cast her final curse. Upon me."

Annabelle was silent. Even the word "sassenach" spoken with a pronounced Scottish accent did not distract her from understanding that she had nearly married a real monster, one who had no interest in the wellbeing of common people, a bit like the Backhems crossed with the owner of Wally-Marty.

"This is it," said Haggis with sadness in his handsomely Scottish voice. "I have no more secrets. I can and will answer any question you have – truthfully. If you want to know about my lovers, ask away – I have none. You won't be surprised to hear that any rumours about my reunion with Margerithe, whose real name is Sarah, are lies she's been spreading. The movie tanked, by the way. When I told her that I was giving away my entire fortune, Margerithe demanded a divorce. I had to remind her that we were already divorced. This was how much she loved me as a person. She actually forgot. Have you forgotten the nights we'd spent together, Annabelle?"

"Evenings," she muttered and Haggis blushed furiously. "But I remember the nights too. The nights when you would squat over your tray and turn into haggis. I would cry my eyes out, but I would first cover you with a metal bowl, so you wouldn't know. I only blamed myself for not loving you the way I should. Paolo! I want a big cake with lots of whipped cream! The cheap one, though! So, anyway, as I was saying, I blamed myself and that was why I left you. I felt that you deserved a woman who would truly love you as you were. And clearly I wasn't that woman."

Haggis was silent.

"Angus," said Annabelle. "Ah, scr– penetrate it, Haggis, you do not deserve my politeness. You hurt lots of people. You caused hurt to your sister, who will never be the same... except between six a.m. and midnight. You got your brother killed,

Haggis. And you killed my feelings, you have broken my golden heart. I have slept with Seamus O'Shaughnessy, I shall tell you, because I tried to get over my love for you. It didn't work. I moved here to Paris to escape my feelings, but I found out that they travel along, no matter where you go; you can change your address, your friends, your shoes, but not your soul. This is why I don't believe you. I had Seamus O'Shaughnessy swear to me that he was a changed man, but all he did was use me to make Geraldine O'Shaughnessy jealous when she asked for divorce. Before you ask, it didn't work. In fact it allowed her to demand 99% of his possessions, as she had very good proof that he's been cheating, and his lawyer settled at 98%. I know this from *Daily Daily* which you can read online even in Paris. Seamus is now selling his body in Berlin at the back of the train station and using lots of heroin, says *Daily Daily,* and he had to forge a letter from his non-existent lawyer he couldn't pay. They printed it. It said 'My lawyer says that you have to stop'. I mean, what the F-word, Haggis...? Where are you?!"

The whisky, despite the addition of a caffeinated drink, nearly caused her to say the F-word aloud, but it was worse. During her tirade Annabelle was waving around the glass with her drink, nearly spilling something that cost her monthly wage per drop, and she was not paying much attention to her ex-fiancée. Who was now gone.

Shocked, she cast a look at her watch. It was one minute past eleven.

Annabelle froze. She knew what she would find on the chair. What she didn't realise but soon found out was that she would have to gently unwrap the clothes around the haggis and she couldn't cut them with the caviar knife and/or the egg knife. (*bijou* was so luxurious that even the fizzy drink came with its own straw, which was organic and made of still-growing bamboo.) And then, as if ordered, which technically was correct, Paolo showed up with the cake and the giant knife, so sharp that she could cut air into slices with it.

"Is your gentleman friend in the men's powder room?" he inquired, as Annabelle briskly kicked the chair to hide the pile of clothes covering a sobbing Scottish dish under the tablecloth, then practically teleported back to her seat, already arranging her facial muscles into something resembling a smile.

"Oui," said Annabelle in French, excited that Paolo gave her such an easy escape. "That's exactly where he is! Please tell me there is no microphone in this, or I'll throw it on the carpet. And you know how expensive this carpet was."

"He'll pay," shrugged Paolo.

"No," said Annabelle cruelly. "You will. I will destroy your Tim of Fundland collection."

"Non! I beg you, Annabelle! I couldn't possibly live a moment longer without my sacred Tim of Fundland collection...!"

"Then remove the microphones," she said and Paolo, grinding his teeth politely, removed no less than four of them. Annabelle took a close look and pointed at the fifth one. Paolo sobbed. He must have been promised tons of French Euros by Jean-Pierre and/or *La Daily Du Daily*.

She sent him away to the kitchen, requesting a styrofoam container to take some food home. Paolo nearly cried until Annabelle explained she was joking and the usual platinum and diamond box would do. Then, once she cut through the clothes with a knife so sharp it actually cut the chair in halves and the haggis landed on the floor with a surprised yelp of agony, she placed the Scottish dish she used to love in the box before discreetly letting herself out. But not before she found the sacred credit card and simply left it on the table, retreating with all the rest rolled into a very expensive ball of fabric and golden cuffs under her arm. The cake, which she intended to throw in the face of Haggis Angus's human form once he was finished, remained untouched.

Chapter Eleven

✦

"What on Earth is this?!" asked Jacqueline in French upon seeing the platinum and diamond box full of haggis.

"Rotten egg," barked Annabelle, holding on to the box protectively.

"I know it's your food, I'm asking about the clothes! Is this Armando di Tomfordo I see?! Oh non, they are all cut...! Who would have done such an awful thing!"

"A monster," said Annabelle shortly, then took out Haggis's wallet and sat on her couch.

The problem was that when she told others (which she never did) that she had roommates, she meant that literally. They were her *room* mates. All four of them stayed in the same room, which had two couches. Two of the girls worked at night. Jacqueline, who liked her beauty sleep, worked during the day. And so did Annabelle, obviously. They only met for breakfast and late dinner, mostly consisting of French cheese and French wine. The girls refused to eat baguettes and croissants, explaining they were "les carbs" which made people fat. Even though Annabelle knew that it was eating too much that made people fat, and if they were not too lazy to exercise – not that she exercised, but the love she used to feel towards Haggis caused her stomach to shrink – they could eat all the "les carbs" they wanted.

She had four and a half hours, roughly, to decide what to do with Haggis in form of haggis. His clothes were useless. It was clear that she couldn't possibly fix the ones she cut into pieces. Haggis in her jeans? His waist, wrapped around his ripped six-pack abs, was the same size as hers, but his muscular thighs... oh, realised Annabelle, she sort of drifted away mid-thought... so his thighs, the size and muscularity of which didn't matter in this emergency situation, would never fit in her jeans even if she had a premonition causing her to only ever wear cargo trousers. Which she didn't.

It wasn't just that she had to hide the actual haggis. He would soon return into his human form. Naked. Skint. Annabelle couldn't afford to buy new clothes for him either, especially not in the middle of the night. Since one or more of the girls were always in, there was no way they could miss the presence of an excruciatingly beautiful and thoroughly naked billionaire... ex-billionaire in their room.

Annabelle quickly ran through the images of her work colleagues stored inside her memory. Was any of them half as gorgeous... no, half as large as Haggis? Especially around the legs? Only Jean-Pierre, she realised in shock, then remembered that she had forgotten the whisky bottle which could have been sold at 75% of the price on an auction website. Annabelle did not berate herself too much, since everyone would have been unable to concentrate on financial matters when faced with a gorgeous man turning into a traditional Scottish dish wrapped in Armando di Tomfordo, but...

"Are you alive?" she whispered, lifting the lid of the box and scowling at the aromatic contents when Jacqueline went to visit the ladies' powder room, also known as a porta-potty – ugh, poor Potty – located two kilometres away from their flat. Jeanette had once experienced explosive diarrhoea and she was still shaking and crying when she talked about it.

"Aye," squelched the haggis quietly. "Can you get me to my room at the hostel?"

"You're staying at a hostel?"

"Where else? I can't afford anything... oh no, there will be twenty-nine other rough sleepers in there. Can you get me to... to..."

"There is only one sensible solution," said Annabelle determinedly. "You have your plane ticket, which I know because I accidentally examined the contents of your wallet. We simply need to commit a crime of breaking into a second-hand clothes store, one that is too poor to have an alarm..."

"Annabelle...! Surely you are not suggesting...!"

"I am. So, one that is too poor to have an alarm system. We will then leave the platinum and diamond box behind as an apology. It will be six a.m. when you shift back. You will just leave. I will stay behind to explain everything."

"You will get arrested," blobbed the haggis after a moment of stunned silence.

"I don't care," said Annabelle, trying to remember how much whisky exactly she drank. No, that wasn't it. She was not drunk in the slightest and even if she were the sudden transformation of Haggis would have sobered her. "I will help you. Because I believe you. Even though you're so poor, yet wearing Armando de Tomfordi."

"Armandi di Tomfordo," corrected the haggis automatically. "I'm sorry, Annabelle, but those are the only clothes I had. I have overalls and an extra pair of socks on my farm."

"What time is your flight?"

"Ten past ten."

"Then it will be twelve thirty," mused Annabelle, who understood the rules of French air traffic very well by now. "Which means you should just about make it to the airport," continued Annabelle, who also understood the rules of Parisian traffic. Especially in the morning. And afternoon. And evening. And night. "I will try to carry you to a second-hand store that is as near the airport as possible, but we don't have that much time... Do you know what, let's just go now. The night is young," she joked, laughing bitterly. This dinner aged her so much she felt practically like a wise old woman. In passing, she glanced at a mirror and found herself surprised at the fact that her hair hasn't gone white when the dinner was so rudely interrupted before she had a chance to throw the cake at Haggis.

"Cargo trousers," she muttered not long after, using the screen of her smartphone as a light. "Size 42. Really? Jeans. Oh, that's my size. Mmm, let me just try them on real quick... yeah, I'll take those. Jeans, jeans, jeans, jeans, jeans. Jeans. Leather. Not your size, but I wouldn't mind... I mean, *never* mind." On their way Annabelle found a bottle of red wine, as often happens in Paris, and was now heroically making her way to the bottom. "Haggis," she suddenly said, her tone strained like the relationship between Seamus and Geraldine O'Shaughnessy. "I found a kilt."

"Is it my clan's tart- colours?"

"Haggis! You will wear it."

"I need a pin, socks, shoes, a sporran..."

"You don't. You need to get the hell out of this store at one minute past six and catch a taxi."

"Annabelle, I can't afford to pay for the taxi."

"You... what? Oh my God," she groaned, despite being agnostic. "How were you going to travel then?"

"You said you left my card behind. I have five French Euros left in my wallet."

Annabelle straightened up, holding on to the kilt, wrapping it protectively in her feminine arms. This was true. "Then I guess I have to go with you and pay," she said. *Then I guess I won't be eating much in the next two weeks*, she thought.

"Annabelle... I am a fool. I had hopes. Great hopes. I bought two tickets to Scotland. In case you would like to... join me."

She dropped the kilt on the floor. Disappointingly, it didn't make any sound whatsoever. Annabelle briefly considered picking up the wine and dropping that, but the bottle wasn't empty yet and French wine was French wine.

"Please," begged the haggis. "You will have no obligations. You can stay at the farm as long as you like. You don't have to do any work, although it would have been helpful and I know that with your golden heart you will not allow me to do everything with my own bare hands. We won't have much food, mostly dried horse meat, but I will come up with – with something. I will sell my body... no, not like that, I meant selling a kidney. Apparently mine are in top shape. I went for a complete health check-up before giving away all my money, I would never have been able to afford it afterwards. I will sell both kidneys and walk around with an artificial one if you agree to come with me."

Romantic, thought Annabelle despite herself, then took a sip of wine. Although it was more of a gulp, really. But Seamus said similar things, he was a changed man, didn't even take steroids any more, yada yada. What was the result? "Non," she said in French. "But I will get you to the airport. Once you shift back and put on the kilt. That's my condition, I don't care about your clan colours. I want to see you in a kilt for once in my life, Angus."

The haggis gasped squelchily. So did Annabelle. It was the wine talking, the wine of honesty and raw truth. She cared. She cared enough not to eat for two weeks due to paying for a Parisian taxi and to save his life and well-being. Yet she was also basic and superficial, wanting to see him in a kilt... She had to face the truth. And... and maybe his farm... non... oui, mais non...

The clock struck five a.m. – of course, she had the hours wrong, London time etc. – and a naked man stood in front of her. A *lot* of a man. Annabelle swallowed, unable to tear her eyes from both his incredible, steroid-free abs and his incredible, steroid-free manly appendage, hanging in a way suggesting that the kilt might be a bit too short in the same way that her little shrunken black dress was for her.

"Sassenach," said Haggis Angus MacBrawn softly.

"Haggis. Get dressed. I'll go and get a taxi," said Annabelle, then retreated. Even in the faint light, even in her three-quarters-of-a-bottle-of-wine slightly tipsy state she knew that if he were to ask her to have les sex, she would have les agreed. To put it mildly.

Chapter Twelve

It would have been quiet in the taxi had the driver not been listening to "Jacques le Taxi", which was a hit in the 80s recorded by a very famous French woman.

Haggis held Annabelle's hand the entire time and she couldn't find it in her to take her hand away from him. She was busy thinking. She already figured out that she would simply go back home with a train, then walk the remaining eighteen kilometres, which would mean only one week without food. Maybe eight days, since the train ticket also didn't come free. But Annabelle's mind was mostly obsessed with one thing.

She still loved him. Despite all her attempts not to, Annabelle still loved him. Yet he hadn't turned human until the time came. So either there were more secrets or she didn't love him the right way after all. Maybe she only wanted his body... well, she *did* want it, Annabelle admitted, consumed by the guilt which came from having been raised by nuns. Especially by the awful sister Bernadette. Who was dead. Ha ha, thought Annabelle joyfully, then realised she wasn't being very nice at all. Sister Bernadette might have looked like a child of a potato and Godzilla, but she was a human being. Or so the gossip said. Haggis was cursed due to all the people he hurt and even his charity efforts, perhaps slightly overblown, didn't lift the veil of sadness of the suffering of those innocents. Despite the fact that sister Bernadette was dead she did not deserve being called "awful"... oh, realised Annabelle. She was in actual fact quite drunk due to not having consumed any food but some caviar. So those thoughts were okay, since everybody knew that being drunk, especially in Paris, made it okay to think of nuns as "awful".

"We're almost there," said the driver in English, having recognised the famous Haggis Angus MacBrawn, whose face appeared on the front page of *La Daily Du Daily* captioned "COMPLETE IDIOT GIVES AWAY LITERALLY EVERYTHING WHAT IS THIS WE CAN'T EVEN". "Can you pay? Being poor and all?"

"I will pay," said Annabelle.

"Roar," jeered the driver. "You can definitely pay."

"I might be poor," said Haggis, "but I can still kill with one punch."

The driver did not demand money for the trip, explaining between apologies that he was feeling especially charitable, inspired by Monsieur MacBrawn's well-known kindness towards his fellow humans.

"We're early," said Annabelle in disbelief. Despite her knowledge of Parisian taxis she had miscalculated the time and as a result they had extra two hours. "I mean, you are early..."

"Come with me, Annabelle," whispered Haggis seductively.

"Non, je regrette everything to do with you," she resisted weakly.

"You can have a horse."

"I don't..." Her voice broke. Annabelle would have sold her own kidney to own a horse. "G-go and wait in line or something, Angus."

"I love you," he said softly.

Annabelle turned around and walked towards the exit marked "Les Trains". Once she was in le train she started to cry and didn't stop until she reached their (hers and her flatmates', not les trains') toilet, which did not deserve the name "ladies' powder room" at all, located two kilometres from the apartment, used it thoroughly, then continued walking home, biting her lip, determined to squash any feelings she still had for Haggis MacBrawn.

As long as his vertically inclined male extension was, it could not ruin her life again.

Even though his legs were so muscular even their muscles had muscles.

Even though she might have accidentally kept his underwear, which she was going to put in a plastic bag so that the musky smell of woodsmoke, whisky, and *man* would stay there as long as possible, until she realised that was a gross thing that only disgusting old men on the Internet did. So she bought an elegant Louie Vittong bag instead, since it happened to be on sale at 99,95% off.

Annabelle simply had to forget his growl; the Scottish words like "sassenach" and "ye ken" which practically made her orgasm a few times during dinner and only her nun-instilled manners allowed her to contain the sensual explosion; his eyes, his tongue, which she thought she had already forgotten but apparently that was not the case, his manly hands, his voice... okay, she sort of mentioned that already, but still. He *truly* repented, unlike Seamus O'Shaughnessy, who probably simply ate one hamburger too many and his abs hid under a layer of fried meat and melted cheese for two hours.

What would sister Bernadette say, wondered Annabelle, dragging her sore feet. You will not get dinner for seven days due to impure thoughts, you good-for-nothing. That's what.

Chapter Thirteen

JEAN-PIERRE GAVE HER THE CARD, INFORMING THAT THE client forgot it, and that he accidentally found out there were only 73 Scottish pounds left on it. Annabelle accepted the card, then put it gingerly in her wallet. Not that she wanted a constant reminder of Angus. But she actually did.

Paolo didn't speak to her for entire four hours before asking her, as gay men do, whether she would like a manicure and a new haircut. Annabelle was definitely in the mood to get a new haircut, so she agreed. Jean-Pierre good-heartedly chuckled as her hair flew around the kitchen, falling into both raw ingredients and ready meals which would soon be served to the Queen and King of a big European country. Annabelle's hair, coloured by Paolo twenty times in the last three weeks, was currently the colour of gold and putting gold in food was all the rage.

When Annabelle's smartphone vibrated, she gasped, grabbed at it, flipped it open and discovered a message. From a man. From a very attractive man, in fact.

Seamus O'Shaughnessy.

"Dear Annabelle," read his text message. "As you can see, I never lost your number. I didn't lie. I was a coward, though. When I saw us on the cover of *Daily Daily* I panicked, thinking that Geraldine would take all my money away in the divorce. Which she did. I am now a poor man, but not poor enough not to be able to come to Paris and invite you for a pizza (but not in the bejou restaurant heh). Perhaps I could somehow convince you to give me the 3rd and last chance, 3rd time lucky, eh? Pls let me know. With cordial greetings, yrs forever, S'O'S xxx".

S'O'S, thought Annabelle, amused, then put the phone back and focussed on Paolo's complaints. Apparently in her excitement she moved so fast he cut off half of the hair on her left side, which meant that she would either look like Phil Oakley from a 70s band "The Human Ocean Mile", or get a crew-cut.

"Do what you want," sighed Annabelle, who would soon use horrible curse words like "crap" upon discovering that she was now a proud owner of a mohawk, which was a punk rock hairstyle that went out of fashion in the late 1960s. She was overwhelmed. Not just by S'O'S's offer. By the realisation that she got so excited by a mere possibility of receiving a message from Angus that she allowed Paolo to ruin her hair.

She took her revenge upon looking in the mirror by not permitting him to do her manicure. Jean-Pierre couldn't stop laughing until he burned the French fries, which made him cry instead.

Seamus. Angus. Seamus. Angus. It was almost as if Annabelle was a romance heroine, constantly forced to choose between two men. She was an avid reader of romances, especially ones featuring Scotsmen, so she knew how it worked. The good guy versus the bad guy. But which one was which? Both insisted that they have changed. Both have committed evil deeds. Both were undeniably hot.

If one of them had a motorbike, it would have been very easy to figure it out. Only the bad boys ever owned motorbikes. But by now according to *Daily Daily* Seamus could only afford the Tube and a cheap *train* to Paris, and if Haggis owned anything motorised it must have been a tractor.

Suddenly Annabelle's eyes opened in a metaphorical way, since they were already open.

She knew which guy was which and what she had to do.

"Come over," she texted back, not bothering to give him her whereabouts. A moment later her smartphone buzzed helplessly with this exact question. Annabelle cackled and sent him the address of la Eifla tower.

What she did not expect was that Seamus would show up seven hours later instead of seven days or half past never. Annabelle just accidentally happened to have gone outside to get some fresh air before standing in the kitchen and complaining about how disappointing it was to actually meet a King and Queen in the real life. (Not that she would actually get to meet them, since Jean-Pierre was a bit overexcited about royalty, even though it wasn't the real thing, i.e. the British one, and insisted on serving them himself. But she would have been able to see them thanks to the many hidden cameras.)

"Annabelle?" he (Seamus, not Jean-Pierre) asked, somewhat surprised. "You look so different."

Annabelle, suddenly very self-conscious, blushed. Her hair was not even a real punk mohawk, it was more of a quaff, which wasn't a real word for hair, but sounded better than "coif".

"It's the new shoes," Seamus continued, amused. "Guchi?"

"Armandi di Tomfordo," lied Annabelle. "Let me guess. You came here to beg me for a last chance, which would be your third. You intend to win my heart. You are very sorry about everything you've said and it was a big mistake of yours."

"Y-yes. How do you know?"

"You wrote all this in your text message," explained Annabelle, greatly enjoying the sight of Seamus O'Shaughnessy's handsome jaw dropping nearly to the ground, which must have been very uncomfortable. Yup, she thought. That was how romances always went. She would now have the upper hand before giving up her inconsequential job to spend the rest of life with the very rich...

Oh.

Seamus wasn't very rich. Neither was Haggis. This was very confusing.

"Well," she announced to the bewildered Seamus, "buggered if I know."

"Pardon me?"

"Nothing, nothing. I'm going to text Jean-Pierre and tell him I'm going home early. He's busy with the King and Queen anyway, long story, so he won't see the message. Then you can take me for a French pizza."

"Is it la pizza or le pizza in French?"

Annabelle glanced at him with slight disgust. "I can't believe you don't know."

"So which one is it?"

"I have no clue either. Let's just go."

She switched off her smartphone and put it on the bottom of her handbag in case Jean-Pierre would telephone her, despite being surrounded by actual, if not real (British) royalty, and demand her to come back to work.

Chapter Fourteen

"Take your clothes off," commanded Annabelle.

Seamus had no idea what struck him, she thought with glee. He did not read romances. Annabelle was in complete control of the narrative, every single movement choreographed, every word repeated a million times in a million books that she read – for Annabelle was, despite her lack of formal education, an avid reader with great memory and brisk intelligence. Which was evidenced by the fact that she learned French so fast that she barely noticed it, going from "yes" to "oui" in what seemed to be a few seconds. Yet she was having a great time. There was nothing fake about it, nothing artificial or cliched. Not when *she* was in this situation. And Annabelle knew exactly what would happen in the chapter before last.

The sex. The bad boy sex. Not the "I am a virgin, please be careful" sex, but the really good one with bondage and various other things. The romantic depictions of "other things" varied depending on the nature of the novel she was currently reading, but they were clear on one thing: the bad boy sex always made the heroine's cave of pleasure turn from a moist, warm hideaway into a roaring waterfall. Annabelle's lady garden was definitely ready to roar for the one last time.

"But Annabelle," whispered Seamus.

"Am I unclear? Take your clothes off."

As Seamus undressed, rather clumsily and not at all like a Chipanddale would, Annabelle tried to focus. But his body, now still muscular but padded with soft curves which were apparently not fake after all (this was known as a "dad-bod"), was diverting her attention from any thought resembling a sentence. He was nowhere near fat, but also nowhere near the ripped guy talking to her about protein supplements. He was just right. In fact, mused Annabelle, noticing how much his ginger hair has grown... he looked like a cover model from the books she adored. There was even a bit of stubble on his masculinely square jaw. His nose, adorably broken during his many years of rugby practice. And those fierce eyes that promised the world and delivered incredible orgasms.

At some point between the pizza and the Irish coffee Annabelle became a fully liberated woman who knew exactly what she wanted, and that something was Seamus O'Shaughnessy.

"I'm going to tie your eyes with this blindfold," announced Annabelle, "which I just so happen to have in my handbag. Then I will handcuff you to the bed and perform acts of sexual nature which will make you beg for more, but I will be relentless... ah, whatever, get on the bed, Seamus."

His body was a work of art. Slightly unfinished, due to not being ripped any more, so a bit like a work of art which got neglected just before the final stage, but still. It would be hers to do anything she wanted with in just a moment. In fact, it already was, mused Annabelle to herself, observing Seamus grinding his teeth, determined not to show how much he was enjoying himself – or perhaps suffering, judging by the guttural sounds his throat was producing. Somewhere between a lion and a... a man, disappointingly.

"Touch it," he begged.

"Hmm," answered Annabelle, looking at his pole of pleasure, looking like it was extremely ready to dance around. She never took pole dancing classes, which meant it would be her first time, which practically made her a virgin again...

Suddenly Annabelle was unsure. What if romances lied? What if there was no HEA, which meant Happily Ever After? What if the only thing she would get out of this would be a few good orgasms and a scolding from Jean-Pierre...? Her heart fluttering like a caged bird, Annabelle realised that the good-humoured Jean-Pierre *might* actually fire her if something would go wrong with the King and Queen of a large European country. Her own hair landed in their food. Annabelle knew that if Jean-Pierre wouldn't be able to convince them that it was always meant to be like this, she would be blamed. She wouldn't just get fired, she would never get a job in Paris, possibly in all of France, since the gay mafia had its threatening tentacles everywhere. She would have to go back to Brownhole Street, where she used to live with a varying number of Polish flatmates, then beg Brenda...

No. Annabelle would not beg Brenda for anything.

"I never put a condom on a man," she purred. "Does it hurt when I do this?"

"Aaarghhhh!!!!"

"Oh no," she gasped. "I didn't mean to hurt you."

"It's not that– it's just that– it's been a while. Annabelle, I want you so bad."

"That's nice," said Annabelle, smiling. "Oh. Do you know, I have to roll it out a bit to figure out which side is which. Or doesn't it matter?"

"It does...! AAAAHHH!!!!!"

"Now I definitely hurt you," she cried. "My lovely Seamus, I didn't intend to... What is that? Did you just..."

"We-we-we will need a new condom."

Annabelle frowned, then went to wash her hands. It must have been quite a while indeed if a few gentle, practically incidental movements of her hand and an attempt to put a condom on caused a spurt of sticky white liquid to stain the bedsheets and her freshly manicured fingers... ah, non, she forbid Paolo from giving her a manicure. Then it was okay.

"I need a short break," groaned Seamus.

"That's okay," answered Annabelle, who had an app on her smartphone, one that enabled her to read books. "I'll just catch up."

"With what?" demanded Seamus, but she didn't answer, switching the machine on, then entering her password to start it up. Annabelle's smartphone was very well protected, as she did not want her secrets to be known. Same as Seamus, Haggis, even Jean-Pierre, who would definitely not tell the King and Queen that there was hair in the real French French fries. Jean-Pierre wouldn't even tell the (not real) royals that it was Annabelle's fault, or Paolo's, he would just fire them afterwards. Everyone had secrets and most kept it on their smartphones...

Her smartphone vibrated sexily, but Annabelle put it away, tiptoed towards the pile of Seamus's clothes and dug out his own smartphone. She placed it on her breast, ensuring the fingerprint reader was located correctly. "Ooohhh," she said somewhat flatly, then doubled up. "Ooohhh. Touch me here, Seamus. Ooohhh yeaaahhh. Right here. A bit to the left. Good boy. Now get your rest."

"What's going on?!" repeated the bewildered musclebound, if slightly padded around the waist ginger rugby player, as she went through his messages.

She was saved in his phone as "Virgin".

Annabelle gawked at the smartphone incredulously. *Virgin?* Did he never update his contact list? She edited the contact, changing it to "A woman of the world", then continued snooping, aware not to press the button which would block the smartphone, disabling her from being able to go on until she made him touch the fingerprint reader again. (It was a very modern smartphone which could read fingerprints.) Above her name was *Bae* – she didn't even have to check to know who it would be. After all, Annabelle had read many romances and knew that the limited cast of characters meant it could only be one out of three. Brenda. Geraldine. Margerithe du Lacq.

She was completely wrong.

Bae, miss you so much. Want to taste you again. Send me a cock pic.

Annabelle gasped when the "cock pic", as they were known among modern youth, loaded. At least it didn't seem familiar, because if it was Haggis's she would definitely become a nun despite being agnostic.

You're such a stallion, Rob Stallion. I want to ride you without a saddle all night long.

"Seamus?" said Annabelle sweetly.

"I'm falling asleep," he groaned.

"Oh, I'll wake you up," she promised, then sat on top of him. Seamus groaned again, but in a very different way. Annabelle playfully pinched one of his chesticles and he yelped. "I think I figured out why your wife left you."

"I don't want to talk about her, sweet Annabelle, please!"

"Because you are a gay homosexual!" announced Annabelle triumphantly. "I found your messages... accidentally... the ones you've been exchanging with Rob Stallion. Really? I mean, really? Do you have no taste?"

"Those are jokes, Annabelle! Just locker room stuff! We're blokes, blokes make jokes, it even rhymes! Please don't pinch me again!"

"Of course not," agreed Annabelle before brutally punching his fertility globes hanging below his currently softened trunk of masculinity.

"Nooo!" cried Seamus.

"Can you explain 'cock pics' to me? Because I've never quite understood that phenomenon. Can't you just ask how big it is? They all look the same, although yours is quite small, steroids or not."

"Uncuff me!"

"Although," continued Annabelle mercilessly, "Rob Stallion's is a bit... how do I phrase it... have you seen curly fries?"

"Uncuff me now, bitch!"

"So it's exactly like curly fries, but not totally, do you know? It's more meaty."

"Bitch!"

Annabelle tsk-tsked. "You are not helping yourself at all. But I have this amazing idea. My workmates are gay, all of them. I will order a few bottles of bubbly here and tell them to come over after work, since there's a very special party."

"Bitch!" repeated Seamus, clearly unable to remember any other words due to the shock of the lifetime he was currently experiencing.

"Oh, Seamus, why do I always have to end up telling you off? Although no, the last time wasn't that bad. Until it was. I don't really have good words for it. Do you think I could get a paparazzo or two to come here? They like taking pictures of us, apparently. Is there a number in your smartphone?"

"Bitch!"

"How funny, it's under P." Annabelle pressed a button. "Hello? This is Seamus O'Shaughnessy's smartphone, his wife speaking. Yes, Geraldine, that one. He is now in a hotel room, I will text you the address, he is with his awful lover whomst you have no doubt seen on the cover of *Daily Daily*. I can't reveal much, but her breasts are still perky for her age, even though they are small, and her hairstyle is a work of art, a harbinger of fashion."

"Hairstyle!" groaned Seamus. "I thought it was shoes!"

"Honestly," said Annabelle, turning towards him, "for a gay man you should have better perception skills when it comes to women's looks. Paolo knew at first sight. Although that's unfair, because he did it to me and will suffer for a while longer. Anyway, oh, I was on the phone. Yes, still here. Will you hurry up? He finishes really fast, like, literally thirty seconds. Don't take a taxi or you won't be there before tomorrow afternoon. Can't wait to see the pics! Todeloo!"

Seamus was crying and sniffling.

Annabelle pressed the same button as before.

The one that opened the Weather app.

Then she threw the phone on the bed, next to Seamus's immobilised body and went downstairs to instruct the porter that Mr O'Shaughnessy wished to be woken up at five a.m. tomorrow morning and asked to absolutely not be interrupted until then.

It wasn't until she was briskly walking away that she realised she was still holding the keys for the pink, furry handcuffs she had accidentally purchased just in case she needed to arrest somebody. Annabelle shrugged, then threw the keys into the nearest garbage bin. Those handcuffs were so thin they barely deserved the name. Surely the porter would have no problem cutting through that "chain".

Then she checked her phone, her heart beating so fast it was practically hardcore techno.

Chapter Fifteen

⚜

THREE DAYS, SHE TEXTED BACK. LET ME KNOW IN THREE days.

He responded in the morning to confirm that everything was going perfectly fine. Two days, she texted back, feeling her heart fluttering inside her chest like a caged bird with a generalised anxiety disorder.

Annabelle told Jean-Pierre that she was leaving. He berated her gently, then laughed, patted her head, said that the King and Queen of a large European country were nowhere as exciting as the real (British) royals, then handed her a thick wad of banknotes, which were unfortunately all small nominals. Still, it looked impressive and should be just enough.

Waiting was a torture for Annabelle. Two more days...! Two entire days! How could she wait so long? It was her own idea, but it sounded better than it felt. Every hour seemed to last a week, which was very reminiscent of the piety lessons with sister Bernadette. Annabelle tried to get some sleep, but then Jacqueline and Jeannette got into a loud fight about which of them "worked" with a bigger celebrity. Annabelle was very close to telling them that both of them were completely unknown outside the middle-aged *Les Westenders* audience before realising they meant a different sort of "bigger" and she just chuckled to herself quietly. If they only knew.

She went for a short walk to take a look at the papers and, to her lack of surprise, the front cover of *La Daily Du Daily* presented Seamus O'Shaughnessy in his fully handcuffed, dad-bod-y glory. Except for the actual bit which he would probably insert into a glory... she couldn't quite get herself to think it out loud... glory opening at a homosexual establishment. It was covered with a black bar. (The masculine bit, not the glory opening at a homosexual establishment.)

It was a *very* small black bar.

Annabelle laughed heartily. She knew that the designer must have slightly altered the photo. After all, she saw the naked Seamus from up close, in fact very close. That bar should have been larger. Not a lot larger, but still. Poor Seamus. The British *Daily Daily* would be reprinting this in 3... 2... 1...

Unfortunately she couldn't find any other deserted wine bottles, which were probably all taken by some tourists who didn't think about others (Annabelle) and their needs. Very egoistic, thought Annabelle huffily. She got out Haggis's card, one that was so luxurious it needed neither a number nor the owner's name, and used it to buy a lottery ticket, understanding clearly that it was their only chance not to live in poverty. For Annabelle has already decided what she wanted, and it was neither Seamus nor any other gay homosexual. She wanted a real man. As long as he was willing to open himself to her completely, in a non-sexual way, because in the sexual way she would be the one willing to open completely, but that was a completely different topic.

Chapter Sixteen

❦

Her plane landed in Scotland. At a Scottish airport. Filled with Scottish men. Not a single kilt in sight, Annabelle sighed quietly, interrupted by Angus (Haggis) dressed in dirty overalls and apparently nothing else, dropping to his knees in front of her, presenting a discreet, if elegant ring.

Some Scottish people around her gasped in delight and started filming the scene using their smartphones. Annabelle hoped that the recordings would end up on YouPipe (a video website), so that she could pick the one where she looked best and anonymously send it to that bitch Brenda.

Then Annabelle remembered she was being proposed to and looked down, half-unconscious from desire.

"Yes," she whispered, unsure whether he had already asked or not yet.

"I love you," professed Haggis. "Even though those overalls, some pigs, sheep, and a very dirty stable that you as a woman will clean every day unless you refuse to do any work which would be perfectly fine with me are all I have, I have found this ring, which belonged to my grand-grand-mother, then my grandmother, then my mother, then to Margerithe, but very briefly..."

"What?! Are you giving me a second... a... let me count... a fifth-hand ring?!"

"It is a family heirloom," he cried. "My sweet Annabelle, thank you for agreeing to join me in the holy matrimony despite the fact that I am both poor and a bad man!"

But Annabelle couldn't hear him anymore, for her gaze accidentally wandered towards somebody else.

Her eyes, slightly blurry with excitement, first focussed on the muscled feet. Then the long socks. Then the knees. Followed by the kilt. Then still the kilt, because, let's face it, it was a *kilt* and this is a Scottish romance novel. Once her eyes unglued from the sporran, her gaze wandered up. Her cave of mystery turned from a slightly moist establishment into a place where it rained inside, making her slightly worried about a potential stain around the personal regions of her jeans.

"Moanmoan the Samoan," she groaned whisperingly.

"Annabelle," cried Angus.

"Hello," said masculinely Moanmoan the Samoan, extending his hand over Angus's head and shaking Annabelle's. "I couldn't be more delighted that you have agreed to marry my great-grand-uncle's-second-wife's-estranged-son's-son."

"Can I stand up?" asked Angus and despite the static electricity connecting Moanmoan the Samoan's hand with Annabelle's, they disconnected to allow Angus to stand between them. "Thank you for agreeing to drive us to my small farm, Jax."

"Jax...?" whispered Annabelle.

"That's what my close friends call me," said Moanmoan, raising his brow seductively. "But first... ah! There you are, my wife of seventeen years, whom I would never cheat on because family is the most important thing for me after my Academy Prize!"

A woman who was not Annabelle, Brenda, Margerithe, or even Paolo wearing a dress wrapped herself around Moanmoan's neck. As if torn out of a trance, Annabelle wrapped her own body around that of Angus. "Would you wear a kilt for me...?" she whispered into his handsome, although not as much as Moanmoan's, ear.

"Annabelle... you know what happened to my brother. I couldn't. It would be too heartbreaking for me. I promise to buy a Scottish slang dictionary and read it to you every night."

A dirty stable, thought Annabelle. Pigs and sheep. And overalls. Not a kilt in sight.

But she could see and feel a *lot* of Angus in those overalls. His brutally masculine arms. His well-pumped, steroid-free pectorals, developed during the work he was performing at his small farm, which she now knew for a fact was not the one with twenty-five horses. She could even feel one of his chesticles, despite the thick fur that covered his impossibly masculine body, rubbing itself seductively against her neck. "Are you wearing anything under those overalls?" she whispered.

"No," he whispered back.

"Is there any hay in your dirty stable?"

"Of course. Lots of it."

Annabelle hardly noticed when her arms wrapped themselves around Angus's neck and her legs around his waist. "Take me. Home. Then take me. Let's do it all night, so that I can see whether I know you exactly as you are now. But first, let's eat something. Make sure it's not a traditional Scottish dish."

"Jax?" said Angus.

Moanmoan unwrapped the greedy arms of his wife of seventeen years from his masculinely tattooed neck. "I'm ready whenever you are," he growled towards Annabelle.

She was ready. To her shame, she was also thinking about celebrity divorces. Then, with a quiet sigh, she took Angus's bare arm and allowed the men (and Moanmoan's greedy wife) to lead her towards the parking lot, into Moanmoan's Lamportini racing car, cheering up when she realised that the YouPipe movies featuring her would now also feature Moanmoan. Brenda would die of envy.

Unfortunately, Annabelle was ready to die from lust...

TO BE CONTINUED!!!

Acknowledgments

I couldn't be more excited to know that you have just finished reading my second novel, "Haggis MacBrawn's (a shade) Darker Secret"! It is thanks to my fans, like you, that I find motivation among my daily chores to author novels like this one. The title of which is not related to a well-known novel by a different author who has earned a trillion dollars from her work. I am a big fan. And aspire to write as well as she does. But the title of my novel is accidental and has nothing to do with that other one.

Anyway, because this is the "thanks" part. I would like to thank Mr Bezo's (I am worried about being sued, so as you might have noticed I changed the names making them completely unrecognisable) for publishing my work. My sweetest baby, who is NOT my husband but my delightful dog, for being so wonderful and fulfilling my life-long dream of having a little bundle of joy in my arms. (My husband Gunther is not little at all, which you will be able to read about in my memoir.)

I am very thankful to Ms Pellington 21 from a well-known social network I am perusing for all the help she has provided to me. It is thanks to superfans like Ms Pellington 21 that I have sold a double-digit number of copies of my first novel, "Haggis MacBrawn's Dishy Secret". Also, I hope you paid for this one and didn't pirate it, which I hear unfortunately happens a lot, so if you have read my novel legally, I am so super grateful! And if you pirated it, you have no shame and should be arrested.

You can discuss anything you want with me here: https://twitter.com/karenauthor1

Aha! I almost forgot to mention that this is a second part of a trilogy and the third novel is coming very soon to your smartphones and e-readers!

HAGGIS MACBRAWN'S (NO LONGER A) BIGGEST SECRET

PART THREE OF THE EDIBLE HIGHLANDER SERIES

Dedication
This novel isn't dedicated to Gunther either, the lazy bar steward.

For my editor
Thank you so much for agreeing to work on my book, (insert editor's name)! I can't pay you a fee, because my husband spends all our money on Prongles (they are a snack that normally spells with "i" but I don't want to be sued) and beer (beer is beer and all I can say about Gunther's is that it's supermarket's own brand with "Strong" added at the end), but since my books are always big hits on the bestselling books' charts, I am delighted to please you by offering 2.5% of my royalties (this means profits) which, I assure you, will make you rich. Please edit the book by Friday when it is published by Mr Bezos. Best regards, yours truly,
Karen xxxxxxx

Presage

My darling, darling fans!

I know you were both so concerned at the long hiatus I have imposed upon you after the first two books in my now finished (in the Epilogue) masterpiece, *The Edible Highlander Saga*, and awaited this latest instalment with baited breath. I can only apologise and blame everyone but myself.

Firstly, I've had to care for my husband, Gunther, through a serious case of 'manflu' (between the three of us, this is a code word we use for a very sensitive medical operation, which he insisted upon even though I told him I was happy to ignore his 12 centimetres and there was no need for me to have to ignore 14 of them). Secondly, once his 14 centimetres recovered, Gunther enthusiastically proceeded to you-know-what. His enthusiasm turned out to be *very infectious* and so I discovered he has acquired interest of 4 (four) maidens (sluts) in our small town. I discovered this, because my niece is a nurse and also a very discreet person who only shares everything with me and nobody else. I send thanks to those 4 (four) maidens for giving him something to do outside the house while I GRIEVED.

Thirdly, the most sadly, which is why I grieved, my beloved doggie Ernesto has passed away to the great doggie sky. (I am myself not a person of faith, but Ernesto was a devout follower of religion. He always told me about it.) Gunther, who thought himself as kind as he is smart, provided me with a replacement in form of a shit-zu. It is a very expensive brand of Japanese dogs, but it also makes a lot of high-pitched noise. I quietly replaced the shit-zu with a Lassie (not a Scottish lassie, but the one from the movie, only it was actually a different one because it is a very old movie) and he never noticed. Doggie God bless you, Gunther, while you and your 4 (four) sluts are recovering from your *infectious* enthusiasm for your 14 centimeters. This has been very hard for both of us (Ernesto and myself) and I'm sure you (my Fans, not Gunther) appreciate my need to withdraw from the hurly burly of writing bestselling novels during this time.

Secondly, there was that ghastly misunderstanding in Thailand. It's important my loyal fanbase understands you shouldn't believe everything you've read in the *Daily Daily* or *Persons*. (Even if it's been lodged at court, as my successful appeal against that dreadful, unfounded conviction demonstrates.)

Anyway! The wonderful news is I'm now free to devote my time to writing novels once more! As Lassie sits next to me, faithful (unlike some) and loving, I channel her lovingness, if not faithfulness, into my third soon-to-be-published (while you are reading this it is clearly already published) novel, *Haggis MacBrawn's (no longer a) Biggest Secret*!!!

Yours literarily

Karen McCompostine (award winning (when I win one, this book will already be published, so I am simply sparing everyone's time changing this in the future and are we not, after all, all really winners in this strange game called life?) Author and feminine romance Icon)

Chapter One

"Oh, Annabelle, I don't know what to think," declared Liza Bonbonet snottily, pausing to blow her nose with considerable vigour into an already uncomfortably moist handkerchief.

Annabelle Elle Ellendeling, lost for words even though she was very good with words in most situations, looked around the elegant, if understated, gold-plated kitchen of Liza's home. It was larger than the farmhouse she now lived in with her fiancé, the handsome and beautifully toned former billionaire Haggis Angus MacBrawn. Annabelle and Haggis enjoyed (although Annabelle was not entirely sure whether "enjoyed" was the right word) a simple life in the High Lowlands of the Lower Highlands of Scotland, ignoring the small complication which meant that every night on the stroke of midnight (GMT) a terrible curse meant Haggis transformed into a werehaggis until 6:00am (GMT). The very thought brought a greasy smell to Annabelle's pretty nostrils, making her nauseouser than she already was. Poor Haggis – it wasn't his fault, she thought guiltily, due to the guilt she was feeling.

Her new best friend Liza (new because Annabelle's old best friend, the very hilarious Brenda had treacherously and not at all hilariously betrayed her in the most treacherous way, making Annabelle out to be a shameful homewrecking slut in some dreadful stories run by that awful excuse for a newspaper, the *Daily Daily*) shared her home with Moanmoan the Samoan, the glamourous acting couple bringing glamour to the beauty of the High Lowlands of the Lower Highlands of Scotland. Speaking of beauty, *Daily Daily* and some other *Nature Publications of Climate* complained a lot about how elegantly the ancient (which meant older than twenty-four years old, as Annabelle knew from her own example) woodland had been gently bulldozed to make space for their three storey concrete home which was mostly made of glass. (As if Scotland was short of trees! What it was short of were Moanmoans the Samoans and Lizas Bonbonets, glamourous acting couples.) The thing that really should have been complained about, thought Annabelle judgementally but in the nicest way possible, was that the house, featured in *Gopping Designs*, was designed by the the loveable Kevin McStorm, who seemed to have a thing for huge windows and an allergy to curtains. Or walls. Even in the loo. Despite living in a hut (which Haggis and she agreed to call a "farmhouse" because they believed in positive thinking) which he (Haggis) had made of turf and rubble, using his own hands, as Haggis MacBrawn was no longer a billionaire and rarely even a thousandaire, Annabelle found her house to be more homely, even though she had to go to the ladies' powder room in the woods, but the woods provided more cover than glass.

But Annabelle reminded herself this was not the important part.

"I know I should be happy," continued Liza sniffily. "My beloved, world-famous, if not critically acclaimed Moanmoan and I, who is beloved, world-famous, and critically acclaimed, live in this lovely house with its huge windows paid for by the millions we've earned from appearing together in the highly successful and critically half-acclaimed movie *Aquasplash*. I have you, Annabelle, my new best friend and neighbour. Even though we've only just met if feels like I have been friends with you forever. Yet, there's something wrong."

"Really?" said Annabelle, her voice rising in pitch. She took a sip of her coffee, pretending that was the reason, although she should have sipped it before the pitch rose, since the beans had been eaten and excreted by rats in order to add to the flavour. It was the sort of fancy coffee actors loved to buy to show they were rich and successful, unlike the instant NotCafé Annabelle drank at home.

Annabelle cleared her throat, her voice rising in pitch even further. "Goodness me, Liza, my voice is rising in pitch," she said, which was called lampshading, so Liza wouldn't notice. "It must be because these amazing coffee beans have been eaten and excreted by rats in order to add to the flavour because you and Moanmoan are so rich and successful, and it's so unlike the instant NotCafé I drink at home."

"Honestly, I can't tell the difference between this and NotCafé," Liza replied with a non-mascara-smearing-tearful shrug, which made Annabelle wonder whether unscrupulous people sometimes took advantage of the rich and famous. Poor (rich) Liza looked distraught. Oh, thought guiltily Annabelle, that was not because of the coffee.

"So," continued Annabelle, pleased that Liza no longer had any suspicions whatsoever about her high-pitched voice, unless she was acting like someone who had no suspicions, but that was enough, "what makes you think something is wrong?"

Liza stood and did that thing actors sometime do where they walk around with a coffee cup whilst talking and never spill a drop, unlike normal people who would drench themselves just by standing up. "I think, my dear best friend Annabelle who I can trust more than anyone else in the whole world, that Moanmoan is having an affair."

"No!" gasped Annabelle in a squeak.

Liza nodded at her friend with beautiful, round, sad eyes that were like a pool of sadness, if sadness were a thing that was sort of like a liquid and sort of like an eye. Or, indeed, two of them, since Liza had two eyes.

"Yes. It's in the little things. A sadness in his smile when he smiles at me. A distance in his gaze when he gazes. All the bunches of flowers he brings from a mysterious place I do not know. Those extra boxes of condoms that arrive with the weekly shop. It's hard to put my finger on it, but something is going on, Annabelle, I'm sure of it."

Annabelle carefully steered their conversation on to more normal things, like how expensive it was to get a *Lamportini* sports car serviced in Scotland, and how it was nice the environmental protesters had stopped throwing eggs at the windows of their tasteful three-story concrete home with a gold-plated kitchen. When Liza left to go to the shops Annabelle was grateful for the excuse to return to the farmhouse. She felt a squirmy, guilty thing, a lot like guilt, squirm inside her as Liza gave her a hug goodbye. As Annabelle walked down the path to the farmhouse she could not stop herself from thinking about (dead) Sister Bernadette. Squirmy didn't quite cover it. Because Sister Bernadette was very judgemental and unlike Annabelle, in a very not nice way at all.

For her treacherous ex-best friend Brenda was right. Annabelle was indeed a shameful slut, even if all of the details of the reports in the horrid *Daily Daily* had been wrong. For Annabelle was currently having a torrid affair with Moanmoan the Samoan, even though it broke the #1 romance rule in romantic novels (And here, Dear Reader, I am breaking the so-called fourth wall to make sure you understand just how cutting edge *this* romance novel is going to be, since I have greatly developed as an author due to the circumstances I outlined in the Presage, so hold on tight and grab those tissues! For your eyes. Not for creepy reasons I wish to not hear about.).

Chapter Two

❦

Haggis MacBrawn greeted Annabelle with a cheery wave as he worked out in the fields where they grew the things they grew on the farm. He was dressed in the typical attire worn by all ex-billionaire Scotsmen who now live on farms, long socks covering his shapely calves, a tight kilt that showed off his muscular thighs, a sporran that flapped seductively and a pristine white shirt of the 'slim fit' cut that most men called Gunther can only eye jealously in the department store before moving on to options such as 'regular' before realising that they are, in fact, only able to wear 'large'.

"Annabelle," he masculinely called out in that brawny Scottish brogue that still made Annabelle's knees go weak. She was, after all, only a woman, thoroughly exposed to all seasons of *Outoflander* which was a television series staring Scottish men who spoke with Scottish accent, and now she was living the dream, although she was only living it at certain times of day and not really during the night.

"It's good to see everything is growing so well, irrespective of the season," she replied, hugging him even though he had been a long way off mere moments ago. Such was the power of love. But only his. Annabelle blushed shamefully, knowing she was a hussy and she didn't deserve the love of this incredible man, who had done some good things and some bad things as well, but repaid for them (literally) and was now a modestly kilted farmer with not a single billion to his soul.

But Annabelle was not a material girl. (This is not a quote from the famous singer Maradonna, because if it was, then I would have changed it, because I don't want to be sued.)

"Soon the things we're growing will be grown and ready to go to Ivor McClunge to be used as ingredients to make his soon-to-be-award-winning whisky, *McClunge's Finest*," Haggis declared as the sun rays embosomed him romantically through a midge-infested sky.

"I do worry, though, Haggis," said Annabelle worriedly. "Whisky takes a long time to ferment in those barrels, even though it is sold in bottles, which makes no sense, but I wouldn't know that, because I am a mere woman who drinks sherry. It could be years before *McClunge's Finest* can be bought by customers who don't want to go blind. I'm delighted that your business acumen is playing the long game and you've waived your payment for our crops of things we grow in this field for a stake in Ivor's whisky enterprise, but we will be poor for many years as a result of the long business game you are playing over such a long time with such acumen."

Haggis gave a Scottish laugh (for they were in Scotland and not France like in the last novel) that declared their love was all that was needed. "Our love is all that is needed until then," he declared. "Besides, we have your income from your job in the flower shop in the village. We can manage on that for now, wee lassie." Annabelle loved it when he spoke in the Scottish dialect and felt even more of a hussy at the same time, because she was conflicted as a character. She would have been much less conflicted if Moanmoan the Samoan was infected by Scottish brogue due to living in Scotland and not even having walls, but unfortunately he wasn't.

"I suppose," she said sadly despite not being a material girl, but her guilt made her sad.

Haggis gave a sigh, looking wistful. "Aye, we'll manage. It's a good job my work out here is nearly done. Soon, I must be home, even though it's still the morning. I must squat over my tray and transform at midnight (GMT) into a haggis." He looked deep into her eyes and Annabelle blinked as a greasy smell which she was imagining because it was actually smell of manure wafted between them. "It astounds me how lucky I am to have found someone to love me, just as I am, without reservation or qualm, despite the fact I become a Scottish dish that divides opinion on the nightly basis. I'm truly the luckiest man alive. Ye ken?"

"If only there was a way to lift the curse," Annabelle said, stroking his manly cheek, knowing there was a way to lift the curse, but she wasn't doing her part.

"Hmm," said Haggis frowning unhappily if lovingly. "So much has gone on, it's sometimes difficult to remember all the specifics of the magical curse that condemned me and my poor wee sister, Potty, to become nightly shifters. [Nigel, make sure "shifters" doesn't get misspelt. – Karen] [Sure beans – Ed.] Perhaps I misunderstood the rules of the curse made by that foul witch, Jane Smith (curse her common name, which makes her so difficult to track down). After all, I was a billionaire who did lots of mergers and acquisitions, not magic. I thought the true love that we share, without flaw or blemish, where you love me just as I am now my secret and my even darker secret have both been revealed would be enough. Yet somehow, I'm still condemned to become a haggis. Ye ken?"

"I ken it very much," Annabelle told him in flawless Scottish, since she had a natural affinity for languages, picking them up as easily as Liza picked up her ratty coffee in order to pace around the kitchen. "We'll unlock the mystery, Haggis, I promise."

Haggis smiled at her with those beautiful blue eyes of his,

which was rather disconcerting as most people smile using their mouth, but Annabelle would have loved him exactly as he was if not for the fact that she didn't. "Never mind the curse, my love. I'm happier than I've ever been in my life, even if we are temporarily crushingly poor due to my long term business strategies. Let me make you a sandwich before you go to work."

"That would be lovely," Annabelle replied, though her heart was heavy. Heavy from all the secrets she'd locked away inside it, secrets that made her a hussy, and thus continued to condemn her fiancé to transform into his squelchy sheep intestine wrapped shifter form. So heavy they were in her heart, she leaned over to the left (where her heart was located) a little bit as they walked down the path to their rustically charming farmhouse that remained a hut no matter how positively they thought and how hard they manifested.

Chapter Three

Annabelle worked at the completely coincidentally named florist's shop of Fleur du Amour, which served as a cruel reminder of her betrayous ex-best friend Brenda, who ran the cafe Cafe du Amour where Annabelle had previously worked and where she had first met Haggis. It was like there was a shortage of ideas of what to call things, which was crazy because there are lots of words and most of those are English. But also Annabelle spoke fluent French and that reminded her of France, where she had also met Haggis who travelled internationally. Oh, thought Annabelle bitterly despite the sandwich being with jam, the times!

Annabelle donned her florist's apron and placed the jammy sandwich Haggis had lovingly made for her on the counter. She waited for something to happen and it immediately did, which she heard the unmistakeable growl of a *Lamportini* sports car wending its way through the glens of the High Lowlands of the Lower Highlands of Scotland. Annabelle felt that growl deep in her soft-walled cave of pleasure. Even though it was not a mystery who was coming, because only one person in the High Lowlands of the Lower Highlands of Scotland owned a

Lamportini. But it did growl anyway. Such was the power of Moanmoan the Samoan.

The florist's shop bell jingled seductively as Moanmoan (who Haggis, inexplicably, called Jax, which seemed disrespectful despite their friendship, after all, Annabelle did not call her best friend Liza Bonbonet "Limbo") strode inside. Tall and muscular, his six pack was clearly visible through his tight-fitting T-shirt (it was a six pack made of muscles, not the sort available in cheap supermarkets, wrapped in plastic, I looked up some pictures but could not insert them here as explanation because of intellectual property rights, but I did have a hot flush and had to fan myself for a bit). Annabelle dragged her eyes from Moanmoan's body up to his handsome, roguish face, framed by a thick, luxuriant beard in which a ferret could frolic happily for a week. If only Annabelle could stop her lips from gluing to his for an entire week. Which she couldn't.

"Can I help you? As a customer in my shop and not in any other way, of course," said Annabelle loudly, just in case any of the villagers should overhear them.

"I would like some flowers please," said Moanmoan badboyishly.

"Really," remarked Annabelle, who worked in a flower shop, which only sold flowers, but she did not fall for Moanmoan because of his intellect. "What kind?"

Moanmoan raised his eyebrow, which wriggled like an inexplicably sexy caterpillar. "The kind that come in bunches, so I can take them home to the woman I so unfortunately married seventeen years ago on a youthful whim. She likes flowers, whilst I like you, Annabelle." He placed his manly, tattooed hands on the counter. Their fingers were a bit like huge, fat sausages but ripped and not greasy in any way, and did not smell of haggis or manure, but of Channel perfume for men.

Annabelle chewed her lip, knowing it would be impossible to resist Moanmoan's charms, although she sort-of wished she called him Jax like Haggis did because that would be so much easier to say. "What about those over there?" she asked, waving in the general direction of all the flowers.

"Perfect," he growled without even looking at the buckets of bouquets. Annabelle's garden of mystery became both less and more mysterious at the thrum of that single word. "I think some of them need watering, though."

"Really?" Annabelle gasped at being critiqued for not doing her job right.

"Yes, really. They need a good hosing." He explained. This made Annabelle feel mansplained because he was a man and she reacted with irritation many of my readers will understand. Unless they are men.

"Well, if *you* want to grab that watering can over there I'm sure –"

"No," Moanmoan interjected, his eyebrows competing with each other in the seductiveness contest (the one on the left was winning, but it was a close race, although at short distance). "No, Annabelle, I'm being sexily flirtatious. What I mean to say is I have my own, special hose right here."

"Gosh," said Annabelle, who had a weakness towards men who were good with words.

"It's very hot in here," said Moanmoan as his strong fingers reached out to stroke her arms and suddenly Annabelle was not at all irritated. "Perhaps you'd like me to take off some of those clothes you're wearing so you can cool down. You can keep your pinny on, though."

Annabelle was powerless to resist those eyebrows and also his powerful arms that he dragged her into, not that she needed to be dragged an awful lot, only over the counter that divided their hungry bodies. It appeared like the water (metaphorical word) filling his hose was under great pressure and she possessed the key to the tap. Soon, possibly in the next paragraph...

But no. Annabelle's dreams were brutally interrupted as the shop bell rang and her new best friend Liza who she'd known for a month walked into the shop. Although she did not know where Annabelle worked, so that meant she was not here to visit her best friend (Annabelle). Who gasped and shoved Moanmoan down behind the counter, out of sight. Liza approached with a friendly smile and Annabelle reciprocated with slight nerves on her face and very delicate nerves that Moanmoan was examining very closely and naughtily underneath the counter.

"I saw my beloved husband's car outside the shop," spoke Liza. "I just wondered if you'd seen him?"

"No," said Annabelle, inwardly cursing as her voice wobbled in highness as Moanmoan's lush, bearded face began to explore her delicious candy store like a ferret would explore his beard.

"If you do see Moanmoan please tell him to give me a call on my expensive *ePhone*," said Liza, who was examining the buckets of bouquets with an expression on her face that Annabelle would describe if she currently had mind to describe things, but it was not a happy expression. "Maybe he's gone down to the betting shop again?" she (Liza) wondered aloud.

"Maybe," squealed Annabelle, whose betting shop was winning left and right (and deep).

Liza looked at the sandwich on the counter before she left. "I can tell Haggis made this for you, Annabelle," she remarked in a way suggesting she knew things about Haggis's sandwiches that made them different from sandwiches made by other people. "I see jam. Yum yum." This rhymed in her American accent and Annabelle let out a high-pitched sound that she was ready to describe as laughter because Liza was nearly as hilarious as Brenda if this was a joke. "Don't let it go stale."

"Ohhh," Annabelle replied throatily, looking down at the bread. The edges were already curling up because this sandwich was really a metaphor for Annabelle's relationship with Haggis. But the jam was sweet and hot (when they made it) and

Moanmoan made her feel all sweet and hot too, of course after Liza departed, several times, whilst in the florist shop and the edges curled exactly like Annabelle's toes when she emitted sounds of ecstasy for numerous times. Moanmoan deserved his name, she thought absent-mindedly, much more than "Jax."

Chapter Four

"I love you, Annabelle, ye ken?" Haggis squelched, late that night as he squatted in his tray in haggis form.

"I love you too," Annabelle replied, curled up on the bed like her toes earlier during the day, the tray full of Haggis on the floor beside her. She felt terrible, especially when the accusatory smell of onions wafted over her.

Something would have to be done. They couldn't carry on like this.

She would speak to Moanmoan the Samoan. This wasn't fair. It had to stop. She was engaged after all, Haggis' fifth-hand ring on her finger. Enjoying the delights of Moanmoan's chiselled masculine rippling toned and artfully tattooed flesh (Annabelle thought he shaved, and yet his skin was so smooth. She thought he probably used moisturiser as well. Actually, thinking of how lucky his moisturiser was and how moist her secret delight was wasn't helping.). How did she become such a monster of desire fuelled with lust? Enjoying Moanmoan was all well and good but Haggis had given up everything for her, even though it was actually quite annoying that he was no longer a billionaire and he hadn't needed to have done any of that in her opinion. It would have been nice to be asked, Annabelle opinionated, since as his fiancé she should have had a word (or a paragraph) on the topic of his numerous horses turning out to be a hut that barely fitted a bed, Annabelle, and a bowl filled with a shifting ex-billionaire.

It's just lust, Annabelle thought in the stillness of the Scottish night (a fact about Scotland: Scottish nights are still, so that Scotsmen's bun-buns don't accidentally get exposed by a gust of wind, which would be awkward to everyone but me while I was doing my research), the werehaggis slorpily snoring (snorping?) next to her. I, she told herself in the voice of Sister Bernadette, then realised that would be wrong pronouns because Annabelle was speaking to herself and Sister Bernadette was still dead, so she changed the tone to her own when she was berating a gorgeously muscled rugby player Seamus O'Shaughnessy for his naughtiness, which now made her think of Seamus's winning pole. I, Annabelle repeated, somewhat unfocused now, am an empowered young woman of the 21st Century and I am NOT a slave to my passions.

Except while Annabelle was not a feminist because she was not a lesbian homosexual and also shaved her armpits, she had a feeling that being an empowered young woman meant that she should follow her passions, as wild and shocking as they were. Ideally she would follow them inside a *Lamportini* car with lights romantically switched off.

The dreams Annabelle had that night were confusing in a very moisturising way.

Chapter Five

❧

Annabelle stood by the windows in Liza and Moanmoan's tastefully decorated home, which was visible from space, late the next night. She was not wondering whether due to the lack of curtains and herself being quite naked she was also visible from space. But if she was, Annabelle, as an empowered 21st Century woman, whose breasts were still quite perky for her age, would not let space perverts shame her into clothing, because this wasn't *The Footmaid's Story*.

Moanmoan, whose name Annabelle repeated many times in the previous hours, was sprawled on the king-sized bed (which was too small for him because kings were not that tall, apparently) with hands behind his head and a satisfied expression on his handsomely bearded face. All of his tattoos looked freshly moisturised by the layer of erotic sweat that had been produced by their throbbing exertions, the mere thought of which caused Annabelle's cupcake to be sprinkled with yearning. Love was like that. It was possible to yearn for someone who was just a few steps away as you stood naked by a window visible from space. Moanmoan's prize-winning (if there were prizes for this sort of thing, which there probably are, come to think of it) orchid of wonder was on full display and Annabelle found it difficult to tear her longing gaze away from the enormous stamen which formed its jaw-dropping centrepiece. (She turned away from the window in the meantime.) Cupcakes and orchids did not really go together, she thought, overthinking it, and she might have to come up with a different metaphor for Moanmoan's special physical attributes. [Or is it a simile, Nigel? I never know – Karen] [I'll check in the dictionary and let you know – Ed.] [Shouldn't editors just know those things? – Karen] [You do your job and I do mine (wink emojicon) – Ed.]

"Won't Liza be back soon?" asked Annabelle worriedly as her heart filled with guilt, unlike her special cupcake that still felt the effects of the orchid that filled it repeatedly earlier.

Moanmoan shook his head and his long hair flew in waves like a horse's mane when there is wind from the side. "No, she's still out paragliding."

"In the dark?" said Annabelle, who was surprised.

"She's an expert paraglider," Moanmoan explained for the benefit of the reader, because this is an important plot point later on. "She did all her own stunts in *Aquasplash*," he added.

"What about you?" Annabelle asked, already impressed at the thought of what he was going to say, promising herself to watch *Aquasplash* but fast-forwarding the bits with Liza in them.

"Oh no," laughed Moanmoan, "I'm not stupid. Some guy called Jeff did them for me. I do not remember his second name because he is not important for the book."

"Even so, I'd better go home before Haggis misses me. I don't like to lie to him," Annabelle added sadly, although technically it wasn't a lie as long as he didn't ask, which meant she really had to go. Her wide eyes transported this message to Moanmoan longingly, but he looked unfazed by her conflicted feelings.

"We could tell them," Moanmoan replied.

Annabelle's heart fluttered like a butterfly that's ingested far too many amphetamines for butterfly party standards. "Tell them? Surely you can't be serious."

"Is this web of lies and deceit any better?" asked Moanmoan, his eyebrows conducting a quizzical dance to communicate the complex emotions that made him more than just a body most women and quite a few gay homosexual men (if not the majority, actually, because Moanmoan was something of a gay icon, not unlike I, the author) would die merely to be near. Let alone do all the things Annabelle had been doing, and then Moanmoan was doing, and then they were like a shampoo, because you have to wash and repeat, except they didn't wash. So this is not really a very good metaphor, but I am sure you know what I mean.

"I came here to end it, Moanmoan," Annabelle told him, determined to do the right thing and not be the slut her ex-best friend Brenda had made her out to be. Bitch. In *Daily Daily*, no less. Annabelle was practically a virgin back then, except for some exceptions. Brenda, Annabelle decided, would never appear in this book again.

"End it? You call that ending it?" Moanmoan laughed deeply, his majestic stamen quivering in quite an alarming way.

Annabelle coughed. She seemed to be out of practice at ending it. Although not at finishing. This she was practicing with alarming regularity.

Moanmoan shook his shaggy head, the forest of his beard framing a set of gleaming teeth normal in America but which people in the UK find positively terrifying, especially in the dark. "Annabelle. Don't you understand?" he explained assertively. "I've been married to Liza for seventeen years but that means nothing to me now I've met you. It's you I love. I know you feel the same way. Neither of us can fight this powerful feeling, so why try? We could have a life together. I'm a millionaire after making so much money filming *Aquasplash*. I could give you everything – far more than Haggis. Be honest, if you really loved him wouldn't you have already married him?"

"It's not that easy with all the organic things we have to grow on the farm using the best and most environmentally friendly techniques," Annabelle replied, her heart now feeling like the butterfly was snorting a line of cocaine drugs for extra fizz. Which Annabelle wouldn't know how it felt, because she did not use drugs and also wasn't a butterfly, but it felt like that, somehow. "We're still planning the wedding and all my time is spent running *Fleur du Amour*."

"I'm your only customer," Moanmoan pointed out, flinging his arms wide and gesturing at the bouquets in vases, as they were too rich and famous to put them in buckets unless ironically, throughout the whole glass house, so she could see all of them at once.

"Even so, Moanmoan, this is nothing more than lust. I am a modern woman of the 21st Century and I have... responsibilities... and a duty to Haggis... and... Goodness me, how can it be getting bigger?"

"That's the effect you have on me," Moanmoan told her, his thornless, juicy cactus swaying pendulously from side to side with hypnotic power. "It's the magic of love, my darling Annabelle. Who are we to resist?"

Who indeed? Was what Annabelle thought as Moanmoan gently took her by the hand (he stood up earlier before flinging his arms, I forgot to say) and led her back to the king-sized bed.

It was already past midnight when Annabelle finally, and reluctantly despite her hurry, extracted herself from Moanmoan's strong arms. She ran to the toilet, cursing when she realised it was surrounded by nothing but glass. She mustered all her dignity as she took a ladylike doo-doo [You can't say "crap," that's not ladylike – Ed.] [FINE, Nigel, mansplain crap at me – Karen] in the full view of the late-night traffic pouring down the A99. Clearly Kevin McStorm was a complete idiot and so were the many magazines that covered (if only) his design and the awards that he won for it.

After hurriedly dressing and kissing Moanmoan goodbye,

Annabelle trudged back to the farmhouse, pondering on his words. Was he right? Was this love rather than lust? She knew deep inside, quite deep indeed, but then, maybe she was simply overpowered by desire as strong as Moanmoan's strong arms. Was this why Haggis was still transforming into a savoury Scottish dish every night? Had she ever loved Haggis, or had it really been his billions from all those mergers and acquisitions that caught her attention? Was she really that shallow? This thought and the one before arrived in the voice of Sister Bernadette and now Annabelle felt shame, but not enough shame not to warmly recall the shenanigans of the never enough hours just before.

Deep in those thoughts, Annabelle opened the door to the farmhouse as quietly as she could so as not to disturb Haggis, who would be sleeping in his tray. She gasped with surprise when she saw a surprising sight that surprised her. For, sitting there at the kitchen table, because in the meantime Haggis made the house bigger and now there was a kitchen, was a young woman.

"Hello Annabelle," she said in a Scottish accent, because she was Scottish. Which made Annabelle gasp in French, hoping the Scottish woman won't understand. "It's lovely to finally meet you."

Chapter Six

❧

Annabelle stared at her visitor, thinking the woman looked familiar. "I'm sorry, I don't think I know you," she spoke worriedly. "What are you doing in my house?"

"Och. I have a key," the woman told her with a warm smile. "I'm family, after all."

"Family?" Annabelle asked, bemused.

The woman nodded. "Yes, we're soon to be sisters-in-law, Annabelle. I'm Potty MacBrawn."

Annabelle gasped. "Potty MacBrawn. Haggis's wee sister, who lives all alone, deep in the forest of Scotland because she was similarly cursed and now faces life as a... as a..."

"Werepotty," Potty supplied, sensing Annabelle's discomfort. If you were going to be a shifter, it was fair to say that the ability to transform into a small, portable commode was pretty low down the list of options (not that people who are cursed are generally given the chance to pick, because the point of the curse is to be inconvenient). Annabelle shuddered, remembering Haggis telling her how, upon changing back in the morning, Potty had experienced some traumatic moments before her self-imposed exile. "Also, I would prefer if you avoided the word 'wee'." Potty shivered and so did Annabelle, in strong empathy although she had never experienced this sort of thing, because she was not a freak.

Annabelle had a flash of understanding, a bit like a lightbulb lighting up above her head, representing the idea that was forming in her mind. Due to her flash of understanding. "But wait. It's after midnight (GMT). Shouldn't you have transformed into ... well, into a potty?"

"Until recently, yes," Potty told her with a smile of joy and happiness that lit the kitchen where Haggis hadn't installed electricity yet. "Things have changed and the curse has been lifted."

"How? Why? How? Why?" Asked Annabelle.

"The curse can only be removed in one of two ways," Potty explained. "Jane Smith has the power to lift the curse herself, but because of her incredibly common name and the sheer number of mergers and acquisitions Haggis completed as he amassed his billions, she is impossible to find. He fired so many Jane Smiths, they are like grains of sand on the shore of a very, very long beach that has lots of sand on it. So, not very easy at all."

"So, if Jane Smith didn't free you, what happened?" Annabelle's heart butterfly needed to take some downers, not that I (the author) or Annabelle would know what they were.

"Surely you can guess, Annabelle?" questioned Potty quizzically. "The only other way the curse can be lifted is through finding true love. A person who loved me not only as Potty MacBrawn, wee... younger sister of Haggis and the late and sadly departed Tartan MacBrawn, but who truly loved me in my shifter form."

"They loved you ... as a potty?" Annabelle asked. "You don't think that's a little bit problematic?"

"Your fiancé is currently a traditional Scottish dish, resting on a tray in your bedroom and you're asking me that question?" Annabelle blushed deeply as Potty continued truthfully. "I was living in a remote forest as you know, to avoid any possibility of being... occupied... whilst in my shifter form. It was a lonely life, so I was grateful for online shopping."

"It's a miracle you could get an online connection deep in the remote forests of Scotland," Annabelle pointed out factually. "We can't get any kind of internet signals here at all!"

"Yes, it was incredibly convenient," said Potty in that woman-of-the-online-world way. To think, thought Annabelle, that she (Annabelle) had a Tweeter account once and was followed by many followers. "Anyway, I would order the things I needed and each week my only human contact was with the supermarket delivery driver. At first it was a different person each week. Then, I noticed that one particular driver kept turning up more and more often. Eventually, the driver worked up the courage to tell me that I was so attractive and desirable, the Mamazon manager permitted the folly of always assigning this route to this one special driver."

"That's a bit stalkerish, wouldn't you say?" Annabelle observed worriedly. She had read about this sort of thing in *Daily Daily* but it only happened to famous people, such as Liza or Moanmoan, and ended with a prison sentence, rather than true love.

Potty pulled a (human) face. "I thought it was romantic, although I was also filled with despair. For I knew that," she said with a note of sadness, but not longing, "no matter how attractive I was and how well moisturised my skin might be, all that would change when I transformed into a small plastic commode. For many weeks, I tried to hide the truth but in the end, I gave in to my carnal desires. After we'd made passionate love, I knew I was soon to lose the object of my affection. Midnight (GMT) struck as we lay in bed, and I changed into my werepotty form, sobbing with anguish as I waited for my new lover's reaction."

"And what happened?" Annabelle asked, her long pause introducing dramatic effect, although not on purpose, but because the vision of a sobbing potty required a bit of recovery time.

"I loved her all the same," said another all-to-familiar voice. Even though Annabelle decided it would not appear in the book ever again! She (Annabelle) turned to face the known uninvited visitor who had been sitting in the lounge (Haggis also built a lounge in the meantime) all this time.

"Yes," Annabelle's ex-best friend Brenda told her with a triumphant smile. "We are proud and out female gay homosexuals!"

Chapter Seven

ANNABELLE'S JAW HIT THE FLOOR IN A METAPHORICAL WAY, AS otherwise she wouldn't have been able to speak and the rest of this novel would have taken on a very different tone. Which I would never do to my readers, since I am not interested in bloody gore and horror. Factually, her jaw remained firmly fixed on her face, where she gawked at Brenda like a fish. [Actually, perhaps that's where I should have started this chapter? I'll make a note to fix this when Nigel does my professional edits as I am enjoying a glass of sherry and a bourbon cream biscuit. Maybe two – one for my sweet doggie Ernesto! [Who had departed as I was during the work on this novel. But I left it as a homage.] – Karen] [TMI, which means too much information – Nigel] [I mean, Ed. – Ed.]

Annabelle gawked like a fish whose jaw had just hit the floor – actually it was the riverbed, since the fish lived in freshwater, but this is a metaphor (or a simile) so it doesn't matter. Brenda looked at her with a smug, self-satisfied look in her eyes. Potty took Brenda's hand and thus proved Annabelle was looking at two homosexual women, who were very much in love in a lesbian sapphic way. Thus rescuing poor Potty from being a potty.

"Brenda, you bitch!" Annabelle said. This was because she had never forgiven Brenda for her betrayal, although the moment was romantic.

"Annabelle, take that back," said Potty, coming to Brenda's defence, like people in love do, which made Annabelle's insides squirm with guilt.

"No," said Brenda. "No, I deserved that because I betrayed my best friend and sold her story to the *Daily Daily*. I am a bitch, even if I'm the bitch you now love wholeheartedly and unashamedly."

You are a better person than me, Annabelle remarked inside of her, not feeling triumphant at all when the two kissed and Annabelle had to look away, because this went on for some time. She made herself a cup of tea and sat down at the kitchen table. After a while she got the biscuit barrel and nibbled on a chocolate nobcock for a time. Delicious. It reminded her a little bit of Moanmoan, although she wasn't sure why. Maybe everything elongated would forever make her think of Moanmoan, Annabelle thought, her absent-minded gaze that was avoiding sapphic love landing on a broomstick.

Eventually the sapphic love scene, which I was going to insert here but I am not familiar with being a gay homosexual woman and I would never lower myself to ask a "ghost writer" to write this for me, came to a shuddering climax that caused Annabelle to shudder with many mixed feelings. Annabelle was relieved when Brenda and Potty joined her at, rather than on, the kitchen table. (Also because they were wearing clothes.)

"I need to know more," said Annabelle. "I know why Potty was living in the remote forests of Scotland but what are you doing up here, my treacherous ex-friend Brenda, working as a supermarket delivery driver? What happened to Cafe du Amour, where we used to work together and you always made me laugh with your hilarious jokes until you betrayed me and sold my story to the *Daily Daily*?"

"Alas, I was forced to sell Cafe du Amour," said Brenda,

sighing tragically. "After the truth about your story broke and it was revealed you weren't a slut at all and Seamus O'Shaughnessy was actually a gay homosexual, there was a backlash. No one visited Cafe du Amour anymore due to my now well-known treacherousness. I have been punished for my greed with ostracism and poverty, Annabelle. I had no choice except to put the business up for sale. Thus devastated, all I could think of was the friendship that I had destroyed, all for some hard cash. The friendship with you," she made specific. "I came out here searching for you, taking a job as a local Mamazon delivery driver to meet as many people as possible, providing they had reliable access to the internet."

"But we had no broadband at the farm," said Annabelle understandingly. Her heart softened like the nobcock she dipped in the tea.

Brenda nodded. "But imagine my surprise when I found myself falling in love with none other than Haggis MacBrawn's wee sister." Potty frowned at this understandably, but Scottish brogue was something that nobody could resist. "It was fate, Annabelle, and now it has given me a chance to reach out to you again."

"I didn't know you found women to be of erotic interest," Annabelle remarked. "Much less romantic," she added hastily.

Brenda shook her head, in contrast to having nodded before, because it was an emotional and confusing situation where all the emotions were involved. "I didn't realise for a long time Annabelle. I never found you attractive, but Potty awoke something in me, something I never realised, but I knew it was true as soon as I felt it for the first time."

Annabelle blinked, her nobcock hardening somewhat, metaphorically that is. Just when she was beginning to feel forgiveness towards her ex-best friend Brenda, with whom she had laughed at so many (Brenda's) jokes, Brenda was being a bitch again, so coldly declaring that she didn't find her attractive and, even if she (Brenda) hadn't realised at the time she was a gay woman, it still bruised her (Annabelle's) pride.

Potty gave Annabelle a piercing look that reached Annabelle's very core. "So, that's our story. When Brenda's love was undimmed after my transformation the curse was broken, and I changed from being a werepotty back into the body of a regular person with a really strange name." She paused. "Actually, I now go by Poutine. It's a French name." Which Annabelle, of course, knew. "I came to tell Haggis the news. That there was hope. Yet when I got here, I realised something. I think you know what I mean."

Annabelle shook her head. "No, I don't think I do."

"No, you do," insisted Potty.

"No, I don't."

"No, you do. You are in what they call denial, Annabelle. It's undeniable."

Annabelle gasped. For the second time in two consecutive books, her eyes were opened metaphorically, since they were already open.

"Now you understand," said Potty, with a sad smile.

"Yes," Annabelle replied, "for my eyes have just been opened. In a metaphorical way. Providing a window to my soul to my eyes that I have in my face. You're talking about him."

They all looked at the bedroom door. From inside, the soft sound of squelching snores drifted into the kitchen, together with the smell of onion and grease. For in that bedroom slept an unloved werehaggis, whose curse had not been lifted at all by Annabelle's love which she couldn't see through the window in her soul, because it wasn't there.

All the women sobbed over how sad this was for Haggis, because the physical exertions they have engaged in (although not at the same time and place) made them very emotional.

Chapter Eight

❧

Haggis was delighted to learn Potty had been freed from the curse of the werepotty, which was a pretty horrid curse when you stopped to think about it, especially when you stopped at a surprise potty in a Scottish forest and didn't know better. He arose at 6:00am (GMT) when he transformed back into his human form. Annabelle listened to his delighted humming in the shower (actually Haggis did a lot of work on the farmhouse in the meantime *and* had enough human brains to put up walls), washing away the smell of one dish Annabelle would never, ever order in any restaurant, even if it was French. He'd given up everything (which Annabelle never truly forgave him for, which she did see through the window to her soul, and it explained way more than she would like to, since apparently she was a material girl after all) for her and Annabelle had nothing to give in return, except for a freshly cleaned bowl that she didn't even clean yesterday, because she was in another man's tattooed arms.

Potty and Brenda headed back to Potty's remote home in the Scottish forest, holding hands, and Haggis departed the house to begin working in the fields doing various things to the things that grew in them so that one day they could be put into barrels. Annabelle watched him from the window, in his smart tartan with his sexy sporran bouncing away in that alluring way sporrans do during field work. She gave a deep sigh, longingly wishing things were different. But they were not different, although they were also not the same, which was simultaneously confusing and completely clear, leaning further towards confusing the longer she thought about it.

With her heart heavy once more and a definite lean to the left in her stride, Annabelle left the farmhouse with a shower and a kitchen table that she felt she didn't deserve, to go to work at Fleur du Amour. Haggis rushed up towards her from the field and enveloped her in his Scottish arms.

"You've a wee face like a slapped arse, my love," he said, though his manly Scottish accent, which dripped with masculinity and testosterone, couldn't pierce the metaphorical cloud he couldn't see (because it was a metaphor) that hung over Annabelle's weary head. Unlike Potty's piercing look earlier. Which could, if it (the look) was still available. Potty's piercing abilities were uncanny.

"Oh, Haggis," she sighed as seductively as she could, "you can slap my arse later if you wish. But not too hard, because I am not one of those *60 Shadows* women who enjoy the sort of behaviours inexplicably causing the novels in which they are described to become bestselling books and movies." Annabelle thought about this for a moment. "Slap away," she instructed.

"That's not what I meant," he replied, with a carefree laugh, brown eyes sparkling with joy and no slapping. "Potty is no longer a cursed shifter. You should be happy for her!"

"I am happy for her," confessed Annabelle truthfully. Which was becoming a rare thing for her. "Well, as happy as I can be about someone I've never met before in my life because they've been living the life of a hermit in the forest, save for some online shopping."

"Then why the sad face, wee lassie?" he purred in Scottish,

like a Scottish lion whose sporran was being lifted by an unmistakeable lever of interest.

"Haggis, doesn't what happened to Potty make you wonder ..." Annabelle trailed off, wondering if she should say anything.

"Why the sapphic love between your ex-best friend Brenda and Potty should have banished the curse, whilst I continue my existence as a werehaggis, even though you're the love of my life and my fiancé?" Haggis asked with such alarming clarity it was as if the book was about to end right there. But it was (the book) not a murder story so it didn't.

"Well, yes," admitted Annabelle miserably.

"Ah well, ye ken, love is a strange thing, Annabelle Elle Ellendeling," he said, using her full name for no apparent reason, which Annabelle found alarming. "I think I know why."

"Are you going to tell me?" she asked, afraid of the answer but still asking him to answer it anyway, which was a bit dumb if you stop to think about it but then again Annabelle wasn't always the sharpest knife in the drawer and was often led astray by her feminine passions and lusts.

"Yes, my darling Annabelle," Haggis said as Annabelle pondered the question of whether Potty and Brenda were feminists underneath their clothes, simultaneously wishing she had looked and that she hadn't had that thought at all. "I'm just building up to it, that's all." He said, which made her feel guilty because she had not thanked him for building a shower and walls. "Their love started in full revealing glory of many shapes. As ye ken, ours was shadowed by secrets, hidden in the shame of my bowl for too long. Now that all our secrets have been stripped away, like your clothes will be soon because my sporran is becoming very uncomfortable, we're living our simple lives as a farmer and a florist. Our love is sprouting from the ground like the flowers you sell and the things I grow so that one day in the far, far future Ivor McClunge can ferment them in his barrels. In the meantime, this ground of secrets that our love is blazingly sprouting from, not unlike what I carry underneath my sporran, weighs heavy on our arms. I," he spoke, and his eyes avoided hers, which Annabelle could tell even though his chin rested on her shoulder, but such is the power of female intuition, "have no other, even bigger secrets. I'm just a poor, simple Scotsman in a well-fitting kilt earning an honest wage, that is, once my alcoholic investment pays off. The love that exists between Potty and Brenda is the pure, sapphic kind and that ended the curse. Their flower has hardened into a brave oak that disemboweled the sun. One day," he said with great certainty that Annabelle didn't feel, "I will find myself never having to squat over a tray ever again."

"That's what you think?" said Annabelle, incredulously confused by the number of florid metaphors, especially the disemboweling oak, which was something she hoped Potty and Brenda didn't actually do, because it sounded dangerous.

"Aye, lassie, it is. It's either that or you're having a torrid affair with my close friend Jax. Hahahaha! Imagine that!" Haggis laughed with light joy, unsuspecting and pure.

"Ha ha ha ha ha ha ha ha," laughed Annabelle in response, hoping it sounded more genuine than it looked on the page.

And then there was a slap of the arse, as per her own request, but she couldn't quite get into it.

Chapter Nine

❧

THE BELL OF FLEUR DU AMOUR JINGLED HORNILY WITH THE promise of passion as Moanmoan the Samoan (who, Dear Reader, we must also remember is known as Jax and is Haggis MacBrawn's close friend) strode into the florist. This time he had arrived on two motorcycles at once, his legs spread widely and arms crossed on his pectorals, which was simultaneously a very masculine thing to do and arose a worried question inside Annabelle, who wondered whether he could have babies ever again after having done that to his nether regions.

"Annabelle," Moanmoan growled, but not in the way dogs growl, which would be weird. He did it in Samoan, Annabelle suspected.

"Moanmoan," she breathed breathily, flushing with embarrassment at the thought of their passionate and uninhibited lovemaking the day before in a house that served as an exhibitionist cinema situated by a busy main road. It was almost like Moanmoan and Liza were a pair of wanton exhibitionists. Which, being famous actors, they obviously were, Annabelle realised, deeply regretting that she had not been born in the entertainment business. Not because she wanted to be an exhibitionist, though.

Moanmoan's eyes undressed her, which wasn't as easy as it sounds since eyes don't have opposable thumbs. But he was special like that. "You're pink about the cheeks, Annabelle, and you're leaning a bit to the left. Did our passionate lovemaking leave you with a bit of a limp?"

"Shush," shushed Annabelle, turning a shade of scarlet, like the letter. (This is a literary reference some of you might not understand. It means she felt like a hussy caught red-gardened.) "Keep your voice down. No one suspects a thing, even though your house as absolutely no privacy whatsoever and you really need to think about the position of your toilet next to the A99."

"Yeah, Kevin McStorm was drooling over the place on *Gopping Designs*," mused Moanmoan amusedly. "I'm sure I saw him lick the kitchen island when he thought no one was looking. But he doesn't have to live there all the f-asterisk-cking time, does he? And it still smells of eggs sometimes as well, when the wind blows from the east."

"Listen, Moanmoan," said Annabelle, screwing up all her courage into a tiny ball and hurling it at the gigantic wall of lust that threatened to topple down and crush her into a squishy sort of hussy flavoured human jam that nobody would want to put in a sandwich. "I meant what I said yesterday."

"What, that you'd never seen a bigger one?"

"No!" Annabelle exclaimed. "I'm not talking about your ridiculous rat shit [doo-doo – Ed.] coffee maker. I mean this has to end. You're married to a loving wife who's greedily been married to you for seventeen years like some egoist which I am not calling her, and I have a fiancé who's given up everything to be with me, which was very stupid of him, but this is what love does to people and shifters. This affair has to stop," she spoke heavily like her heart. But they were hurting those they loved the most, Annabelle said to conclude.

"Annabelle, I've already told you," Moanmoan insisted masculinely. "You're the one I love."

"Well, I don't love you. I've just been using your body. For all the sex." This was a lie, Annabelle thought, but he did not know that. Or that Haggis built a kitchen with a kitchen table inside while they were bonk-bonking on the down low. Yet instead of guilt, she was filled with heat, already undressed by his eyes above which the lonely caterpillars performed their mating dance, which was not really something she approved of, as caterpillars were technically babies of butterflies like the one using cocaine drugs inside her heart right now. She, Annabelle told herself in third person, was sex-obsessed. Even by caterpillars, although they were really eyebrows. However, she was also a confident, independent woman with a future with her farmer husband and she was not about to throw all that away for some rando famous millionaire actor who possessed *Lamportinis* in all sorts of colours judging by her somewhat hazy memories that were hazed by other things he possessed, and by that she meant neither the two (out of who knew how many?) motorcycles nor the glass house.

Poor, very rich Liza. She was Annabelle's best friend for five weeks now, which should count for something, and definitely would, if Moanmoan shifted into a kale smoothie every midnight (GMT).

"I see," said Moanmoan, stroking with his muscular fingers a beard so lush birds could happily nest in it and raise a clutch of fledglings in warmth, comfort and safety. Although I thought that last bit (with kale smoothie, not the birds) was a good ending for a chapter, but I forgot there was this bit here still left. "That's a pity."

"Why's that?" Annabelle asked reluctantly, knowing this was exactly what the manipulative and so well-equipped he could serve as a tripod actor wanted her to do.

"Because the movie company, *Warmup Brothers*, is about to announce they're making *Aquasplash 2, A Drip Too Far* and I'm going to the launch party in Edinburgh tomorrow. I have a spare ticket for the event and I'm staying at the five-star *Razzle*

Hotel on the Royal Mile. It has a very large bed and a toilet with actual walls."

"But surely Liza should be coming with you as your *Aquasplash* co-star?" Annabelle asked, voice quavering.

"She has a clash with a competitive paragliding competition in Poland," Moanmoan explained. "She'll be gone for several days. Leaving me alone."

Not alone, Annabelle thought sluttishly, if she (Annabelle) had something to say about it.

Chapter Ten

❦

Annabelle left Haggis the following morning, explaining she was closing the shop and going away for a few days at a bouquet tying convention in Edinburgh. Haggis looked at her with those distinctive eyes of his, one blue, one green, each one full of undeserved love and trust. She was crushed by the shame and guilt of how much she didn't feel any shame or guilt.

"That sounds like a great idea, my wee little sassenach." He said. "It's important to keep up with all the latest trends when it comes to tying bouquets if you're in the florist business. Tie one for me whilst you're over there and I'll look after all the things we're growing, here on the farm. Funnily enough, Jax was telling me he's up in Edinburgh too for this launch party for a new film. You two might bump into each other whilst you're there!"

Annabelle almost asked who Jax was, so distracted she was by bumping into each other, which was something that she was intimately acquainted with when it came to "Jax."

As Haggis disappeared in the depths of the fields that grew future single malt, Moanmoan discreetly picked up Annabelle in his *Lamportini* (it was the colour of her *Victorian Mystery* underwear, which was black, like his favourite tipple

Gumminess which he was indulging in, but not during driving which would be irresponsible, and Annabelle couldn't help but wonder, as her underwear lost its dryness somewhat, whether he had so many *Lamportinis* or employed someone to repaint it every morning). They set off, driving at perilous speed through the High Lowlands of the Lower Highlands before reaching the twisting turns of the road that wended its way through the Low Highlands of the Higher Lowlands, which is where, as everyone knows but I shall write it down anyway because I didn't do my research for nothing, the great city of Edinburgh is found. Nothing excites a woman more than a man driving a high-performance sports car he can barely control with reckless disregard for the speed limit and the safety of other innocent road users. So thought Annabelle, pleasantly aroused at the perspective of soon becoming pleasantly aroused, once she stopped being sick into her plastic carrier bag.

With a squeal of tyres and smoke billowing out from the exhaust (of the car), Moanmoan drew up outside the front door of the *Razzle Hotel*. Annabelle staggered out with all the grace she could muster as she emerged from the passenger seat clutching her bag of sick. Which Moanmoan gentlemanly handed to the doorman whilst tossing the keys to the valet when he approached to park their car. Avoiding the doorman's judgemental gaze, because what could *he* know about being driven in a high-performance sports car the driver could barely control with reckless disregard for the speed limit and the safety of other innocent road users, Annabelle followed Moanmoan inside the hotel on shaky legs. She remembered the good old times (but not that old, because Annabelle was still in her prime) when her best friend Brenda held her hair when Annabelle was sick from too much pop music on the dance floor. Since she could scarcely ask Liza to do that while Annabelle was being mercilessly cruised around in Moanmoan's *Lamportini*, she desperately needed a shower for her hair.

"We have time before the evening gala," Moanmoan

asserted as he opened the curtains – a marvellous invention – and took in the majestic city of Edinburgh with a satisfied smile that beamed whiteness all over Edinburgh's majesticity. But before he proceeded to explaining what they had time for, Annabelle dashed into the bathroom, feeling like Cinderella if Cinderella was prone to motion sickness and didn't know which out of the thousand bottles in the bathroom the size of Luxembourg was shampoo.

Luckily, all it took for Annabelle's face to regain its normal non-green colour and her discreet dry-heaving to stop were three wee (she thought in Scottish) double gin-and-tonics in the hotel bar. The press were there for the lavish event the *Warmup Brothers* were putting on, but Annabelle was confident she wasn't the focus of their attention. They spent a lot of time snapping pictures of Moanmoan and the Backhems, who were also there for some reason no one was quite sure about. Especially as the bar didn't serve ice cubes with dressing (water) on the side.

They (the Backhems) didn't seem to know *Aquasplash 2, A Drip Too Far*, was a film, so some people started saying they'd been invited to the wrong event but they still added glamour to the occasion, because they were very glamourous. Although Liza Bonbonet was away at her paragliding meeting in Poland her son (and Moanmoan's step-son) Lemme Crave-Itz, world-renowned musician who played the guitar noisily with both of his hands, also grabbed the attention of the press. Some women were screaming in poorly-disguised lust at his firm jawline and beautifully clipped beard. The hussies, Annabelle thought in disgust, holding on to Moanmoan's sequoia of muscles (his arm).

Over at the bar, Annabelle made herself look inconspicuous in her iridescent cocktail dress made of peacock feathers, making small talk with various film executives and a veterinary surgeon from Aberdeen called Nigel, who will never be mentioned again in this story. With remarkable timing, Moanmoan slid onto the bar stool just as Nigel [Stop this, Nigel

– Karen] [He's leaving – Ed.] vacated it to try and find some chips. [See? All gone – Ed.]

"Fancy finding you here," Moanmoan muttered. "Would you like to go somewhere more private?"

Annabelle fluttered her eyelashes, arousingly wooed by his clever chat line. "That would be nice, but I've only just finished dry heaving," she explained truthfully, because Annabelle decided to become a person who tells the truth at least some of the time. "Perhaps some air first?"

Moanmoan offered Annabelle his arm with a winsome grin (she let go of it earlier before sitting by the bar) [of the arm, not the grin, Nigel, fix this – Karen], framed by a beard that put a young, chiseled, heavily tattooed, double-motorcycle-striding Father Christmas to shame. Together they took in the vibrant night time scene of the Royal Mile, and Annabelle felt much more herself by the time they returned, except "herself" apparently included drowning her *Victorian Mystery* underwear with tangible lust.

One minute after they'd left, Nigel [You should mention that Nigel was very handsome – Ed.] [Shut up Nigel and stop inserting yourself into my book. – Karen] [I am the editor and this means I get to do the edits because that is what editing means. – Ed.] [Then name your handsome character ED, Ed. Except you won't. Because you are fired!!! – Karen (I must remove this with my new editor before the publication)] came back from the chippy across the road, looking wistfully at the empty chair where the lovely girl in the modestly understated peacock dress and hair that was wet on one side had been sitting while not holding Moanmoan's arm, which Nigel didn't know about, because he left before that.

Back in Moanmoan's hotel suite he took a relaxing shower to "wash away the stink of paparazzi," which was really a remark intended as social commentary on the state of the world today. Annabelle was very impressed by his mind, which had depths beyond those she could see through the murky waters of his celebrity in *Aquasplash*. She herself reclined on a sofa, kicking off her high heels as she inspected the coffee table. Moanmoan had brought a few books and magazines with him, further proving that he was an intellectual, and she felt her heart flutter (just a normal flutter this time, since the (metaphorical) butterfly had come down off all those illegal drugs that should never be taken (this is more commentary on our modern world where, with all its challenges, drugs can seem like the perfect escape, my Fans, but I can assure you (as my experience in Thailand proves) that they are not. Absolutely not. But we, or rather I, digress)).

(I took a paragraph break here because my digression confused even me, my new editor has to fix this before publication. I'm going to put a note in my calendar to hire one. Editor, as in.)

She found herself in state of great excitement upon finding a book named *A Noisy & Unsubtle Revenge* written ("written" Annabelle thought hopefully) by TOM HARDY. But, in a plot twist, and also because I would never use the real Tom Hardy in my books because I don't want to get sued, it turned out that there was no single photo of Tom Hardy (the real one) in it, only letters and sentences. With crushing disappointment, only now noticing that the book had a woman on the cover that did not look anything like Tom Hardy even at the least flattering of angles, Annabelle tossed the book away in disgust. A cheap trick to try and attract attention, she thought in disgust about the author pretending to be Tom Hardy while not being Tom Hardy but a woman writing sentences that were not about Tom Hardy at all. She would next have berated herself for not being an intellectual like Moanmoan himself, but with impeccable timing Moanmoan emerged from the bathroom in a cloud of fragrant steam (because as she could now tell from the scent he had an excellent self-care regime involving moisturising also body parts that did not belong to her, safely stored inside *Victorian Mystery* underwear, which more men should really take to heart, not the underwear but the excellent self-care regime and the moisturising, and while at it they should really lay down their *Prongles* and pick up a protein if they wanted to achieve attention of their lady companions, but enough about my husband Gunther).

"Does your tummy feel at ease now, darling?" Moanmoan said masculinely in a throaty way that had Annabelle's well-tended potting shed trembling with yearning for his moisturised self.

"I have," she breathed at him seductively and toothpastely (there were actually two bathrooms and I simply didn't bother writing about her ablutions), the peacock feathers of her demure cocktail dress shimmering in a way that was also seductive. Even fully dressed, Annabelle thought about herself in third person, but proudly, she was a born seductress. But then, in addition to his tattooed muscles gleaming because of his thoughtful and considerate moisturising routine, the towel which was wrapped around Moanmoan's waist dropped to the floor, leaving so, *so* much for Annabelle to admire. Some men were born lucky, she thought, very, very lucky, and so were some women, for instance herself.

Annabelle rose from the sofa and stroked his manly chest, the tips of her fingers dancing over this bulging pectoral muscles, tracing his broad chest, tiptoeing over his six pack which was found on his trim stomach, sliding around his hips, caressing his strong back (which was also not hairy and moisturised, because Moanmoan had very good reach, which could and should be misinterpreted), exploring his lower back and then, finally, encountering his lower lower back, which was round, smooth and extremely, satisfyingly firm, like a watermelon, but made of testostestorene. Suddenly, Annabelle felt like she wouldn't mind a nibble or two. What was the Samoan national dish? Was it called Moanmo–

Nakedly, Moanmoan drew her into his moisturised muscles that his arms consisted of, stroking her hair and looking deeply

226

into her eyes. "That peacock feather cocktail dress was an interesting choice this evening," he said, inexplicably changing the mood, even though there were two cocks in the sentence. Or maybe because, because two cocks and Annabelle didn't belong in one sentence, since she wasn't a freak, but wait for my next book.

"What? This old rag?" Annabelle sang cocquetishly. "It's just something I had specially made when you gave me those tickets for the launch party," Annabelle explained, hoping her explanation didn't make her sound the way she felt, which was like a poor relative trying to impress an audience that was very difficult to impress.

"Were you trying to impress me, my love?" whispered Moanmoan (Bugger, it didn't work, thought Annabelle.) "If so, it's working, as you can probably tell." (Oh my, it worked, thought Annabelle.)

Her hands moved fluidly absorbing some of the moisturiser which was good because Annabelle felt slightly dehydrated, returning to the six pack on Moanmoan's trim stomach before sliding down to find... dear Reader, she found it. Gardenly metaphors failed to describe the implement longing to tend to her potting shed of desire. His well-loved shovel? It did not sound ideal, especially as it was not even usable as a shovel. Garden hose? She tittered at that one, immaturely and knowingly, that as a woman she should not be acting (even in her thoughts) as if she were an overexcited (this she was) highschool girl (which she was, but a very long time ago). Grouter? Shears? Annabelle decided on a wood-splitting axe, realising she was overthinking this.

"You're overthinking this," Moanmoan growled wood-splittingly, confirming Annabelle's thought that she was overthinking this. He was so smart, she thought, and knew women's thoughts. Like Nel Bigson in that movie called *What Woman Thinks* only without the stockings. "Let me help you by removing that hastily thrown together elegantly understated (like our gold-plated kitchen, the countertop of which you must remember intimately by now) shimmering peacock feather dress."

Buttons popped and zips zipped as Moanmoan freed Annabelle from the dazzling, if animalistic (fittingly, as so were her desires) garment. Hooks were wiggled ineffectually as Moanmoan battled with her bra, because his fingers were a bit overmoisturised for the difficulties posed by bras. But he got there in the end. Annabelle kicked her panties away, where they landed on an unlit lamp in the corner (it was fortunate it was unlit, as otherwise this would have created a fire risk and hotel fires are actually the second biggest cause of death in Scotland, which is a remarkable statistic that almost beggars belief).

Moanmoan nuzzled at Annabelle's breasts, which were still perky despite her advanced age, and she emitted melodious sounds of pleasure. Despite knowing it was wrong and Sister Bernadette would berate her for enjoying the delights, since they were being dispensed by a man married to his very egoistic to keep him on a short leash wife of seventeen years and she was the fiancé of a former billionaire turned farmer. Yet in that moment, in the most expensive suite of the *Razzle Hotel*, where the famous and glamourous (and neither of those things and also not handsome Nigel, I decided to take revenge over Nigel for writing himself into this book) were currently being entertained downstairs in the bar by Lemme Crave-Itz's shadow puppet routine, Annabelle felt the most famous and glamourous of them all. Did the Backhems get to enjoy Moanmoan's luscious growth of well-tended facial fur? She did not think so, although now she was a bit worried. Annabelle admired closely, as she took Moanmoan's face in her hands, his eyes of an indeterminate colour (because the lights were on low and that lamp housing her *Victorian Mystery* panties was unlit, which was the responsible thing to do) and also the erotic thunderbirds of his eyebrows dancing in pleasure to the rhythm of the butterfly of her heart. Yet again, she had to ask herself this question, despite the moment being so bad for questions, and also this paragraph very long already. Was this love or was she just giving in to her carnal lusts and desires?

Annabelle found that she didn't give a shit (take this, Nigel, with your doo-doo) [Note to my new editor (insert name): please remove all remarks about Nigel which I am inserting due to my nerves being shot – Karen] about the answer as Moanmoan gently laid her back on the bed and the very tip of his trusty trowel grazed the mysterious entrance that led inside her potting shed. It was the biggest trowel she had ever seen and her eyes bulged when she realised Moanmoan wasn't done yet.

"I love you," Moanmoan told her as he unlocked the gate of her potting shed with his award-winning towel.

He said the L-word, Annabelle would think if she could think. But she couldn't, having given in to her craving for troweling, as the door to her potting shed slammed open and all the pots inside turned out to be ready for spring. As a gardener, Moanmoan planted seedlings all over the shed over and over, but he did it through a protective rubber, because they were responsible adults. Due to gardening being very time-consuming and the necessity not to cross certain plants in wrong pots because this, as Annabelle knew being somewhat a gardener herself even though mostly in buckets and already cut, which Moanmoan was not, it took a very long time of frolicking in the flowerbed they have lovingly (for he said the L-word, even if Annabelle couldn't think about it at this not-at-all difficult time) blossomed with their implements and [what's the romantic word for manure, dear editor? I forgot – Karen]. And at the end, Annabelle whimpering of fulfilment, she finally achieved the goal she set for herself, nibbling playfully on Moanmoan's lower lower back's firmly rounded fruit.

Both finally sated, they lay together naked amongst the tangled bedclothes. Annabelle let out a long, satisfied sigh. This had been the perfect day. Except for being violently sick earlier.

But it felt so much earlier that it was practically many years ago. Time passed differently when you were in the L-word, she now thought and remembered, and was about to say it back when Moanmoan flicked on a light in a casual way and reached for the book written by the woman on the cover whose name Annabelle knew was not really Tom Hardy because she had checked.

"My mind's racing, due to the excitement of all our passionate lovemaking," he explained as he leafed through the pages, while drinking a can of Gumminess. "A paragraph or two of this and I shall be asleep without snoring, because my body is too attractive for snoring. But first we will curl up, with me being the big spoon, and our night of sleep will be blissful together." Which was what lovers did after lovemaking, Annabelle thought, using the L-word twice inside her thoughts, empowered by this freshly announced feeling that now she knew was definitely:

LOVE.

Chapter Eleven

THE FIRE ENGINE DROVE AWAY FROM THE *RAZZLE HOTEL*, sirens blaring and lights flashing. Annabelle wasn't sure why they'd done that, because they were leaving after putting the fire out, although the acrid smell of smoke and burned peacock feathers still hung in the Edinburgh air.

She was standing outside the entrance to the hotel. All her clothes had been destroyed in the fire, which had started in their suite. Annabelle would never admit to that, although she knew for a true fact, that it was the combination of Moanmoan flicking on the light and her *Victorian Mystery* which she now no longer possessed being draped over that lamp. Annabelle now understood why hotel fires are the second biggest cause of death in Scotland. She thanked God in case He existed, as having nothing to lose because if He didn't, then He didn't care, and also she only did it in her thoughts.

Moanmoan had been more fortunate. He'd managed to grab his suitcase and rescue most of his clothes (which were designer clothes and therefore expensive in a way that could solve world hunger if those monies were repurposed, which is a reflection on the state of society, but importantly they were saved, and so neither Moanmoan nor the society suffered financial losses) (except for the owners of the hotel but they probably had insurance and let's face it, nobody cares for financial losses of insurances), so he looked his usual, smart, well-dressed and handsomely toned self as he stood next to Annabelle, thanking the parking valet when he returned with Moanmoan's *Lamportini*. Annabelle looked less glamourous than she had the night before, dressed in veterinary scrubs borrowed from Nigel (who never wore anything else because in addition to not being handsome he was also VERY POOR, ha ha Nigel) [Please remove this remark, my dear editor (insert name), because it makes me look petty, which I am not – Karen] after he'd seen her trying to maintain her modesty with a scorched bath towel. This caused Moanmoan to growl jealously and so Nigel couldn't dispose of his veterinary scrubs quickly enough so that Annabelle could cover her modesty (he wasn't looking, but she felt very naked when she was naked).

"We'd better go," said Moanmoan as he stowed his luggage in the car and climbed into the driver's seat. There were hundreds of press outside as a result of the blaze, cameras clicking and flashing as Annabelle, currently costume-playing as a veterinarian, embedded herself inside the *Lamportini*, clutching her purse. (The purse didn't burn.)

"I think we were fairly discreet, considering," Moanmoan mused as he navigated the busy streets of Edinburgh.

Annabelle turned on her *Sansunk* phone because she couldn't afford expensive *ePhones*, and gasped when she saw several notifications from *YouPipe*. She opened this first one with a beating heart. The movie's title was MYSTERY BLAZE, MYSTERY WOMAN and there was Annabelle, dressed in her scrubs, clambering with little elegance into Moanmoan's car. (The hotel, despite being burnt, had very fast Internet.) As she scrolled through the comments, knowing she shouldn't be doing it because she had read many warnings in articles in magazines about comments under *YouPipe* movies, Annabelle realised that people could be both imaginative and cruel. But, she thought pleased despite this, she was officially a woman of mystery and not some average-looking woman in scrubs.

MOANMOAN THE SAMOAN STEPS OUT WITH WOMAN OF AVERAGE BEAUTY DOWN EDINBURGH'S ROYAL MILE said *Persons*. Which Annabelle knew she should have avoided but she couldn't. Annabelle was relieved she was dressed in a proper outfit (the one with peacock feathers) in these photos, at least. She found the use of the word "average" to be vicious and offensive to poor Moanmoan, suggesting that he would be seen dead (metaphorically) in public with a woman of average beauty. Which he would not due to being a celebrity actor whose muscles had muscles under playfully dancing tattoos on his skin. She, despite not being a feminist, would not let *Persons* shame her into striving for unattainable (unless you were yourself a famous celebrity, such as Moanmoan's selfish wife of seventeen years, Liza Bonbonet) beauty goals. Which is another example of the cutting-edge social commentary this book is filled with. Because those are important issues needing to be tackled.

Well, Annabelle thought as she finished tackling, at least they don't call me a slut!

And then. The *Daily Daily* entitled their "article" WOMAN PUTS ON PEACOCK DISPLAY AS SHE STRUTS HER STUFF WITH AQUASPLASH 2 ACTOR MOANMOAN – DRESSED LIKE THAT, SHE'S BOUND TO BE A SLUT! The pictures, which she focused on easily, because the *Daily Daily* was not the sort of publication that abused words, were more flattering than those in *Persons* and Annabelle decided to hang them on the walls, except – this was a conundrum – she couldn't do it in the farmhouse, since that would be cruel for poor, not rich Haggis, and Moanmoan's award-winning stupid house had no walls. This was a metaphor, she suddenly understood, for celebrities' lives being constantly observed without an ounce of privacy being given to them. And now that she was on the cover (on the Internet, but soon) of *Daily Daily* herself,

Annabelle felt their pain. Which bounded her with Moanmoan even closer, so close actually that she didn't even vomit because she was so delighted (despite being called a strutting slut) by their closeness.

Whilst the gorgeous, understated, shimmering peacock outfit was currently ash somewhere in the ashes of the hotel, she had photographs of it. Annabelle sighed. At least, she thought reasonably through the pink cloud of love and the grey cloud of losing her outfit and also being shamed, she wasn't being named.

Annabelle had to read the website TeaAmZed with her eyes closed. ANNABELLE ELLE ELLENDELING'S RAUNCHY SHAG WITH AQUASPLASH ACTING ACE MOANMOAN THE SAMOAN WHO IS MARRIED TO LIZA BONBONET WHO CO-STARS IN THE MOVIE BUT COULD NOT BE PRESENT DUE TO A PARAGLIDING COMPETITION IN POLAND WHERE SHE PERFORMS HER OWN STUNTS LEAVES HER (ANNABELLE ELLE ELLENDELING) IN NEED OF A HOSING DOWN!!! ROYAL MILE PICTURES ON PAGE 2. SNEAKY PICTURES OF THEM SHAGGING LIKE DEMENTED RABBITS ON PAGES 4-17. THE RAZZLE HOTEL FIRE DAMAGE IS "CATASTROPHIC AND LIVES COULD HAVE BEEN LOST DUE TO A PAIR OF PANTIES" SAYS FIRE BRIGADE CHIEF! Hotel fires are the second biggest cause of death in Scotland it also added, which Annabelle had to squint at on her Internet, because nobody cared what fire brigade chiefs who were not even attractive had to say or about deaths in Scotland unless they happened to celebrities, which fortunately they did not in this case.

HAVE YOU SEEN THIS LOST DOG? screamed the *The Edinburgh Eye*. Well, Annabelle thought relievedly, three out of four wasn't bad. Although they could have meant a female dog which was called a "bitch," but there were actual pictures of the dog, and not of Annabelle – huffing at "average beauty" – whilst not realising for a moment that she too was being drawn into the murky world of celebrity culture, despite her poor upbringing and modest work as a florist kept in business by the very hottie expensively humping (the *Lamportini* did so) next to her at dangerously illegal speeds.

"Much reporting?" Moanmoan asked with little interest, as he was used to being on covers of magazines and online websites.

"A little," Annabelle replied in a little, but not at all average, voice.

The good thing, she thought, was there was no broadband or even online signal in the farmhouse and Haggis couldn't afford an *ePhone*, or even a *Sansunk*, so there was a chance, no matter how slender, that she could field those baseless accusations he would not know had a base so he wouldn't accuse her of them. (This was why their inability to order online shopping was an important plot point earlier in the story, even though it looked at the time like this was all about Potty. I had learnt this when I took a creative writing course online, because I, myself, have Internet. And they sent me a diploma.) However, it would be all too easy for Liza to check her *ePhone* whilst paragliding in Poland. A shocking image crossed Annabelle's mind of Liza reading the whole, sordid story whilst doing a daring loop the loop, losing concentration and plummeting to her death in the famous mountains of Poland that she couldn't remember the name of, but that didn't matter because everybody knew about them. Of course, were Liza to die then Moanmoan would be free and since Annabelle wasn't yet married... which she thought shamefully.

Annabelle shuddered, and not in a good way. Was *this* what she had become? A murderous, if passively and not due to her fault, glass-home-wrecker? She had turned into the hardened bitch that she accused her ex-best friend Brenda of being, consumed by lust to the point way beyond simple betrayal. No,

Annabelle thought of herself, now being consumed by guilt, which reminded her she hadn't eaten anything for many chapters now, except a nibble on Moanmoan's national fruit, but she didn't really eat it, because she wasn't a freak and also he was very expensive. No, no, she added. She was better than this and would prove it after the *Lamportini* stopped performing macho power slides and then she realised she wasn't vomiting exactly because she hadn't eaten anything, which in retrospect was a very smart decision, thus proving Annabelle was smart. She was bound to find a way to clear both of their smeared reputations.

Wisely, she realised that this happened all the time. As a celebrity, Liza Bonbonet's photos were always photo shopped into unflattering positions. (Suddenly, Annabelle felt feministic anger in sympathy for poor, rich, photo shopped Liza.) Everybody, except for everybody who had seen her in the hotel, the tailors who worked on her no longer existing shimmering, but elegantly, outfit, and the peacocks, but they were dead, and also Nigel whose veterinarian scrubs she was now wearing but this could be easily explained as a lavish gift to finish the bouquet-tying course, knew that tabloids did this all the time.

They took to the twisting road which winded through the Low Highlands of the Higher Lowlands, before blasting along more roads, this time in the completely different High Lowlands of the Lower Highlands, which is the place in Scotland where Annabelle and Moanmoan both lived. The landscape was very descriptive. And Annabelle's conscience so dirty it needed a long bath. Her heart was heavy again and she was leaning to the left, which would have placed her on Moanmoan's shoulder except they were in Great Britain, where – as most of my readers might not know – cars are mirrored horizontally, so she just hung limply on the door in the security of the safety belt. Feeling nauseous despite not having eaten, because she found herself nauseating and she was inside herself all the time.

Chapter Twelve

※

The tyres of Moanmoan's car crunched over the gravel road leading to Annabelle's farmhouse in a shamefully satisfying (and slower) way.

"Well, it's been a memorable trip," said Moanmoan with a grin. "And memories are what memories are made of, after all."

Annabelle took her head out from between her knees, as this was the only position which worked to prevent her nausea caused by being inside herself as she didn't want to spoil Nigel's fresh veterinary scrubs, even though she would never see or even think of him again during this story. "Yes, thank you for the gala tickets." She spoke. "I'm sorry that with all the press reporting, Liza, your (here she wisely avoided an adverb, not to seem like a smaller person) wife of seventeen years, is going to find out we've been having a blazingly fierce affair and she will be very sad." A tear circulated inside Annabelle's eye.

"Liza doesn't get sad," Moanmoan ignored her concerns with a wave (of hand). "Liza is vicious, as evidenced by her doing her own stunts while paragliding in Poland. And you've been her best and most trusted friend for at least five and a half week now." Moanmoan pointed out, as he steered the car around a wandering bison, creatures which roam freely in this remote part of Scotland where it's difficult to order from an online shop. Scotland, you see, is a rough place to live in, and this is why it needs so much whisky. "I think the pain of your betrayal will cut deeply." Annabelle was shocked by how casually he blamed her and not himself. "But don't worry. I'll be here and I'll stand by you no matter what. Because of our love." Now Annabelle was joyful in a guilty way, because this was what love was all about, standing by her (or lying down) at all times, in the face of vicious – she shuddered attractively – Liza.

When they reached the farmhouse Haggis couldn't be found. Annabelle wasn't too worried though, because this probably, if not even obviously, just meant he was out working in the fields where they grew things, that, she thought bitterly, they were selling for *nothing* to Ivor McClunge as ingredients for his whisky distillery, where they distilled whisky in barrels. She sighed, thinking life would be easier were it not for Haggis's long-term business strategies, which played the long game and left them penniless (except for the money she earned when Moanmoan bought the entire contents of her flower shop except for the buckets and the counter, which made him her sugar daddy, some might think, but that was a thought Annabelle decided not to have).

No, Annabelle wasn't too worried that Haggis was out working, but she was very worried indeed, in fact possibly even extremely, by the presence of a black *Soil Rampager* waiting for them. It had four wheels, one on each corner, each one the size of a pony, alloys blackly glittering in the morning sunshine. Annabelle recognised the car immediately as the one belonging to Liza Bonbonet. (Because she had seen it before when she visited Liza and then Liza went to shop.) Liza had clearly driven in some haste, making use of the *Rampager*'s off-road capabilities to drive straight through the fields surrounding the farm, gouging a deep trail of devastation and ruined crops behind her, even though it was far quicker to drive on the road which led to Liza's house with its cutting-edge transparent architectural design. Liza was leaning against the muddy *Rampager*, arms folded and a cross look on her face, which confirmed Annabelle's suspicions that it belonged to Liza.

"She looks cross," said Moanmoan as he stopped the car and climbed out using his muscles.

"She does," said Annabelle, feeling rather self-conscious as he joined the pair, still dressed as a vet. "I wonder why?" she said hypocritically, blushing.

"Liza," Moanmoan called out in a friendly voice, throwing his arms wide. "Such a wonderful surprise. I thought you were away for several days in that international paragliding competition in Poland. Yet, here you are!"

"Yes, here I am," said Liza. Whose lips were pressed into a firm, thin line of disapproval, which made it quite hard for her to talk.

"Did you miss me?" Moanmoan asked, arms dropping down to his sides.

"Clearly more than you missed me," Liza incomprehensibly said with her firm lips.

"Did the paraglider have both the range and speed to get all the way from Poland back to this remote part of Scotland in the same time it took me to drive here from Edinburgh in this high-performance sports car?" asked Moanmoan.

"Yes," replied Liza with an explanatory nod.

"Sooooooo," Moanmoan drew out the word, which is why there are all those extra 'O's, because he was stalling, "did you happen to catch up on the news? About the *Aquasplash 2, A Drip Too Far* launch party at the *Razzle Hotel*?"

"Where nothing happened," Annabelle added hastily, "and we were not in it, especially not in the most expensive suite."

Liza made a noise a bit like a cement mixer toppling into a sock factory, which left Annabelle none the wiser although, if she'd had to guess, at that moment she would have plumped for a probable 'yes' on that score. Although she wasn't plump. (Or of average beauty.)

Moanmoan looked at Annabelle, his sexy caterpillars of eyebrows contorted in a slow dance of confusion. "Do you know Liza's native language of Polish where this might have meant 'no' or 'yes'?"

"Alright, it's a yes," said Liza, deciding to speak properly in the interests of moving this scene along. "I have to say, Moanmoan, after seventeen years of blissfully happy marriage except for the times when we were desperately unhappy, I'd have expected more from you." She turned to Annabelle, whose stomach did a paraglide-like somersault, which would be quite a sight to see, if Annabelle was transparent like Liza's and Moanmoan's house. "And Annabelle! We've been best friends for a whole month," she said hurtfully underestimating the length of her friendship, "confiding in each other about everything except for my irresistible compulsion to shoplift despite being a multi-millionaire, but we're not here to talk about that today. We're here to talk about your relationship with my husband, which the press online have laid bare for all to see even though I was only using the Polish internet. How *could* you, Annabelle?" She did not sob this last sentence, unsettlingly.

"Liza, what can I say?" Said Annabelle.

"We need to talk properly, Annabelle Elle Ellendeling. Get in the car." Liza nodded towards the *Soil Rampager*.

Annabelle swallowed and looked at Moanmoan in search for help. But whilst he was standing by her, in certain distance because he was really standing closer to Liza together with his arms hanging by his sides, he did not look like someone ready to help. "I think maybe we should talk to Liza together, don't you?"

Moanmoan shook his shaggy head. "No. Not really." His tone was ominous, suggesting that Liza was indeed very vicious.

"Oh," said Annabelle. She had no option other than to climb into the *Soil Rampager* next to Liza before the pair of them drove off.

Chapter Thirteen

LIZA AND ANNABELLE DROVE AT SPEED THROUGH THE FIELDS, a wake of churned mud in their wake, crops that would not become whisky – so Annabelle felt – launching into the air, splashing through streams, shearing through sheep pens, clattering through fences and scrawping through hedgerows. No hedgehog was safe as the *Rampager* did what it was designed to do and took a pointless route through pristine (but no longer when it routed through it) countryside.

"Would you like to talk?" asked Annabelle as she was flung from side to side as the car bounced over an ancient cairn. Which is a Scottish word for a pile of rocks.

"No. I would prefer this part of our journey to be in uncomfortable silence," Liza told her, reversing to make sure she knocked over a standing stone dating back to Neolithic times before continuing their journey.

Their journey continued in uncomfortable silence, despite all the noise.

Eventually the *Rampager* blasted through another fence and slewed its way in a torrent of mud and dead wildlife down onto the drive outside Liza and Moanmoan's house. A dead pheasant slid off the bonnet as Annabelle slid off the front window because Liza braked so viciously. Moanmoan's *Lamportini* was already there, having driven the direct route home on the road. However, Moanmoan was nowhere to be seen, making himself scarce so the two possibly ex but hopefully not, hoped Annabelle, best friends could have their moment in private. Coward. He might have an incredible six pack in his stomach under the skin and bulging pectoral muscles that could crack coconuts but when it came to the fierce anger of a woman scorned, Moanmoan had met his match. And married it.

"Are we going to have coffee?" Annabelle asked, gingerly stepping over the dead pheasant, which was ironic, since she was dressed as a vet and should be bringing the pheasant back to life instead.

Liza gave her friend the kind of grin you see in movies, where the bad guy has something awful planned but the good guy has no choice other than to go along with their heinous scheme so that (a) we get to find out what the bad guy had planned all along and (b) you have the opportunity to wonder why the bad guy gets off on that kind of stuff and what happened in their childhood to make them act in this way, because it isn't exactly normal, is it? (Also when I say "guy" I don't mean that in a male way, because Liza was of female gender... [dear editor (insert name), please do something with this paragraph before I get cancelled – Karen])

"I'm sorry," said Annabelle. "I didn't quite catch what you said."

"That's because I only grinned at you and I didn't say anything," Liza replied, chillingly.

"Oh." Said Annabelle, who was only partially consolated by realising she was the good guy in this comparison.

"Now I shall answer your question, Annabelle. No, we're not going to have coffee, although if we were I wouldn't waste my rat-excreted beans on you. All you'd get from me is NotCafé, which is far cheaper but still better than you deserve. To think of all those times," said Liza angrily, "when I listened to you talk about your ex-best friend Brenda, and how she was a bitch, and yet, in a moment of even greater irony than all those wild animals who looked into your eyes and died during our brief but murderous car journey thinking you were a vet, you were the real bitch all along."

"I'm so sorry I'm a bitch, Liza. However, I feel compelled to point out that although you spoke for quite a long time there, you didn't actually answer my question."

"Didn't I? Oh, sorry about that. To answer your question, Annabelle, we're going paragliding," Liza explained, even more chillingly than before, if that were possible. Which it was.

Soon, because it was parked next to the house too, Annabelle sat awkwardly in the seat of the paraglider as Liza spun the propeller to start the engine, which spluttered angrily, which was how Liza felt so they were united as one while Annabelle felt like an outsider despite being inside, into life.

Liza climbed into her seat behind Annabelle, wearing a warm flying suit of the kind paragliders wear, clipping her harness together. She flicked several switches on the dashboard of the paraglider, even though she wasn't at the front. But Liza was that sort of person, realised Annabelle, who unlike Liza knew fear of paragliding even though she had never paraglided before. The jet engines which powered paragliders fired into life. They also sounded angry and this was another metaphor for Liza's feelings. By now, Annabelle was pretty certain that Liza was angry.

Liza leaned forward and tapped a red button in the middle of Annabelle's harness. "Don't fiddle with that." She suggested.

"Why?" Annabelle asked mortifiedly.

"It's the quick release mechanism that's on your harness that you won't find on mine. If this is pressed once we're at 50,000 feet, which is not the normal cruising altitude for paragliders unless you perform your own stunts, which I do, you'll fall to your death and there will be nothing I can do to save you."

"Oh." Answered Annabelle sepulchrally.

"Ready?" Liza called out viciously.

"No!" said Annabelle. There was a lot of fear in her high-pitched voice. "Why are you wearing that warm flying suit and I'm still dressed in these flimsy veterinary scrubs which I borrowed doesn't mind from whom because he will definitely not appear in this book again? Won't it be cold at 50,000 feet?"

"You won't be up there too long," Liza replied, with a smile which might have been comforting but wasn't.

Before Annabelle could protest the paraglider roared into life, propellers spinning, jet engines flaming, wings flapping. It sped off down the previously unmentioned runway outside Moanmoan and Liza's ladylike doo-doo generating (how did Liza do it? wondered Annabelle to take her mind off the runway) challenging house, the paraglider clawing its way into the air moments before they reached the busy traffic on the A99. A driver honked his horn as one of the paraglider's wheels ran over the roof of his car in a filmic way and then they were airborne.

"Got away with it again," Liza shouted loudly. "Stupid place to put a runway, really! They should move the road." She spluttered indignantly, as a person who is so rich that she knows they should know better and they do too, but they're socialists who keep roads in inconvenient place on purpose to inconvenience rich people.

"Oh my," said Annabelle as the wheels retracted into the wings, which continued to flap furiously as they gained altitude.

"There's nothing else like the graceful, quiet peace that comes from paragliding," Liza screamed over the roaring noise of the propellers and the jet engine as they powered their way into the sky.

Annabelle looked down at the High Lowlands of the Lower Highlands of Scotland, where she lived, the patchwork of fields and other things you find in the countryside receding at an alarming rate. They seemed to be Very High Lowlands of the

Very Low Highlands now, in fact. She could just about see her little farmhouse. Liza and Moanmoan's house still stood out, stark white (it had a white roof on top of all the windows) against the rolling green of Scotland, since it was visible from space. For which NASA awarded them a special award as it helped cosmonauts find Scotland and then it was very easy to navigate further on.

"This is where I feel free," Liza declared delightedly. Which was not a feeling Annabelle possessed. "Nothing up here but the birds and enormous commercial and passenger carrying jet aircrafts, which can't see us on their scopes because I don't have a valid licence or carry any of the legally required transponders. Fortunately, I have an innate gift when it comes to flying, which is why I compete in all those international paragliding competitions. When you're a famous actor, one of the benefits is no one ever asks you for the paperwork." She shared.

"I can see why you love it so much," Annabelle replied, trying not to retch. Fortunately she still hadn't eaten anything. Which made her feel like a celebrity, except the thin veterinarian scrubs on loan from Nigel [I SAID NO MORE NIGEL – Karen] [Sorry for yelling, my new editor (insert name), but wouldn't you feel the same if there were all those Nigels in your novel? – Karen] and she was starting to lose all the feeling in her limbs.

"I do my best thinking up here," Liza told her. "When I was over in Poland, which is a country in the European Union that I come from, I knew I needed to talk to you. Up here, away from the hurly burly cosmopolitan life we share in this remote and inaccessible part of Scotland, we can get away from it all. I want to have an honest conversation with you in complete privacy, in my own special place."

"You mean you wanted to talk to me after you saw all those things on *YouPipe*, and *Persons* and the *Daily Daily* and *TeeAmZed*?" asked Annabelle, shiveringly, rather hoping that Liza might have missed the last one, so it really wasn't a good idea to have mentioned it in the first place. But she was very anxious.

"No, I mean before then," Liza replied, enigmatically.

"Before? I don't understand."

"There's something I need to tell you, Annabelle. Something I should have told you long ago as my best friend of a month – almost six weeks now, in fact, due to the inevitable passage of time."

"What?" cried Annabelle, slightly liberated from the fear of Liza knowing, but not from the fear of Liza in general. "What is it you should have told me?"

Liza opened her mouth full of American white teeth to speak, but as she was sitting behind Annabelle, this was really just speculation on Annabelle's part. What Annabelle didn't need to speculate about was the huge *Boing 769* passenger jet that was flying straight towards them.

Chapter Fourteen

LIZA BONBONET DID ALL HER OWN STUNTS IN *AQUASPLASH*, as we'd established much earlier in the novel. She had cat like reactions although she didn't have four feet and the instincts of a humming bird in flight, deftly spinning the steering wheel and applying the paraglider's handbrake. The wheels in the wings squealed and it was enough to slow the paraglider's speed a fraction. The *Boing 769* performed an evasive loop the loop, a memorable moment for Karen's (unrelated) hen party bound for Magaluf, I'm sure. Which she deserved for reasons I will explain in my memoir, *The Life of the Artist*, title subject to change. Liza barrel-rolled the paraglider in response, although, since that meant they carried on in exactly the same direction as before, it was really the *Boing 769* pilot who avoided them, whatever Liza might have thought, Annabelle thought. Often, though, there's simply no telling people and if they believe something, that's it, she mused in that moment in time when time stops and you see your entire life in front of your eyes, but she closed them. They believe it, even when all the evidence points in the other direction. It's just how some people are. So she concluded.

Then Annabelle wondered if this was the moment when her

life ended. She blinked her eyes open and found it wasn't, gripping the harness as if her life depended on it. That was when her thumb strayed onto the red rapid release button of her harness. (!) There was a misleadingly innocent click and, as the paraglider continued to spin through the sky, Annabelle was flung from her seat with a terrified wail.

Annabelle wondered if *this* was the moment when her life ended. She blinked and found it still wasn't, as they were at the typical cruising altitude for a paraglider driven by Liza of 50,000 feet and it actually takes quite a long time to fall that distance back to Earth. Annabelle spread out her arms and legs, stabilising her fall and looked out across the High Lowlands of the Lower Highlands of Scotland, where she lived. It all looked so beautiful, although it was a deadly kind of beauty of the kind that would soon kill her, when she arrived back home (or thereabouts) at considerable speed without a parachute.

Annabelle reflected that she was only in this position as a result of her wanton lust. Haggis should have been enough for her, even if he did smell of grease and onions. She wasn't just a hussy, but also a superficial one. The grease, after all, had moisturising effects she did not appreciate before it was too late, as in now. She uttered a little sigh, trying to come to terms with her situation. If everything was about to end, it was better to be at peace with her decisions. That evening in the *Razzle Hotel* certainly was a night to remember and every single piece of her lady garden still ached in a satisfied way after such relentless potting and seeding, and a bit of digging, if she were to be honest.

At least I'll die knowing I have that memory, thought Annabelle. It's something I can treasure forever – well, for the next five minutes or so, at least.

There was a strange buzzing noise in the air. Annabelle looked round and saw Liza leaning out of the paraglider. She'd engaged the autopilot and was hanging off one of the wings, with one hand, the other stretched out to reach Annabelle.

Annabelle reached out and the tips of her cold fingers brushed those of Liza, sending Annabelle spinning away. Somewhere, music was playing dramatically, like it does in the movies, but neither of them could hear it. Annabelle managed to stop tumbling, eyes wide as the paraglider autopilot carefully tracked her fall through the sky and brought Liza near once more.

"Come on, Annabelle," called out Liza. "Take my hand like they do in the movies and stop pissing about."

Annabelle stretched out her arm, hand inches from Liza's. The wind roared past them and when Annabelle looked down the High Lowlands of the Lower Highlands of Scotland, where she lived, were much nearer.

"Don't look down, Annabelle." Said Liza. "Look at me! Take my hand. Remember what happened in *Aquasplash*!"

"But nothing like this happened in *Aquasplash*," Annabelle pointed out.

"Can you think of a movie where it did?"

"No."

"Well, look it up on iFDL, the Internet Film Data List, once you take my goddamn hand which I am extending as a gesture of friendship despite the hurt you have caused me but you don't know half of it!"

Annabelle made one more effort, grasping Liza's gloved hand, holding on tight with all her might. Liza dragged her back into her seat, clipped her in and then dropped back into her own chair with a whoop. That was the kind of thing that was easily possible, thought Annabelle as she passed out, when you did your own stunts in movies.

Some time later, but she didn't know how long because she was passed out, Annabelle woke up in her own soft, familiar bed. It was dark, and there was a brooding shadow in the bedroom next to her. She could see the faint outline of a masculine, well-toned body, a kilt revealing a shapely thigh and an excitedly arisen sporran. There was a faint smell of grease in the air.

"Haggis?" she whispered.

"Aye, wee lassie, it's me alright. You've had quite the adventure, haven't you?"

Annabelle sat up in bed and flicked on the lamp next to her. (Which had no underwear on top of it. She had learned her lesson.) She was dressed in comfy pyjamas that people commonly wear in Scotland because it's so chuffing cold, even in that season they comedically call 'summer'. Believe me, dear Reader, I have done my research. So, the veterinarian's, whose name we will not use again, scrubs were gone. Hopefully, Annabelle hoped, it wasn't Haggis who undressed her, although technically she would prefer if it was, but then he might ask questions, especially as the name of the veterinarian, whose name we will not mention ever again, was embroidered all over the scrubs.

"Haggis, I don't know where to begin," Annabelle began insecurely.

"Och, it's alright, dearest Annabelle. I've spoken to Liza. Although we don't have a strong enough broadband connection to order an online weekly shop and I was living in blissful ignorance, typical of former billionaires who become farmers, she showed me everything on her expensive *ePhone*."

"Everything?" asked Annabelle.

"Aye, my sweet lassie, everything."

"The *YouPipe* movie?"

"Aye."

"The story in *Persons*?"

"Aye, lassie. I've read that one."

"The article in *Daily Daily*?"

"Aye. That too. Thought that one was a bit unfair. It was a nice dress – you didn't need to be a slut to wear that."

"And the gossip website *TeaAmZed*?" asked Annabelle mortifiedly, recalling the disgusting words of the website.

"Even *TeeAmZed*, my love. When I said everything, I meant everything. I have to say, I didn't think *TeaAmZed* did a particularly good job, from a journalistic point of view. They were the only ones who picked up on the fire but that part of the story was buried by the classifieds. Did you know, hotel fires are the second biggest cause of death in Scotland? Something should be done about that."

"Yes, Haggis," said Annabelle guiltily and also missing her *Victorian Mystery* panties which were very expensive when you were a florist and not a celebrity, "but perhaps we need to talk about us. About what this means. About what this means for us, before we start looking at fire regulations in hotels." She said jokingly trying to lighten up the situation.

Haggis gave her a sad smile (not that easy to do – try it some time, when you're looking in the mirror and you'll see what I mean, I did a lot of research, Reader). "Aye, we need to talk about us. I know about you and Jax, my close friend, despite the fact we've never been seen together throughout this novel."

Annabelle looked into Haggis's deep, grey eyes, filled with love, and felt her love stirring for this complicated, ruggedly handsome and incredibly masculine man-dish. It was the sort of love you felt for someone when you were shagging someone else and then they found out about it, though. So in a way it was quite awkward, actually.

"Haggis, I tried to love you, I really did," she confessed. "In fact, I know I loved you once, for a time and it was very real. But, despite everything Stephunie Myarse's done to popularise people who are shifters with all those books and movies, it's..." Annabelle coughed, knowing that once she'd said the words, there was no calling them back. But she had to say them immediately, because this book was already very long. "I just don't *like* haggis, even though it's Scotland's traditional dish, and I feel Scottish at heart, especially when I am watching *The Outoflander* and Jiminy Frasier takes his shirt off. It, I mean haggis, not the t-shirt, smells and tastes disgusting and, unfortunately, Haggis Angus MacBrawn, you change into something that" – she swallowed the words "disgusts me" due to not being a horrible person – "disagrees with my palate. Vampires and wolves are really cool but, due to the cruelty of Jane Smith's curse..."

"Curse her common name, making her so difficult to trace," muttered Haggis.

"Yes, curse her and her curse." Cried Annabelle angrily. "She was cruel, Angus. Weretartan. Werepotty. Werehaggis. I'm sorry, but those are absolutely shit things to shift into." She paused. "I mean, absolutely unpleasant, and neither shit nor wee things."

"Thank you for caring for Poutine's feelings," Haggis replied in a sigh. His deep sigh seemed to emanate from his very soul, resonating in his deep, brown eyes – one blue, one green. This was the magic Annabelle had fallen for right after she had learned what "mergers" were. With her heart tight like a scrunchie on a ponytail, Annabelle wondered how close they were to midnight (GMT) and the next, terrible transformation. Which was always disconcerting and shocking despite always being the same.

"You're right," he said at last. "I'm a shit shifter."

"It's quite hard for my delicate English ears to understand you with your incredibly sexy Scottish accent sometimes," Annabelle spoke, being deliberately dense by how cruel Haggis's words were to his self.

"I'm a shit shifter," Haggis enunciated more clearly to her dismay. "If you don't like the taste of haggis and you don't like the smell of haggis (and, let's face it, it doesn't exactly look very appetising, does it? he added in parentheses) then what is there to love after midnight (GMT), when once I return to my human shape I depart to work in the fields where things grow that will later ferment in barrels? I should never have brought you up here, wee lassie, trapping you with me in this remote farm where we grow things. I was being selfish. Ye ken?"

"I ken very much but I'm the one who should apologise," Annabelle told him, taking his hand and giving it a gently reassuring squeeze of apology. "I wanted to give this a try, my nearly beloved Haggis, I really did. Also, Annabelle MacBrawn would be a really bad-ass name to carry around. But as soon as I laid my eyes on Moanmoan the Samoan, your best friend who you call Jax, I was consumed by feelings I simply couldn't control." If feelings, she thought with shame, feeling the cave of her secret awaken at just the thought, were the right word. Well, she was feeling it, so it was. "I'm not proud of it, Haggis, but the truth is, I think I love him. And that's why you're still a shi-shifter, condemned to exist as a werehaggis squatting on a tray. My love for you was never pure enough to break the curse and it had nothing to do with the secrets you were keeping. You deserve better than me." She burst out with tears flowing down her face. "You deserve to find that pure love, as Potty and Brenda have found in a sapphic way, which will end your torment."

Haggis arose from his chair and ran his fingers through his Scottish hair. "There's more," he said, looking away from her, which made the statement much more dramatic. In the distance, a thunderclap was heard from the cloudless sky.

"More? More what?" There was no way Annabelle could stomach even more Scottish cuisine, even if she didn't actually have to stomach it, just sleep next to it, which was actually worse when one thought about it, because if she was actually stomaching it, she would only have to do it once.

"More secrets, Annabelle. I think I know, I mean ken, how to end the curse."

"How?" she cried in excitement that was equally happy as it was scared.

"By revealing my biggest secret of all," Haggis told her, dramatically, which was a very good ending for a chapter, which I had learnt in the creative writing school on the Internet. (And I have a diploma.)

Chapter Fifteen

There was a long and dramatic silence after Haggis's dramatic statement. Eventually Annabelle could stand it no longer.

"I can stand this silence no longer, Haggis." She spoke breaking the silence. "If there's a hope you can end this curse then tell me. Tell me your biggest secret."

"You won't be proud of me," said Haggis ashamedly.

"I promise, I won't judge you. I stood by you when I discovered you transformed into a savoury traditional Scottish dish on the stroke of midnight (GMT). I stood by you when you gave away all your billions in the hope of finding reconciliation for all those sackings you were responsible for when you did mergers and acquisitions and those other things ordinary people don't understand." Annabelle hid a sigh, but failed to hide her pride at how well she hid this sigh, and Haggis smiled warmly, because he thought she was being proud of him. Which she was, of course, because Annabelle was a good person. "I stood by you when you decided to become a farmer, even taking on a completely new and demanding career as a florist in a remote Scottish village. You may not want to believe it, but we'd be broke without Moanmoan buying all those flowers for Liza. No one else comes in the shop! It's almost as if this village doesn't have any inhabitants other than..." She thought briefly. "Nobody at all." Because they didn't live in the village themselves either.

"Alright, Annabelle," said Haggis decisively in his trademark Scottish burr that would still melt her panties if they hadn't burnt in a dramatic accident that wasn't her fault. "I'll tell you and then there'll be no more secrets between us. There's a reason why I bought, and manually extended into many rooms including a shower and the kitchen table this particular farmhouse, in this particular part of the High Lowlands of the Lower Highlands of Scotland. I wanted Jax and Liza to be my neighbours, you see, because I've always loved Liza." His sigh was as deep as Annabelle's horror at her realisation of this. "When she married Jax they moved to America and I didn't see them for many years, but then when *Aquasplash* was a global mega hit they became millionaires and built their new home in Scotland. All of a sudden, there was a chance to rekindle our old romance. And I took it." He said with shame, but not enough shame for Annabelle's liking. And so she screamed. "You bastard!" as she threw the bedside lamp at Haggis. It smashed to pieces on the wall behind him, plunging them into darkness of the traditionally still Scottish night (except the thunderclap earlier).

"I thought you said you wouldn't judge," Haggis protested murkily. "You've literally just confessed to having your own affair with my closest friend Jax!"

"Yes, but I expected *you* to be faithful, you heartless brute," Annabelle cried, feeling betrayed. "I feel betrayed, Haggis," she said tearfully, "and you're the one who's done the betraying. Quite a bit of betraying, actually, by the sound of it. For many years!"

"Well, aye, quite a bit, actually," he confessed into the darkness. "But remember there was a long break in the meantime, during which I tried to be an honest man for you. Yet, because

I am a man despite being a werehaggis and I have needs that I carry underneath my kilt exposed to the elements, and the love I share with Liza is eternal and pure now that I told you about it, there's not a lot of work to do on the farm, because all these things we're growing all by themselves, and she was not acting in any films during the days which I spent not telling you where I spent them, so out of guilt I have built a shower and a kitchen table, but otherwise..." Here he ran out of breath. "Haven't you wondered what I was doing out of the house all day long?"

Annabelle reeled from the revelation. Should she have been surprised, even though she was completely surprised? After all, Haggis had been a cut throat businessman, all his life, merging things and acquiring things relentlessly as he amassed fortune upon fortune. You didn't do that unless there was a hard, selfish streak to your nature, and you were a monster devoid of emotions, such as a lawyer. Jane Smith's curse had certainly brought Haggis down a peg or two but perhaps *this* was the real Haggis, the one that had been there all along. Their love had always been doomed. Because he couldn't love anybody. Except Liza. Whose viciousness fitted his. Thought Annabelle, feeling, surprisingly, relieved, although, obviously, angry.

"And Liza's international paragliding competitions?" she asked in disbelief, although their paragliding excursion felt very believable. "Were they just a cover story for your own secret, sordid affair, you male hussy?"

"Sometimes," Haggis confessed guiltily. "At first, that was all it was. An affair. Then one night, when you were away, we overslept and at midnight (GMT) I transformed into my shifter form. You can imagine Liza's reaction."

"Poor Liza," Annabelle said, despite herself. She too remembered the shock of discovering Haggis's true nature.

"The poor girl was terrified but I plopped to her with an explanation what had happened and that it was important we washed the sheets in the morning, which to be fair I was going to do anyway for... er... other reasons. Such as cleanliness. There was sorrow in her eyes, Annabelle, but there was also something else. Her stomach rumbled and she licked her lips."

Annabelle frowned in the darkness. Haggis couldn't see her expression and she began to wish one of them would put on another light, but she didn't want to be to the one to suggest it, since she'd smashed the lamp in the first place. She wanted to maintain the upper hand in this argument, no matter how ridiculous that made everything. But also, she reminded herself, she could now frown and roll her eyes and wiggle her tongue as much as she wanted, and that was a positive side to this situation. So she didn't say anything about another light instead.

(In the movie adaptation, please put one candle in the background, Netflix. Or it will be a very weird scene. I am a literary genius, but that feels too literary even for me. – Karen)

"You're going to have to explain the significance of that to me, Haggis." Said Annabelle.

"She was into me, Annabelle."

"Clearly," said Annabelle with a shudder caused by the vision of vicious Liza licking her lips while surrounded by waft of grease and onion, which, come to think of it, would be exactly what she would expect Liza to be like, deep underneath that rich and moisturised surface, "but what happened, after you washed the sheets?" She did not want to hear anything about what had happened *before* that. Her imagination was doing the hard work which would make her biscuit soft if Annabelle was a man and biscuits were body parts.

Haggis shook his head but Annabelle couldn't see him do that, even though earlier in this encounter, before she'd put on the light, she would have been able to. (But that was earlier and the darkness of the night was not as dark yet as it was now, darkened by the secondary darkness of his sordid secret. Which explained it. I always like to clarify those things, because what I write is a slice of life, and in life those things are more obvious. As you will know due to being a person who is alive, Reader.) Like Annabelle, Haggis realised Annabelle couldn't see any of his gestures during this watershed moment in their relationship, since they were in complete darkness. However, she'd been the one who'd smashed the lamp, so he was damned if he fixed the problem she'd created. He could be petty like that, but then, he'd never pretended to be perfect, except when he did, but the fact that it was pretending made him more imperfect, which was his true nature.

"What I'm saying, Annabelle, is Liza likes haggis."

"I can see that now!"

"No, not Haggis with a capital H. Read my dialogue more carefully. I mean she likes the traditional Scottish dish. The sheep's stomach, the finely chopped hearts, the onions, the seasoning." In the darkness, he watched Annabelle's face turn green and eyes fill with displeasure of her palate. "The lot. Annabelle, I had to fight the woman off and stop her from eating me, and that's not easy in haggis form, I can tell you."

"So, you mean, she loves you in both your human and haggis forms?" Annabelle asked, panically attempting to remove the imagery from in front of her imagination.

"Exactly," Haggis confirmed her guess triumphantly.

Now Annabelle began to understand what he was *really* telling her, coming clean of his sick, depraved secrets that he had not shared with his best friend of much, much longer than six weeks. Such were billionaires, she thought, even when they were skint. Human (and haggis) nature did not change overnight. This made her sad, but was also social commentary, which I would like to point out, so you don't think this is some sort of ordinary romance. "So, you think, because Liza is partial to a traditional Scottish dish," Annabelle spoke aloud, hiding the truth inside her head, "her love for you in both human and shifter form might be strong enough to break the curse? But, if that's true, then why do you continue to transform every night?"

Haggis sighed deeply and dramatically into the all-enveloping darkness that enveloped them, because this was an extremely dramatic moment and we've been building up to this point over three books. I apologise, Reader, for keeping you in the darkness (this is a pun) so long! But here it goes. "This was the final secret. I couldn't love Liza properly whilst living a lie, pretending I also loved you. I think that, by confessing to you and revealing my biggest, darkest secret I can be true in my love for Liza. If I'm right, then on the stroke of midnight (GMT), the curse will finally be lifted."

"What time is it?" asked Annabelle.

"I don't know. I can't see my watch in the darkness. I'll put on a light," said Haggis.

Thank God! Both of them thought, having found an excuse (this will need to be changed in the Netflux movie, over which I demand complete artistic control – Karen).

Chapter Sixteen

THE MINUTES TICKED BY SLOWLY, EACH ONE TAKING 60 seconds to elapse. The betrothed (still) couple's hopeful hearts beat at the rhythm of each second, but faster. Haggis had discarded his shirt, kilt, socks and sporran and now crouched, naked, in his customary pose over the tray. There was a time when his naked body would have sent a thrill of desire through Annabelle, Annabelle thought, and touched her right down in her private olive grove of Mediterranean delights, which were much more delicious than the Scottish ones, despite the brogue and all the hand-waving Italians did when they spoke Spanish, which was how you knew they were Italians. Now, though, Annabelle realised their feelings for each other had changed. If Haggis was right, they were destined to be with other people. Happily loving them in open light of day (and, in Moanmoan's case, walls, or lack thereof, which even if it was a social commentary on the nature of celebrity, Annabelle intended to change as soon as possible).

"What time is it?" asked Haggis, who'd taken off his watch. He had learnt from that unfortunate mistake with flossing too late and it was not a lesson he ever wanted to learn again, but I am going into a digression. Which is an artistic thing to do to make you more aware of how slowly the time was ticking for Annabelle and Haggis.

Annabelle looked at her watch which she didn't take off, because she didn't have to. "11:53pm" she told him.

"Ach. I'm a bit early. I wonder if there's time for a quick cup of tea?"

"It's a bit late for that," Annabelle remarked. "You'll be crossing your non-existent legs all night." If things go wrong, she thought to herself, but did not say it, not wanting to cause Haggis anxiety, in case anxiety interfered with pure love between vicious, cold people (and werehaggises) devoid of all emotion as if they were lawyers.

"Aye, you're right. It's more looking for something to do, you know, I mean, ye ken, to take my mind of things. What time is it now?"

"11:54."

"Annabelle." Said Haggis.

"Haggis?" She asked in response.

"What happens if I still change tonight? Does that mean we've got it all wrong? Have we messed up the one true love that existed between us? Am I cursed forevermore to live as one of the worst kinds of shifters? The edible kind, the sort who'd never feature in a Stephunie Myarse novel, not even one of the cheap spin off ones or one of the novellas no one ever buys?" He raked his hand through his hair in that Scottish way of his.

Annabelle was many things. She'd been a waitress, she'd worked briefly in business as Haggis's assistant, she'd been a waitress again. Then she'd been a waitress once more, but this time in Paris (France) where she'd demonstrated her amazing linguistic capacity. Now she was a florist. She reflected that none of this qualified her to offer an opinion on the arcane magical arts that Jane Smith had unleashed to transform Haggis Angus MacBrawn into a werehaggis. As a result, she chose her next words very carefully.

"I don't ken, Haggis."

"Och, we'll find out soon enough, I guess."

Annabelle glanced at the clock and saw the time tick over to 11:59pm. But now the seconds were doing that thing she remembered from school. Seconds were like runners in a blindfolded cross-country race with an egg on a spoon, the sort they held at school. You'd get the keen, nippy seconds, who'd dash around and maintain a constant pace and they'd run across the finishing line in no time at all. Then there were the less fit seconds, who staggered over the finishing line puffing and gasping, in dribs and drabs. There would be the seconds who would sneak off during the first lap and hide in a bush or the woods, re-joining the race towards the end, throwing water over their faces to look like they were sweating. Finally, there were the incredibly unfit seconds who didn't think to hide for a few laps. (This, sadly, included Annabelle. Her talents lay elsewhere. Mostly in Moanmoan's house, at the moment, which was a very long moment of Annabelle not lying in Moanmoan's house.) Those seconds virtually crawled across the line, the last one taking so long parents would begin to shout abuse at them, because let's face it, nothing is so boring to watch as blindfolded school cross-country races with an egg on a spoon, especially as it's a winter sport because most PE Teachers go into the profession to conduct legalised forms of cruelty on the young and innocent, unable to become lawyers because their imagination when it comes to torture is limited.

But enough about sports. If you want to hear about this sort of thing, talk to my husband Gunther in the language of interpretive grunting.

Annabelle observed the seconds tick slowly by...

Tick – 11:59:57pm
Tock – 11:59:58pm
Tick – 11:59:59pm
Tock – 12:00:00am
Tick – 12:00:01am

She glanced up as midnight (GMT) finally arrived like a

gasping, asthmatic cross-country runner with a beer belly and legs like matchsticks. (Not unlike my husband Gunther.) She blinked, banishing the strange image from her mind as she focussed on the naked well-toned and completely steroid free specimen of Scottish masculinity in front of her, still crouching over a tray in a position that falsely (so Annabelle hoped) suggested he was constipated like Kot Hurrington in the television series *Play of Kingseats*.

"What time is it?" Haggis gasped non-constipatedly.

"Oh, Haggis," she said, heart fluttering ever so slightly in a drug free way that wouldn't get it arrested. There were no more words.

"Yes, wee lassie?"

"You're no longer a werehaggis, my dear," said Annabelle. "The curse is broken!"

Annabelle started to cry as Haggis jumped for joy, the less firmly attached parts of his delicious anatomy bouncing with delight (his, she thought sadly, remembering the times when his special edition single malt was her tip of joy) as he ran around the bedroom. It wasn't the sight of the naked, no longer edible, highlander careening around the farmhouse that caused Annabelle's happy tears to pour from her eyes. It was the absence of the smell of grease and onions.

Epilogue

Haggis sat across from Annabelle, holding hands with Liza in the farmhouse kitchen. Annabelle couldn't deny the existence of the love the pair shared for each other. It crackled like electricity crackles, but in a good way, rather than when there's a serious fault with a piece of electrical equipment, which could be a fire hazard and needs to be dealt with very quickly. Which was the most common cause of death in Scotland, before hotel fires, even. So it was like this, but not lethal, at least not at this moment. One night, Annabelle thought, Liza might find herself *very* hungry and — oh. Haggis no longer became a haggis. Would it count as cannibalism if he were to order haggis in a five-star Mishelon restaurant? This was not a thought she wanted to dwell on, so she didn't.

Moanmoan carried a tray to the table, carefully balancing three hot cups of Notcafé and his usual can of Gumminess. He smiled broadly, his eyebrows weaving themselves into a silent expression of remorse for how he'd cowardly abandoned Annabelle, thus consigning her to a paragliding flight that almost cost her her life, again, from the hands of his vicious wife Liza, although then Liza used those hands to save Annabelle's life, which had to count for something.

Nevertheless, Moanmoan was clearly a dangerous man to be around, she (Annabelle) reflected as she sipped the steaming liquid that hid in plain light, being literally called Notcafé because it would not be served in any self-respecting café where people ordered coffee. She gave a discreet, feminine dry heave as she recalled the drive to Edinburgh in his *Lamportini*. Dangerous was the word, but there were also other words. Ripped. Toned. Muscular. Pecs. Abs. The muscles you have in your arms and legs that don't come so easily to mind. Tattooed. Well-groomed. Handsome. Trowel. She wasn't (very) shallow, but she was only a woman, after all. Men thought they had needs. Women *knew* they did. And Moanmoan was all man – all the masculine, moisturised wholesome man any woman could want for. And he was all hers. Goody! She thought liberatedly.

Haggis looked at Liza. "I'm afraid Notcafé is the best I have to offer you in my humble home, since I am now nothing more than a humble farmer with only my strategically long-term business interests and no immediate earning potential."

"It's fine," replied Liza. "I'm an independently wealthy actor and multi-millionaire. Somehow, between us, we'll make do."

"You mean you want to live in the farmhouse?" asked Haggis, incredulously.

Liza nodded in confirmation of her choice. "Of course. This is the life you wanted after giving up your billions. I can paraglide and act, and you can carry on watching things as they slowly grow."

Annabelle slid Haggis's fifth-hand engagement ring back to him across the table. "I should return this," she said freely as if the ring was a very small handcuff that bound all her hands at once instead of just one finger, "as I think it's fair to say our engagement is officially over."

Haggis nodded, solemnly taking the ring and turning it over in his Scottish hand. In some way, Annabelle thought, he was now more desirable than when she actually had him. Even his Scottish hair emanated more Scottishness than before. Which, she realised as she watched Haggis saying "thank you" to her, was because he had been blessed with true love of a vicious woman who paraglided in the European Union. "Thank you," Haggis said, as Annabelle noticed earlier. His handsome eyes of all colours at once, because love did that, glanced at Liza. "Perhaps one day, Liza, you could wear this sixth-hand on your finger, once you and Jax have come to terms with the end of your seventeen-year marriage. I imagine there are all sorts of formalities you will need can go through before we can all finally be with the person we truly love."

"We're American," Moanmoan said, as if that explained everything, while in fact it only explained the teeth that served as torches in emergency situations. As Annabelle discovered, it wasn't actually possible to find herself in complete darkness with Moanmoan, unless his teeth were hidden from the public by her lips pressing his in a romantic kiss. Which she enjoyed doing.

"We can dissolve our marriages on the internet in five minutes, invoking the unstable actor's relationship laws over in the US," Liza added, seeing the confusion on Haggis's and Annabelle's faces. "Poor Lemmy will be devastated once he finds out from the only publication he reads, *Lemmy's Fan Club Letters with Nudes but Tasteful*." She joked hilariously.

"Not here, you can't," Haggis said with a laugh in his broad, Scottish mouth with normal teeth inside. "We don't even have enough broadband signal here to order a weekly shop."

The four of them rose, putting down their cups of Notcafé, which really was very cheap and extremely nasty. (As you noticed, I changed the name of the brand, because I don't want to get sued, but I speak the truth and you KNOW I do, Notcafé.) Annabelle realised that if she shared her life with Moanmoan, she would never drink cheap coffee again. Only the best of rats would shit hers out. Curtains, she thought moistly from ecstasy brought by the thought of having curtains and also things that she and Moanmoan would be doing behind them (from the inside, not the outside, which would defeat the point). Kevin McStorm could go penetrate himself with his architectural purity that was also social commentary on the nature of celebrity.

The four of them headed outside, just as a car drew up. Annabelle gasped as Brenda and Poutine erupted from it excitedly, rushing over to congratulate Haggis now the curse of the werehaggis had been ended. As Poutine and Haggis laughed, talking in their Scottish dialect as Scottish people do in Scotland, Brenda came over towards Annabelle.

"Annabelle?" she said, tentatively.

"Brenda," said Annabelle, assertively. She did not add "bitch" for which she was proud of herself.

"Annabelle. I know what I did was unforgiveable and I'm a bitch" – your words, not mine, thought Annabelle virtuously – "but there was a time when I was once your best friend, and for longer than the six and a half weeks, approx., that you've been Liza's best friend. I know I'm only the former owner of Cafe du Amour and I can't compete with all these former billionaires and multi-millionaire actors now I live a lowly life as a supermarket delivery driver for the local shop of Mamazon. However, there was a time when we laughed at my jokes because I am hilarious and I only occasionally took advantage of you. Can you find it in your heart to forgive me, so we can become friends again?"

Annabelle sighed, dramatically. "Brenda. You hurt me more than I can say, and you're right, you were a treacherous bitch." Oh no, she realised in alarm. Her purity has not been entirely restored yet and this was the epilogue. At least she didn't think of Sister Bernadette again. Doo-doo! So she did. "But if the last few weeks have taught me anything, it's that...", she said after the pause for those thoughts. "Gosh, now I come to think about it, I'm not sure what the last few weeks have taught me."

Annabelle thought about that for a time, making everything awkward for everyone until Moanmoan stepped in together with his eyebrows and an axe he playfully threw at the target (which happened to stand exactly where he threw the axe) as he had a habit of doing. It was disarming. Luckily.

"Perhaps," he said, wryly, with a wise wriggle of his eyebrows, as he stared at the two ex-friends who were indeed sometimes bitches, but Brenda more than Annabelle, "the lesson here for all of us is that life is too short to bear a grudge, and if we find the right person and we love them, we shouldn't let things like 'doing the right thing' or 'oh, no, I can't, I'm married,' or 'that breaches the pre-nuptial agreement,' get in the way. We should just do what we want, and screw everyone else. Both literally, and metaphorically."

Everyone laughed loudly (perhaps too loudly, and for slightly too long) and agreed this was an excellent life lesson, especially if it meant they could move past the awkward silence between Annabelle and Brenda. Then Liza pretended she wasn't calling her lawyer whispering about pre-nuptial agreement and Moanmoan pretended his handsome skin on his face didn't go all pale.

Annabelle sighed, conciliatorily, without pretending, because she wasn't an actor. "Let's move past this awkward silence, Brenda," she said loudly to drown out Liza's excited whispers about the *Lamportinis* and the house and the room for the pony and the pool table that Annabelle hadn't even seen yet, despite the transparency the house provided. "I forgive you for being a treacherous bitch." So she spoke with great kindness. "Life is too short and you're too hilarious, even though we haven't seen very much of that lately, not to be my best friend."

"Does that mean I'm not your best friend any longer?" asked Liza, challengingly, disconnected from her lawyer after assuring that Moanmoan's motorcycle collection would be sold for parts used in paragliders. Which Annabelle didn't hear.

Annabelle cleared her throat, realising she'd forgotten about Liza completely. "No, of course not. You're my best American friend."

"The best kind of all, then," Liza replied with a white-toothed smile that made the British people recoil in horror. (I did my research by meeting an American person once. Those teeth belong in horror movies and not in mouths of non-American human people. Unless you lost something in a forest and it's too dark to find it.)

Moanmoan put his arm around Annabelle outside the farmhouse as they waved goodbye to Brenda and Poutine, whilst Haggis and Liza walked on ahead. The last thing they saw before Brenda descended into the car again was she taking in the crispy, clean, clear Scottish air just as a cloud of midges decided with incredible bad timing to descend upon the household. To Annabelle's delight, Moanmoan's moisturising routine repelled them, sending every single one of the little bastards arrowing towards Brenda instead.

"Ugh," said Annabelle empathetically as Brenda coughed out the flying minions of Satan. It was a reasonable punishment, she thought. Yes, Annabelle thought. Now, with this act of God, although Annabelle didn't believe in Him, although now she was starting to, their friendship was restored and she wished Brenda nothing more but happiness with Poutine in the depths of Scottish forest.

[I deleted the part where Nigel wrote himself in blabbing about being a kind and humble veterinarian from Aberdeen who has only ever shown kindness to everyone he meets, be they man or beast. Because he said "tough bananas" to me once on a margin and this proves he was not all that kind. – Karen]

Moanmoan the Samoan paused outside the front door of his architecturally insensitive home, turning to kiss Annabelle full on the lips. Her muffin of clandestine secrets jiggled in a way that she hoped was a portent of things to come.

"Shall we go inside, order some internet divorces which mock the sanctity of heterosexual marriage, and begin our new life together, Annabelle Elle Ellendeling?" he said with his white teeth cavorting seductively in American way.

"Yes," Annabelle breathed, squealing in delight as Moanmoan scooped her up in his strong, manly, tattooed arms that he knew how to use for many purposes. He might have been a coward, but he was her coward, and his special can, limited edition of one and only, overflowed with Gumminess she was ready to store inside her special storage capacity. "Yes, let's. I hope Brenda can deliver our new curtains from Mamazon by the end of today."

He carried Annabelle over the threshold, where Annabelle smelled not the smell of onion, grease and strange curses, but strong, expensive coffee, excreted by a rat to maximise both the flavour and the price the gullible and the glamourous were willing to pay. The curses of the Edible Highlander *and* the Inedible Plastic Implement were lifted. Somewhere, far away, a Jane Smith was crying witchily with furious anger. This was the happy end of *The Edible Highlander Saga*, but not of her life with Moanmoan, which continued long and deep into her private chamber of carnal delights on regular basis.

The End

Acknowledgments

Firstly, of course, I thank you, dear Fans (and Mr Bezos, who publishes my novels) for giving me this amazing career as a published novelist!

Secondly, I dedicate this novel (there was a dedication in the beginning but it was a joke to signify this book's humorous tone) to Ernesto. May Brenda deliver it to you if her supervisor allows her to drive her van to doggie heaven. I love you. Ernesto, not Brenda.

Thirdly, I would like to thank my fabulous new editor (insert editor's name) for turning my book into the masterpiece that it is and removing all references to Nigel. What would I do without you? Mmmwah! You are my best friend forever and I don't say this lightly, (insert editor's name).

Fourthly, I thank the Muse. From the pain I have sustained was born this book, my third, but not final!!! Because the literary world won't know what took it by storm, but it will be me, channeling you, my Muse, into those electronic pages.

Fifthly and lastly, I would like to thank Scotland for letting me research it. Extra special thanks to Gareth, Alastair, Blake, Lachlan, Murdock, Rory, Gareth again, the other Rory, Jaime, Clyde, Duncan, Craig, Keith, Gareth again, and Scott which is very ironic but in a delightful way. (Gareth, if you lost my number, let me know and I will call yours. I have it saved in my expensive *ePhone* under "Tripod" which inspired me to write the character of Moanmoan, who is not based on a Holywould actor of any name or persuasion, because I don't want to get sued.)

Sixthly, because I forgot, I wanted to thank Tweeters for

helping me research paragliding. It is thanks to your knowledge that you have so generously shared that I could make it such a visceral experience. I practically felt like I was there, surrounded by the flapping wings and the flaming engines. One day I may paraglide myself and hopefully live to write all about it in my upcoming memoir, *Life of the Artist* (title subject to change)!

Visit my blog here: https://karenmccompostine.wordpress.com/ and I am also on Twitter: https://twitter.com/karenauthor1

Printed in Great Britain
by Amazon